GORE VIDAL wrote his first novel, *Williwaw* (          while overseas in World War II. During four decades as a writer, Vidal has written novels, plays, short stories, and essays. He has also been a political activist. As a Democratic candidate for Congress from upstate New York, he received the most votes of any Democrat in a half-century. From 1970 to 1972 he was co-chairman of the People's Party. In California's 1982 Democratic primary for U.S. Senate, he polled a half-million votes, and came in second in a field of nine.

In 1948 Vidal wrote the highly praised international best-seller *The City and the Pillar*. This was followed by *The Judgment of Paris* and the prophetic *Messiah*. In the fifties Vidal wrote plays for live television and films for Metro-Goldwyn-Mayer. One of the television plays became the successful Broadway play *Visit to a Small Planet* (1957). Directly for the theater he wrote the prize-winning hit *The Best Man* (1960). In 1964 Vidal returned to the novel with *Julian*, the story of the apostate Roman emperor. This novel has been published in many languages and editions. As Henry de Montherlant wrote: "*Julian* is the only book about a Roman emperor that I like to re-read. Vidal loves his protagonist; he knows the period thoroughly; and the book is a beautiful hymn to the twilight of paganism." During the last quarter-century Vidal has been telling the history of the United States as experienced by one family and its connections in what Gabriel García Márquez has called "Gore Vidal's magnificent series of historical novels or novelized histories." They are, in chronological order, *Burr, Lincoln, 1876, Empire, Hollywood*, and *Washington, D.C.*

During the same period, Vidal invented a series of satiric comedies – *Myra Breckinridge, Myron, Kalki, Duluth*. "Vidal's development . . . along that line from *Myra Breckinridge* to *Duluth* is crowned with success," wrote Italo Calvino in *La Repubblica* (Rome). "I consider Vidal to be a master of that new form which is taking shape in world literature and which we may call the hyper-novel or the novel elevated to the square or to the cube." To this list Vidal added the highly praised – and controversial – *Live from Golgotha* in 1992.

Vidal has also published several volumes of essays. When the National Book Critics Circle presented him with an award (1982), the citation read: "The American tradition of independent and curious learning is kept alive in the wit and great expressiveness of Gore Vidal's criticism."

Vidal recently co-starred with Tim Robbins in the movie *Bob Roberts*.

## Books by Gore Vidal

### Novels

Williwaw
In a Yellow Wood
The City and the Pillar
The Season of Comfort
A Search for the King
Dark Green, Bright Red
The Judgment of Paris
Messiah
Julian
Washington, D.C.
Myra Breckinridge
Two Sisters
Burr
Myron
1876
Kalki
Creation
Duluth
Lincoln
Empire
Hollywood
Live from Golgotha

### Short Stories

A Thirsty Evil

————

### Plays

An evening with
Richard Nixon
Weekend
Romulus
The Best Man
Visit to a Small Planet

————

### Essays

Rocking the Boat
Reflections upon a Sinking Ship
Homage to Daniel Shays
Matters of Fact and Fiction
Pink Triangle and Yellow Star
and other essays
Armageddon?
At Home
Screening History
A View from the Diner's Club

GORE VIDAL

# MESSIAH

An *Abacus* Book

First published by E P Dutton & Co, Inc 1954
First published in Great Britain by William Heinemann Ltd 1955
Revised edition first published by Little, Brown & Co, Inc 1965
Revised edition first published in Great Britain
by William Heinemann Ltd 1968
This edition published by Abacus 1993

A CIP catalogue record for this book
is available from the British Library.

ISBN 0 349 10364 X

Typeset by Vivitext Creative Services,

Printed in England by Clays Ltd, St Ives plc

Abacus
A Division of
Little, Brown and Company (UK) Limited
165 Great Dover Street
London SE1 4YA

*For*
TENNESSEE WILLIAMS

# INTRODUCTION

The fate of books is incalculable, to overdo understatement; "Classics" of not so long ago have vanished without trace while even the agreed-upon classics of our traditional literature undergo so many sea-changes in the age of the cathode tube that many – most? – have drowned entirely and now lie full fathom five. If they do not lend themselves to the ruthless Good Taste of Merchant-Ivory, they gather dust on library shelves, attracting only dry rot and the odd scholar in desperate search of a subject for dissertation.

My own books have had many lives and deaths. Recently, I asked the British libraries to give me a breakdown of how often the forty or so books of mine were lent out in a year. Since one's latest book is usually in most demand, I expected *Lincoln* to head the list. But no, *Lincoln* ranked third or fourth. Number one proved to be *Duluth*, a book that enjoyed not only a small sale in the UK, but so outraged most of its reviewers that many confessed that they had, like the first London listeners of Wagner, become depraved and immoral as a result of exposure to so unsettling a work where neither time nor sex followed the usual formulas. Later, the critics did come to the book's rescue but by then a book is usually lost to the university syllabus and so lies four fathom deep. But *Duluth* goes on and on, appealing not only to lovers of the film *Airplane*, but also to the professors at the University of Bologna who regard it as perfect "neo-baroque." The heroine, Darlene

Ecks, now lives for what *seems* forever – or is it just one Duluthian day? – in the Duluth Police Department, strip-searching Mexican aliens while in lustful pursuit of black Big John, drug dealer and master criminal. Meanwhile, the Sapphic sister of the mayor of Duluth, having died in the early pages of the book, has moved on, not to Heaven but to a TV serial called "Duluth," quite different from the real thing. While her late friend, Beryl, crops up in a popular magazine fiction, *Rogue Duke*, where she is a spy as well as a lover of the six-foot-tall Viking world-conqueror, Napoleon Bonaparte, the Scourge of Europe. Then as the spaceship in the Duluth swamp opens . . . There are many surprises.

For those who only want to read books of great social significance, let me say that I recently met a British journalist who said, out of the cerulean blue: "The Spanish translation of *Duluth* is the most popular book in the women's penitentiary of Lima, Peru." *That* is truly significant. For those who prefer to go upmarket, let us cut now to the Royal Lodge at Windsor late one night. The Sister of the Sovereign reads *Duluth* aloud to a small group. Then, laughter at last under control, she turns to the Author and says, "What is there in me so *base* that loves this book?"

*Messiah*, the first of my . . . what shall I call them? Satiric inventions? Masterpieces of bad taste? as Brigid Brophy observed of *Myra Breckinridge*. Well, I won't categorize. *Messiah* suffered the initial fate of *Duluth*. Later, critics rescued it but by then it hardly needed rescue. Tagged as science fiction, the book has been read by millions in paperback, among them "Alice Cooper," the rock singer, as well as the makers of the musical *Hair* who tried for years to transform it into a film.

The story was somewhat in advance of its day: a charismatic undertaker, John Cave, goes on television – this is back in the fifties – and starts a world religion that swiftly replaces Christianity and most of Islam. His message? Death is nothing; hence *no* thing. Since no thing, by definition, is neither good nor bad, death can be seen as a positive good and people are invited to remove themselves from life in pleasant establishments. Incidentally, this was long before anyone spoke of over-population. Happily, film makers have always felt free to quarry my inventions. In the movie *Soylent Green*, in an overcrowded world, one checks into a charming room and, nicely drugged while watching beautiful images of the pre-*Blade Runner* natural world, checks out by taking "Cavesway."

Over the years a great deal has been written about *Messiah* (I am now cribbing from the Preface to a Gregg Press series of science fiction classics). "*Messiah*," writes Elizabeth A. Lynn, "is terrifyingly convincing. Vidal turns the Christian mythology inside out to create a religion based on death, and the frightening thing about it is that he makes us believe that western culture, *American* culture, could accept it, and worse, *create* it." Needless to say, preface and book were written long before the Reverend Jim Jones, of Jonestown, made it all come true by killing off himself and about 1,000 willing followers. John Cave's own end, and that of the narrator, are ironic, to say the least. Lynn quotes from Damon Knight's *In Search of Wonder*: "*Messiah* has a quality so uniformly absent from science fiction novels that it comes here as a shock: conviction, the feeling that the story is in some deep sense true."

With *Kalki* I again, it would seem, am mixing religion and the media, specifically television, in a world that is less far-out than *Duluth*, less here-and-now than *Messiah* (although there is a character in *Messiah* who is 2,000 years old, a woman who has learned nothing in two millennia but the true meaning of monetary exchange rates). The premise of *Kalki* is that one man, in order to save our species from over-population and pollution – plainly, a super-Green before his time – declares that he is the last incarnation of the god Vishnu and that this cycle of creation is finished. Then, with him as progenitor, the human race can start again on a clean planet, empty of the current five billion hungry, restive folk. Again there was outrage in book-chat land. *Any* alternative world to the one that our masters let us live and die in is considered dangerous even if it is wildly comedic and, in the case of *Kalki*, rather worse than theirs. Mick Jagger promptly bought the screen rights. Of all my books, *Kalki* is the one that nice boys and girls in England – the ones with pink and green hair and attractive safety pins through ears and noses – most want me to autograph. I think they like the idea of starting the human race all over again.

*Myra Breckinridge* and the sequel *Myron* were, of course, a source of outrage ("Has literary decency fallen so low?" keened *Time* magazine) but *Myra* proved to be a world bestseller, and Myra became the Hollywood mega-star she was born to be. This time a film *was* made. Although I have never seen it, I do know that despite the iconic presences of Raquel Welch and Mae West, the film was so bad that the book stopped selling for a decade. Only now does Myra return to her rightful place as queen of every heart. Literary critics enjoy writing about Myra and her wild attempts to bring the movies back to Hollywood's Golden Age of the Thirties and Forties when stars were *well-groomed.* In the course of the first book she changes her sex: first out of conviction; then again out of love. Under that hard-boiled exterior is the heart of a tender man/woman.

In the second book, Myra is now Myron and happily married. But a vengeful Myra still lives inside Myron. Late one night, while he is watching an MGM turkey called *Siren of Babylon* with Maria Montez, Myra pushes Myron through the television set and into not only the movie – but the glorious year 1948 as well. For Thom Gunn, "These two books [are] the twentieth-century equivalents of *Alice in Wonderland* and *Through the Looking-Glass.*"

Myra's looking-glass adventure makes it possible for her to turn *Siren of Babylon* into a hit. As one of many visitors from the future who have got caught in the movie while watching it on late night television (they are drawn into the TV set as if it were a black hole in space), she is visible to the "locals" who live back of the studio lot but when she goes *into* the actual movie, she is invisible to the actors. Slyly, she undoes metal breast plates, revealing breasts, slips loin cloths to one side, revealing what she calls "American rosebuds."

Meanwhile, she decides to save the human race through the creation of a new race of fun-loving Amazon studs whom she personally changes from male to female, often with disturbing results. But her best quality, altruistic megalomania aside, is her great good humour, except when Myron surfaces to take over the controls of their common body. They alternate for dominance. He wants to get back home to the present and his wife. She wants to stay in Hollywood to dominate 1948 movies. As Professor Catherine R. Stimpson writes in *My Oh My Oh Myra*, "The agony of *Myron* is the struggle between Myron and Myra, two mutually loathing souls imprisoned in a single body . . . they embody the spectrum of genital possibilities in the late twentieth century: heterosexual biological male who has become a medically created but ardent female, who in turn becomes prosthetic male (the dildo), medically created male. Like the *Satyricon*, Myra/Myron blithely accepts polymorphous sexual experiences . . ." It is good to have Myra back. After all, this is her/his/their age.

Gore Vidal
Ravello, 1993

I sometimes think the day will come when all the modern nations will adore a sort of American god, a god who will have been a man that lived on earth and about whom much will have been written in the popular press; and images of this god will be set up in the churches, not floating on a Veronica Kerchief, but established, fixed once and for all by photography. Yes, I foresee a photographed god, wearing spectacles.

On that day civilization will have reached its peak and there will be steam-propelled gondolas in Venice.

November, 1861: The Goncourt Journals

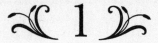

1

I envy those chroniclers who assert with reckless but sincere abandon: "I was there. I saw it happen. It happened thus." Now I too, in every sense, was there, yet I cannot trust myself to identify with any accuracy the various events of my own life, no matter how vividly they may seem to survive in recollection . . . if only because we are all, I think, betrayed by those eyes of memory which are as mutable and particular as the ones with which we regard the material world, the vision altering, as it so often does, from near in youth to far in age. And that I am by a devious and unexpected route arrived at a great old age is to me a source of some complacency, even on those bleak occasions when I find myself attending inadvertently the body's dissolution, a process as imperceptible yet sure as one of those faint, persistent winds which shift the dunes of sand in that desert of dry Libya which burns, white and desolate, beyond the mountains I see from the window of my room, a window facing, aptly enough, the west where all the kings lie buried in their pride.

I am also conscious that I lack the passion for the business of familiar life which is the central preoccupation of our race while, worse still, I have never acquired the habit of judging the usual deeds of men . . . two inconvenient characteristics which render me uncertain whenever I attempt to recall the past, confounding me sadly with the knowledge that my recollections are, after all, tentative and private and only true in part.

Then, finally, I have never found it easy to tell the truth, a temperamental infirmity due not so much to any wish or compulsion to distort reality that I might be reckoned virtuous but, rather, to a conception of the inconsequence of human activity which is ever in conflict with a profound love of those essential powers that result in human action, a paradox certainly, a dual vision which restrains me from easy judgments.

I am tempted to affirm that historic truth is quite impossible, although I am willing to accept the philosophic notion that it may exist abstractly, perfect and remote in the imagination. A windy attic filled with lovely objects has always been my personal image of those absolutes Aristotle conceived with such mellifluous optimism . . . and I have always liked the conceits of philosophy, the more extravagant the better. I am especially devoted to Parmenides, who was so strenuously obsessed with the idea of totality that he was capable, finally, of declaring that nothing ever changed, that what has been must still exist if it is yet remembered and named, a metaphysical conception which will, I suspect, be of some use to me as I journey in memory back to that original crisis from which I have for so long traveled and to which, despite the peril, I must return.

I do not say, then, that what I remember is all true but I can declare that what I shall recall is a relative truth as opposed to that monstrous testament the one-half world believes, entrenching deep thereby a mission at whose birth I officiated and one whose polished legend has since become the substantial illusion of a desperate race. That both mission and illusion were false, I alone can say with certainty, with sorrow, such being the unsuspected and terrible resolution of brave days. Only the crisis, which I shall record, was real.

I have said I am not given to making judgments. That is not precise. It is true that in most "wicked" acts I have been able, with a little effort, to perceive the possibilities for good either in actual intention or (and to me more important) in uncalculated result; yet, ultimately, problems in ethics have never much concerned me: possibly because they have been the vital interest of so many others who, through custom, rule society, more agreeably than not. On that useful moral level I have been seldom, if ever, seriously engaged. But once on another, more arduous plane I was forced to make a choice, to judge, to act; and act I did in such a way that I am still startled by the implications of my choice, of my life's one judgment.

I chose the light in preference to the dreamless dark, destroying my own place in the world, and then, more painful still, I chose the light in preference to the twilight region of indeterminate visions and ambiguities, that realm where decision was impossible and where the potentialities of choice were endless and exquisite to contemplate. To desert these beloved ghosts and incalculable powers was the greater pain, but I have lived on, observing with ever-increasing intensity that blazing disc of fire which is the symbol as well as material source of the reality I have accepted entirely, despite the sure dominion in eternity of the dark other.

But now, as my private day begins to fade, as the wind in the desert gathers in intensity, smoothing out the patterns in the sand, I shall attempt to evoke the true image of one who assumed with plausibility in an age of science the long-discarded robes of prophecy, prevailing at last through ritual death and becoming, to those who see the universe in man, that solemn idea which is yet called by its resonant and antique name, god.

2

Stars fell to earth in a blaze of light, and where they fell, monsters were born, hideous and blind.

The first dozen years after the second of the modern wars were indeed "a time of divination," as one religious writer unctuously described them. Not a day passed but that some omen or portent was remarked by an anxious race, suspecting war. At first, the newspapers delightedly reported these marvels, getting the details all wrong but communicating a sense of awfulness that was to increase as the years of peace uneasily lengthened until a frightened people demanded government action, the ultimate recourse in those innocent times.

Yet these omens, obsessive and ubiquitous as they were, would not yield their secret order to any known system. For instance, much of the luminous crockery which was seen in the sky was never entirely explained. And explanation, in the end, was all that the people required. It made no difference how extraordinary the explanation was, if only they could know *what* was happening: that the shining globes which raced in formation over Sioux Falls, South Dakota, were mere residents of the Andromeda Galaxy, at home in space, omnipotent and eternal in design, on a cultural visit to our planet . . . if only this much could definitely be stated, the readers of newspapers would have felt secure, able in a few weeks' time to turn their attention to other problems, the visitors from farther space forgotten. It made little difference whether these mysterious blobs of light were hallucinations, intergalactic visitors or military weapons; the important thing was to explain them.

To behold the inexplicable was perhaps the most unpleasant experience a human being of that age could know, and during that gaudy decade many wild phenomena were sighted and recorded.

In daylight, glittering objects of bright silver maneuvered at unearthly speed over Washington, D.C., observed by hundreds, some few reliable. The government, with an air of spurious calm, mentioned weather balloons, atmospheric reflections, tricks-of-eye, hinting, too, as broadly as it dared, that a sizable minority of its citizens were probably subject to delusions and mass hysteria. This cynical view was prevalent inside the administration, though it could not of course propound such a theory publicly since its own tenure was based, more or less solidly, on the franchise of those same hysterics and irresponsibles.

Shortly after the mid-point of the century, the wonders increased, becoming daily more bizarre. The recent advance in atomic research and in jet propulsion had made the Western world disagreeably aware of other planets and galaxies, and the thought that we would soon be making expeditions into space was disquieting, if splendid, giving rise to the not illogical thought that life might be developing on other worlds somewhat more brilliantly than here at home and, further, that it was quite conceivable that we ourselves might receive visitors long before our own adventuring had begun in the starry blackness which contains our life, like a speck of phosphorus in a quiet sea. And since our people were (and no doubt still are) barbarous and drenched in superstition, like the dripping "Saved" at an old-time Texas baptism, it was generally felt that these odd creatures whose shining cars flashed through our poor heavens at such speed must, of necessity, be hostile and cruel and bent on world dominion, just like ourselves or at least our geographic neighbors.

The evidence was horrific and plentiful:

In Berlin a flying object of unfamiliar design was seen to land by an old farmer who was so close to it that he could make out several little men twinkling behind an arc of windows. He fled, however, before they could eat him. Shortly after his breathless announcement to the newspapers, he was absorbed by an Asiatic government whose mission it was at that time to regularize the part of humanity fortunate enough to live within its curiously elastic boundaries, both temporal and spiritual.

In West Virginia, a creature ten feet tall, green with a red face and exuding a ghastly odor, was seen to stagger out of a luminous globe, temporarily grounded. He was observed by a woman and four boys, all of unquestionable probity; they fled before he could eat them. Later in the company of sheriff and well-armed posse, they returned to the scene of horror only to find both monster and conveyance gone. But even the skeptical sheriff and his men could detect, quite plainly, an unfamiliar odor, sharp and sickening among the clean pines.

This particular story was unique because it was the first to describe a visitor as being larger instead of smaller than a man, a significant proof of the growing anxiety: we could handle even the cleverest little creature, but something huge, and green with an awful odor . . . it was too much.

I myself, late one night in July of the mid-century, saw quite plainly from the eastern bank of the Hudson River, where I lived, two red globes flickering in a cloudless sky. As I watched one moved to a higher point at a forty-five-degree angle above the original plane which had contained them both. For several nights I watched these eccentric twins but then, carried away by enthusiasm, I began to confuse Mars and Saturn with my magic lights until at last I thought it wise to remain indoors, except for those brief days at summer's end when I watched, as I always used to do, the lovely sudden silver arcs meteors plunging make.

In later years, I learned that, concurrently with the celestial marvels, farm communities were reporting an unusual number of calves born two-headed, chickens hatched three-legged, and lambs born with human faces; but since the somewhat vague laws of mutation were more or less well understood by the farmers these curiosities did not alarm them. An earlier generation would have known instinctively that so many irregularities forecast an ill future, full of spite.

Eventually all was satisfactorily explained or, quite as good, forgotten. Yet the real significance of these portents was not so much their mysterious reality as the profound effect they had upon a people who, despite their emphatic materialism, were as easily shattered by the unexpected as their ancestors who had beheld eagles circling the Capitoline Hill, observed the sky grow leaden on Golgotha, shivered in loud storms when the rain was red as blood and the wind full of toads, while in our own century, attended by a statesman-Pope, the sun did a dance over Portugal.

Considering the unmistakable nature of these signs, it is curious how few suspected the truth: that a new mission had been conceived out of the race's need, the hour of its birth already determined by a conjunction of terrible new stars.

It is true of course that the established churches duly noted these spectacular happenings and, rather slyly, used them to enhance that abstract power from which their own mystical but vigorous authority was descended. The more secular, if no less mystical, dogmas . . . descended variously from an ill-tempered social philosopher of the nineteenth century and an energetic, unreasonably confident mental therapist, a product of that century's decline . . . maintained, in the one case, that fireworks had been set off by vindictive employers to bedazzle the poor workers for undefined but patently wicked ends, and, in the other case, that the fiery objects represented a kind of atavistic recession to the childish world of marvels; a theory which was developed even further in a widely quoted paper by an ingenious disciple of the dead therapist. According to this worthy, the universe was the womb in symbol and the blazing lights which many people thought they saw were only a form of hallucination, harking back to some prenatal memory of ovaries bursting with a hostile potential life which would, in time, become sibling rivals. The writer demanded that the government place all who had seen flying objects under three years' close observation to determine to what extent sibling rivalry, or the absence of it (the proposition worked equally well either way), had affected them in life. Although this bold synthesis was universally admired and subsequently read into the Congressional Record by a lady Representative who had herself undergone nine years' analysis with striking results, the government refused to act.

3

But although nearly every human institution took cognizance of these signs and auguries, none guessed the truth, and those few individuals who had begun to suspect what might be happening preferred not to speak out, if only because, despite much private analysis and self-questioning, it was not a time in which to circulate ideas which might prove disagreeable to any minority, no matter how lunatic. The body politic was more than usually upset by signs of nonconformity. The atmosphere was not unlike that of Britain during the mad hour of Titus Oates.

Precisely why my countrymen behaved so frantically is a problem for those historians used to the grand, eternal view of human events. Yet I have often thought that much of our national irritability was closely related to the unexpected and reluctant custody of the world the second war had pressed upon the confused grandchildren of a proud, isolated people, both indifferent and strange to the ways of other cultures.

More to the point, however, was the attitude of our intellectuals, who constituted at this time a small, militantly undistinguished minority, directly descended in spirit if not in fact from that rhetorical eighteenth-century Swiss whose romantic and mystical love for humanity was magically achieved through a somewhat obsessive preoccupation with himself. His passion for self-analysis flourished in our mid-century, at least among the articulate few who were capable of analyzing and who, in time, like their great ancestor, chose the ear of the world for their confessional.

Men of letters lugubriously described their own deviations (usually political or sexual, seldom aesthetic), while painters worked devotedly at depicting unique inner worlds which were not accessible to others except in a state of purest empathy hardly to be achieved without a little fakery in a selfish world. It was, finally, the accepted criterion that art's single function was the fullest expression of a private vision . . . which was true enough, though the visions of men lacking genius are not without a certain gloom. Genius, in this time, was quite as rare as in any other and, to its credit, it was not a self-admiring age. Critics found merit only in criticism, a singular approach which was to amuse the serious for several decades.

Led by artists, the intellectuals voiced their guilt at innumerable cocktail parties where it was accepted as an article of faith that each had a burden of guilt which could, once recognized, be exorcised. The means of recognition were expensive but rewarding: a trained and sympathetic listener would give the malaise a name and reveal its genesis; then, through confession (and occasionally "reliving"), the guilt would vanish along with asthma, impotence and eczema. The process, of course, was not easy. To facilitate therapy, it became the custom among the cleverer people to set aside all the traditional artifices of society so that both friends and strangers could confess to one another their worst deeds, their most squalid fantasies, in a series of competitive monologues conducted with arduous sincerity and surprisingly successful on every level but that of communication.

I am sure that this sort of catharsis was not entirely valueless: many of the self-obsessed undoubtedly experienced relief when dispensing secrets. It was certainly an instructive shock for them to find that even their most repellent aberrations were accepted quite perfunctorily by strangers too intent on their own problems to be outraged, or even greatly interested. This discovery was not always cheering. There is a certain dignity and excitement in possessing a dangerous secret life. To lose it in maturity is hard. Once promiscuously shared, vice becomes ordinary, no more troublesome than obvious dentures.

Many cherished private hells were forever lost in those garrulous years, and the vacuum each left was invariably filled with a boredom which, in its turn, could be dispelled only by faith. As a result, the pursuit of the absolute, in one guise or another, became the main preoccupation of these romanticists who professed with some pride a mistrust of reason, derived quite legitimately from their own incapacity to assimilate the social changes created by machinery, their particular Lucifer. They rejected the idea of the reflective mind, arguing that since both logic and science had failed to establish the first cause of the universe or (more important) humanity's significance, only the emotions could reveal to us the nature of reality, the key to meaning. That it was no real concern of this race why or when or how the universe came into being was an attitude never, so far as I can recall, expressed by the serious-minded of the day. Their searching, however, was not simply the result of curiosity; it was more than that: it was an emotional senseless plunging into the void, into the unknowable and the irrelevant. It became, finally, the burden of life, the blight among the flowers: the mystery which must be revealed, even at the expense of life. It was a terrible crisis. made doubly hard since the eschewal of logic left only one path clear to the heart of the dilemma: the way of the mystic, and even to the least sensible it was sadly apparent that, lacking a superior and dedicated organization, one man's revelation is not apt to be of much use to another.

Quantities of venerable attitudes were abandoned and much of the preceding century's "eternal truths and verities" which had cast, rocklike, so formidable and dense a shadow were found, upon examination, to be so much sand, suitable for the construction of fantastic edifices but not durable, nor safe from the sea's tide.

But the issue was joined: dubious art was fashioned, authorities were invoked, dreams given countenance and systems constructed on the evidence of private illumination.

For a time, political and social action seemed to offer a way out, or in. Foreign civil wars, foreign social experiments were served with a ferocity difficult to comprehend; but later, when the wars and experiments went wrong, revealing, after such high hopes, the perennial human inability to order society, a disillusion resulted, bitterly resolved in numerous cases by the assumption of some mystical dogma, preferably one so quaintly rich with history, so sweeping and unreasonable in its claims, as to be thoroughly acceptable to the saddened romanticist who wanted, above all else, to *feel*, to know without reasoning.

So in these portentous times, only the scientists were content as they constructed ever more fabulous machines with which to split the invisible kernels of life while the anti-scientifics leaped nervously from one absolute to another . . . now rushing to the old for grace, now to the new for salvation, no two of them really agreeing on anything except the need for agreement, for the last knowledge. And that, finally, was the prevailing note of the age: since reason had been declared insufficient, only a mystic could provide the answer, only he could mark the boundaries of life with a final authority, inscrutably revealed. It was perfectly clear. All that was lacking was the man.

## ❧ 2 ❧

### 1

The garden was at its best that first week in the month of June. The peonies were more opulent than usual and I walked slowly through the green light on the terrace above the white river, enjoying the heavy odor of peonies and of new roses rambling in hedges.

The Hudson was calm, no ripple revealed that slow tide which even here, miles to the north of the sea, rises brackishly at the moon's disposition. Across the river the Catskills, water-blue, emerged sharply from the summer's green as though the earth in one vivid thrust had attempted sky, fusing the two elements into yet another richer blue . . . but the sky was only framed, not really touched, and the blue of hills was darker than the pale sky with its protean clouds all shaped by wind, like the stuff of auguries and human dreaming.

The sky that day was like an idiot's mind, wild with odd clouds, but lovely too, guileless, natural, elusive.

I did not want to go in to lunch, although there was no choice in the matter. I had arrived at one o'clock; I was expected at one-thirty. Meanwhile, avoiding the house until the last possible moment, I had taken a neighbor's privilege of strolling alone about the garden; the house behind me was gray and austere, granitic, more English than Hudson Valley. The grounds swept softly down toward the river nearly a mile away. A vista had been cleared from the central terrace, a little like the one at Versailles but more rustic, less royal. Dark green trees covered the hills to left and right of the sweep of lawn and meadow. No other house could be seen. Even the railroad between the terrace and the water was invisible, hidden by a bluff.

I breathed the air of early summer gladly, voluptuously. I lived my life in seasonal concert with this river and, after grim March and confusing sharp April, the knowledge that at last the trees were in leaf and the days warm was quite enough to create in me a mood of euphoria, of marvelous serenity. I contemplated love affairs. I prepared to meet strangers. The summer and I would celebrate our triumph soon; but, until the proper moment, I was a spectator: the summer love as yet unknown to me, the last dark blooming of peonies amid the wreckage of white lilacs still some weeks away, held in the future with my love. I could only anticipate; I savored my disengagement in this garden.

But then it was time to go in and I turned my back resolutely on the river and ascended the wide stone steps to the brick terrace which fronted the house on the river side, pausing only to break the stem of a white and pink peony, regretting immediately what I had done: brutally, I had wished to possess the summer, to fix the instant, to bear with me into the house a fragment of the day. It was wrong; and I stood for a moment at the French door holding the great peony in my hand, its odor like a dozen roses, like all the summers I had ever known. But it was impractical. I could not stuff it into my buttonhole for it was as large as a baby's head, while I was fairly certain that my hostess would be less than pleased to receive at my hands one of her best peonies, cut too short even to place in water. Obscurely displeased with myself and the day, I plunged the flower deep into a hedge of boxwood until not even a glimmer of white showed through the dense dark green to betray me. Then, like a murderer, the assaulted day part-spoiling, I went inside.

## 2

"You have been malingering in the garden," Clarissa said, offering me her face like a painted plate to kiss. "I saw you from the window."

"Saw me ravage the flowers?"

"They all do," she said obscurely, and led me after her into the drawing room, an oblong full of light from French windows opening upon the terrace. I was surprised to see that she was alone.

"She'll be along presently. She's upstairs changing."

"Who?"

"Iris Mortimer . . . didn't I tell you? It's the whole reason."

Clarissa nodded slyly from the chair opposite me. A warm wind crossed the room and the white curtains billowed like spinnakers in a regatta. I breathed the warm odor of flowers, of burned ash remnants from the fireplace: the room shone with silver and porcelain. Clarissa was rich despite the wars and crisis that had marked our days, leaving the usual scars upon us, like trees whose cross-sections bear a familial resemblance of concentric rings, recalling in detail the weather of past years . . . at least those few rings we shared in common, for Clarissa, by her own admission, was twenty-two hundred years old with an uncommonly good memory. None of us had ever questioned her too closely about her past. There is no reason to suspect, however, that she was insincere. Since she felt she had lived that great length of time and since her recollections were remarkably interesting and plausible, she was much in demand as a conversationalist and adviser, especially useful in plots which required great shrewdness and daring. It was perfectly apparent that she was involved in some such plot at the moment.

I looked at her thoughtfully before I casually rose to take the bait of mystery she had trailed so perfunctorily before me. She knew her man. She knew I would not be difficult in the early stages of any adventure.

"Whole reason?" I repeated.

"I can say no more!" said Clarissa with a melodramatic emphasis which my deliberately casual tone did not entirely justify. "You'll love Iris, though."

I wondered whether loving Iris, or pretending to love Iris, was to be the summer's game. But before I could inquire further, Clarissa, secure in her mystery, asked me idly about my work and, as idly, I answered her, the exchange perfunctory yet easy, for we were used to one another.

"I am tracking him down," I said. "There is so little to go on, but what there is is quite fascinating, especially Ammianus."

"Fairly reliable, as military men go," said Clarissa, suddenly emerging from her polite indifference. Any reference to the past she had known always interested her. Only the present seemed to bore her, at least that ordinary unusable present which did not contain promising material for one of her elaborate human games.

"Did you know him?" I never accepted, literally, Clarissa's unique age. Two thousand years is an unlikely span of life even for a woman of her sturdy unimaginativeness; yet there was no ignoring the fact that she *seemed* to have lived that long, and that her references to obscure episodes, where ascertainable, were nearly always right and, more convincing still, where they differed from history's records, differed on the side of plausibility, the work of a memory or a mind completely unsuperstitious and unenthusiastic. She *was* literal and, excepting always her central fantasy, matter-of-fact. To her the death of Caesar was the logical outcome of a system of taxation which has not been preserved for us, while the virtue of the Roman republic and the ambitions of celebrated politicians she set aside as being less than important. Currency and taxation were her forte and she managed to reduce all the martial splendor of ancient days to an economic level.

She had one other obsession, however, and my reference to Ammianus reminded her of it.

"The Christians!" she exclaimed significantly; then she

paused. I waited. Her conversation at times resembled chapter headings chosen haphazardly from an assortment of Victorian novels. "*They* hated him."

"Ammianus?"

"No, your man Julian. It *is* the Emperor Julian you are writing about?"

"Reading about."

"Ah, you *will* write about him," she said with an abstracted Pythoness state which suggested that I was indefatigable in my eccentric purpose, the study of history in a minor key.

"Of course they hated him. As well they should have . . . that's the whole point to my work."

"Unreliable, the lot of them. There is no decent history from the time they came to Rome up until that fat little Englishman . . . you know, the one who lived in Switzerland . . . with the *staring* eyes."

"Gibbon."

"Yes, that one. Of course he got all the facts wrong, poor man, but at least he tried. The facts of course were all gone by then. They saw to that . . . burning things, rewriting things . . . not that I really ever *read* them . . . you know how I am about reading. I prefer a mystery novel any day. But at least Gibbon got the tone right."

"Yet . . ."

"Of course Julian was something of a prig, you know. He *posed* continually and he wasn't . . . what do they call him now? an apostate. He *never* renounced Christianity."

"He what? . . ."

Clarissa in her queer way took pleasure in rearranging all accepted information. I shall never know whether she did it deliberately to mystify or whether her versions were the forgotten reality.

"He was a perfectly good Christian *au fond* despite his peculiar diet. He was a vegetarian for some years but wouldn't eat beans, as I recall, because he thought they contained the souls of the dead, an old orphic notion."

"Which is hardly Christian."

"Isn't that part of it? No? Well, in any case the first Edict of Paris was intended . . ." But I was never to hear Julian's intent, for Iris was in the doorway, slender, dressed in white, her hair dark and drawn back in a classical line from her calm face. She was handsome and not at all what I had expected, but then Clarissa had, as usual, not given me much lead. Iris Mortimer was my own age, I guessed, about thirty, and although hardly a beauty she moved with such ease, spoke with such softness and created such an air of serenity that one gave her perhaps more credit for the possession of beauty than an American devoted to regular features ought, in all accuracy, to have done. The impression was one of lightness, of this month of June in fact . . . I linger over her description a little worriedly, conscious that I am not really getting her right (at least as she appeared to me that afternoon) for the simple reason that our lives were to become so desperately involved in the next few years and my memories of her are now encrusted with so much emotion that any attempt to evoke her as she actually was when I first saw her in that drawing room some fifty years ago is not unlike the work of a restorer of paintings removing layers of glaze and grime in an attempt to reveal an original pattern in all its freshness somewhere beneath. Except that a restorer of course is a workman who has presumably no prejudice and, too, he did not create the original image only to attend its subsequent distortion, as the passionate do in life; for the Iris of that day was, I suppose, no less and no more than what she was to become; it was merely that I could not suspect the bizarre course our future was to take. I had no premonition of our mythic roles, though the temptation is almost overpowering to assert, darkly, that even on the occasion of our first meeting I *knew*. The truth is that we met; we became friends; we lunched amiably and the future cast not one shadow across the mahogany table around which we sat, listening to Clarissa and eating fresh shad caught in the river that morning.

"Eugene here is interested in Julian," said our hostess, lifting a spring asparagus to her mouth with her fingers.

"Julian who?"

"The Emperor of Rome. I forget his family name but he was a cousin, I think, of Constantius, who was dreary, too, though not such a bore as Julian. Iris, try the asparagus. We get them from the garden."

Iris tried an asparagus and Clarissa recalled that the Emperor Augustus's favorite saying was: "Quick as boiled asparagus." It developed that *he* had been something of a bore, too. "Hopelessly involved in office work. Of course it's all terribly important, no doubt of that . . . after all the entire Empire was based on a first-rate filing system; yet, all in all, it's hardly *glamorous.*"

"Whom *did* you prefer?" asked Iris, smiling at me. She too was aware of our hostess's obsession; whether or not she believed is a different matter. I assumed not; yet the assumption of truth is perhaps, for human purposes, the same as truth itself, at least to the obsessed.

"None of the obvious ones," said Clarissa, squinting nearsightedly at the window through which a pair of yellow-spangled birds were mating on the wing like eccentric comets against the green of box. "But of course, I didn't know everyone, darling. Only a few. Not all of them were accessible. Some never dined out and some that did go out were impossible. And then of course I traveled a good deal. I loved Alexandria and wintered there for over two hundred years, missing a great deal of the unpleasantness at Rome, the *unstability* of those tiresome generals . . . although Vitellius was great fun, at least as a young man. I never saw him when he was Emperor that time, for five minutes, wasn't it? Died of greed. Such an appetite! Once as a young man he ate an entire side of beef at my place in Baiae. Ah, Baiae, I do miss it. Much nicer than Bath or Biarritz and certainly more interesting than Newport. I had several houses there over the years. Once when Senator Tullius Cicero was traveling with that poisonous daughter of his, they stopped . . ."

We listened attentively as one always did to Clarissa . . . does? I wonder if she is still alive. If she is, then perhaps the miracle has indeed taken place and one human being has finally avoided the usual fate. It is an amiable miracle to contemplate.

Lunch ended without any signs of the revelation Clarissa had led me to expect. Nothing was said that seemed to possess even a secret significance. Wondering idly whether or not Clarissa might, after all, be entirely mad, I followed the two women back into the drawing room, where we had our coffee in a warm mood of satiety made only faintly disagreeable for me by the mild nausea I always used to experience when I drank too much wine at lunch. Now of course I never drink wine, only the Arabs' mint tea and their sandy bitter coffee which I have come to like.

Clarissa reminisced idly. She possessed a passion for minor detail which was often a good deal more interesting than her usual talks on currency devaluation.

Neither Iris nor I spoke much; it was as if we were both awaiting some word from Clarissa which would throw into immediate relief this lunch, this day, this meeting of strangers. But Clarissa continued to gossip; at last, when I was beginning to go over in my mind the various formulae which make departure easy, our hostess, as though aware that she had drawn out the overture too long, said abruptly, "Eugene, show Iris the garden. She has never seen it before." And then, heartily firing fragments of sentences at us as though in explanation of this move of hers, she left the room, indicating that the rest was up to us.

Puzzled, we both went onto the terrace and into the yellow afternoon. We walked slowly down the steps toward the rose arbors, a long series of trellis arches forming a tunnel of green, bright with new flowers and ending in a cement fountain of ugly tile with a bench beside it shaded by elms.

We got to facts. By the time we had burrowed through the roses to the bench, we had exchanged those basic bits of information which usually make the rest fall (often incorrectly)

19

into some pattern, a foundation for those various architectures people together are pleased to build to celebrate friendship or enmity or love or, on very special occasions, in the case of a grand affair, a palace with rooms for all three, and much else besides.

Iris was from the Middle West, from a rich suburb of Detroit. This interested me in many ways, for there still existed in those days a real disaffection between East and Midwest and Far West which is hard to conceive nowadays in that gray homogeneity which currently passes for a civilized nation. I was an Easterner, a New Yorker from the Valley with Southern roots, and I felt instinctively that the outlanders were perhaps not entirely civilized. Needless to say, at the time, I would indignantly have denied this prejudice had someone attributed it to me, for those were the days of tolerance in which all prejudice had been banished, from conversation at least . . . though of course to banish prejudice is a contradiction in terms since, by definition, prejudice means prejudgment, and though time and experience usually explode for us all the prejudgments of our first years, they exist, nevertheless, as part of our subconscious, a sabotaging, irrational force, causing us to commit strange crimes indeed, made so much worse because they are often secret even to ourselves. I was, then, prejudiced against the Midwesterner, and against the Californian too. I felt that the former especially was curiously hostile to freedom, to the interplay of that rational Western culture which I had so lovingly embraced in my boyhood and grown up with, always conscious of my citizenship in the world, of my role as a humble but appreciative voice in the long conversation. I resented the automobile manufacturers who thought only of manufacturing objects, who distrusted ideas, who feared the fine with the primitive intensity of implacable ignorance. Could this cool girl be from Detroit? From that same rich suburb which had provided me with a number of handsome vital classmates at school? Boys who had combined physical vigor with a resistance to all ideas but those of their suburb, which could only be described as heroic considering the power of New England schools to crack even the toughest prejudices, at least on the rational level. That these boys did not possess a rational level had often occurred to me, though I did, grudgingly, admire, even in my scorn, their grace and strength as well as their confidence in that assembly line which had done so well by them.

Iris Mortimer was one of them. Having learned this there was nothing to do but find sufficient names between us to establish the beginnings of the rapport of class which, even in that late year of the mid-century, still existed: the dowdy aristocracy to which we belonged by virtue of financial security, at least in childhood, of education, of self-esteem and of houses where servants had been in some quantity before the second of the wars: all this we shared and of course those names in common of schoolmates, some from her region, others from mine, names which established us as being of an age. We avoided for some time any comment upon the names, withholding our true selves during the period of identification. I discovered too that she, like me, had remained unmarried, an exceptional state of affairs, for all the names we had mentioned represented two people now instead of one. Ours had been a reactionary generation. We had attempted to combat the time of wars and disasters by a scrupulous observance of our grandparents' customs, a direct reaction to the linking generation whose lives had been so entertainingly ornamented with untidy alliances and fortified by suspect gin. The result was no doubt classic but, at the same time, it was a little shocking. The children were decorous, subdued; they married early, conceived glumly, surrendered to the will of their own children in the interests of enlightened psychology; their lives enriched by the best gin in the better suburbs, safe among their own kind. Yet, miraculously, I had escaped and so apparently had Iris.

"You live here alone?" She indicated the wrong direction though taking in, correctly, the river on whose east bank I did live, a few miles to the north of Clarissa.

I nodded. "Entirely alone . . . in an old house."

"No family?"

"None here. Not much anywhere else. A few in New Orleans, my family's original base." I waited for her to ask if I ever got lonely living in a house on the river, remote from others; but she saw nothing extraordinary in this.

"It must be fine," she said slowly. She broke a leaf off a flowering bush whose branch, heavy with blooming, quivered above our heads as we sat on the garden bench and watched the dim flash of goldfish in the muddy waters of the pond.

"I like it," I said, a little disappointed that there was now no opportunity for me to construct one of my familiar defenses of a life alone. I had, in the five years since my days of travel had temporarily ended, many occasions on which to defend and glorify the solitary life I had chosen for myself beside this river. I had an ever-changing repertoire of feints and thrusts: for instance, with the hearty, I invariably questioned, gently of course, the virtue of a life in the city, confined to a small apartment with uninhibited babies and breathing daily large quantities of soot; at other times I assumed a prince of darkness pose, alone with his crimes in an ancient house, a figure which could, if necessary, be quickly altered to the more engaging one of remote observer of the ways of men, a Stoic among his books, sustained by the recorded fragments of forgotten bloody days, evoking solemnly the pure essences of nobler times, a chaste intelligence beyond the combat, a priest celebrating the cool memory of his race. My theater was extensive and I almost regretted that with Iris there was no need for even a brief curtain raiser, much less one of my exuberant galas.

Not accustomed to the neutral response, I stammered something about the pleasures of gardens. Iris's calm indifference saved me from what might have been a truly mawkish outburst calculated to interest her at any cost (mawkish because, I am confident, none of our deepest wishes or deeds is, finally, when honestly declared very wonderful or mysterious: simplicity, not complexity, is at the center of our being; fortunately the trembling "I" is seldom revealed, even to paid listeners, for conscious of the appalling directness of our needs, we wisely disguise their nature with a legerdemain of peculiar cunning). Much of Iris's attraction for me . . . and at the beginning that attraction did exist . . . was that one did not need to discuss so many things. Of course the better charades were not called into being, which, creatively speaking, was a pity. But then it was a relief *not* to pretend and, better still, a relief not to begin the business of plumbing shallows under the illusion that a treasure chest of truth might be found on the mind's sea floor . . . a grim ritual which was popular in those years, especially in the suburbs and housing projects where the mental therapists were ubiquitous and busy.

With Iris, one did not suspend, even at a cocktail party, the usual artifices of society. All was understood, or seemed to be, which is exactly the same thing. We talked about ourselves as though of absent strangers. Then: "Have you known Clarissa long?" I asked.

She shook her head. "I met her only recently."

"Then this is your first visit here? To the Valley?"

"The first," she smiled, "but it's a little like home, you know. I don't mean Detroit, but a memory of home, got from books."

I thought so too. Then she added that she did not read any longer and I was a little relieved. With Iris one wanted not to talk about books or the past. So much of her charm was that she was entirely in the present. It was her gift, perhaps her finest quality, to invest the moment with a significance which in recollection did not exist except as a blurred impression of excitement. She created this merely by existing. I was never to learn the trick, for her conversation was not, in itself, interesting and her actions were usually predictable, making all the more unusual her peculiar effect. She asked me politely about my work, giving me then the useful knowledge that, though she was interested in what *I* was doing, she was not much interested in the life of the Emperor Julian.

I made it short. "I want to do a biography of him. I've always liked history and so, when I settled down in the house, I chose Julian as my work."

"A life's work?"

"Hardly. But another few years. It's the reading which I most enjoy, and that's treacherous. There is so much of interest to read that it seems a waste of time and energy to write anything ... especially if it's to be only a reflection of reflections."

"Then why do it?"

"Something to say, I suppose. Or at least the desire to define and illuminate, from one's own point of view, of course."

"Then why ... Julian?"

Something in the way she said the name convinced me she had forgotten who he was if she had ever known.

"The apostasy; the last stand of paganism against Christianity."

She looked truly interested, for the first time. "They killed him, didn't they?"

"No, he died in battle. Had he lived longer he might at least have kept the Empire divided between the old gods and the new messiah. Unfortunately his early death was their death, the end of the gods."

"Except they returned as saints."

"Yes, a few found a place in Christianity, assuming new names."

"Mother of god," she murmured thoughtfully.

"An un-Christian concept, one would have thought," I added, though the beautiful illogic had been explained to me again and again by Catholics: how god could and could not at the same time possess a mother, that gleaming queen of heaven, entirely regnant in those days.

"I have often thought about these things," she said, diffidently. "I'm afraid I'm not much of a student but it fascinates me. I've been out in California for the past few years, working. I was on a fashion magazine." The note was exactly right. She knew precisely what the world meant and she was neither apologetic nor pleased. We both resisted the impulse to begin the names again, threading our way through the maze of fashion, through that frantic world of the peripheral arts.

"You kept away from Vedanta?" A group of transplanted English writers at this time had taken to Oriental mysticism, under the illusion that Asia began at Las Vegas. Swamis and temples abounded among the billboards and orange trees; but since it was *the* way for some, it was, for those few at least, honorable.

"I came close." She laughed. "But there was too much to read and even then I always felt that it didn't work for us, for Americans, I mean. It's probably quite logical and familiar to Asiatics, but we come from a different line, with a different history. Their responses aren't ours. But I did feel it was possible for others, which is a great deal."

"Because so much is *not* possible?"

"Exactly. But then I know very little about these things." She was direct. No implication that what she did not know either did not exist or was not worth the knowing, the traditional response in the fashionable world.

"Are you working now?"

She shook her head. "No, I gave it up. The magazine sent somebody to take my place out there (I didn't have the 'personality' they wanted) and so I came on to New York, where I've never really been, except for weekends from school. The magazine had some idea that I might work into the New York office, but I was through. I have worked."

"And had enough?"

"Of that sort of thing, yes. So I've gone out a lot in New York, met many people; thought a little . . . " She twisted the leaf that she still held in her fingers, her eyes vague as though focused on the leaf's faint shadow which fell in depth upon her dress, part upon her dress and more on a tree's branch ending finally in a tiny fragment of shadow on the ground, like the bottom step of a frail staircase of air.

"And here you are, at Clarissa's."

"What an extraordinary woman she is!" The eyes were turned upon me, hazel, clear, luminous with youth.

"She collects people, but not according to any of the usual criteria. She makes them all fit, somehow, but what it is they fit, what design, no one knows. *I* don't know, that is."

"I suppose I was collected. Though it might have been the other way around, since I am sure she interests me more than I do her."

"There is no way of telling."

"Anyway, I'm pleased she asked me here."

We talked of Clarissa with some interest, getting nowhere. Clarissa was truly enigmatic. She had lived for twenty years on the Hudson. She was not married but it was thought she had been. She entertained with great skill. She was in demand in New York and also in Europe, where she often traveled. But no one knew anything of her origin or of the source of her wealth and, oddly enough, although everyone observed her remarkable *idée fixe*, no one ever discussed it, as though in tactful obedience to some obscure sense of form. In the half-dozen years that I had known her, not once had I discussed with anyone her eccentricity. We accepted in her presence the reality of her mania, and there it ended. Some were more interested by it than others. I was fascinated, and having suspended both belief and doubt found her richly knowing in matters which interested me. Her accounts of various meetings with Libanius in Antioch were brilliant, all told most literally, as though she had no faculty for invention, which perhaps, terrifying thought, she truly lacked, in which case . . . but we chose not to speculate. Iris spoke of plans.

"I'm going back to California."

"Tired of New York?"

"No, hardly. But I met someone quite extraordinary out there, someone I think I should like to see again." Her candor made it perfectly clear that her interest was not romantic. "It's rather in line with what we were talking about. I mean your

Julian and all that. He's a kind of preacher."

"That doesn't sound promising." A goldfish made a popping sound as it captured a dragonfly on the pond's surface.

"But he isn't the usual sort at all. He's completely different but I'm not sure just how."

"An evangelist?" In those days loud men and women were still able to collect enormous crowds by ranging up and down the country roaring about that salvation which might be found in the bosom of the Lamb.

"No, his own sort of thing entirely. A little like the Vedanta teachers, only he's American, and young."

"What does he teach?"

"I . . . I'm not sure. No, don't laugh. I met him only once. At a friend's house in Santa Monica. He talked very little but one had the feeling that, well, that it was something unusual."

"It must have been if you can't recall what he said." I revised my first estimate. It was romantic after all. A man who was young, fascinating . . . I was almost jealous as a matter of principle.

"I'm afraid I don't make much sense." She gestured and the leaf fell into its own shadow on the grass. "Perhaps it was the effect he had on the others that impressed me. They were clever people, worldly people, yet they listened to him like children."

"What does he do? Does he live by preaching?"

"I don't know that either. I met him the night before I left California."

"And now you think you want to go back to find out?"

"Yes. I've thought about him a great deal these last few weeks. You'd think one would forget such a thing, but I haven't."

"What was his name?"

"Cave. John Cave."

"A pair of initials calculated to amaze the innocent." Yet even while I invoked irony, I felt with a certain chill in the heat that *this* was to be Clarissa's plot, and for many days afterward that name echoed in my memory, long after I had temporarily forgotten Iris's own name, had forgotten, as one does, the whole day, the peony in the boxwood, the leaf's fall and the catch of the goldfish; instants which now live again in the act of re-creation, details which were to fade into a yellow-green blur of June and of the girl beside me in a garden and of that name spoken in my hearing for the first time, becoming in my imagination like some bare monolith awaiting the sculptor's chisel.

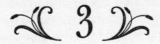

# 3

1

I did not see Iris again for some months. Nor, for that matter, did I see Clarissa, who the day after our lunch disappeared on one of her mysterious trips. Clarissa's comings and goings doubtless followed some pattern though I could never make much sense of them. I was very disappointed not to see her before she left because I had wanted to ask her about Iris and also . . .

\* \* \*

It has been a difficult day. Shortly after I wrote the lines above, this morning, I heard the sound of an American voice on the street side of the hotel; the first American voice I've heard in some years. Except for me, none has been allowed in Upper Egypt for twenty years. The division of the world has been quite thorough, religiously and politically, and had not some official long ago guessed my identity, it is doubtful that I should have been granted asylum even in this remote region.

I tried to continue with my writing but it was impossible: I could recall nothing. My attention would not focus on the past, on those wraiths which have lately begun to assume again such startling reality as I go about the work of memory . . . but the past was lost to me this morning. The doors shut and I was marooned in the meager present.

29

Who was this American who had come to Luxor? And why?

For a moment the serenity which I have so long practiced failed me and I feared for my life. Had the long-awaited assassins finally come? But then that animal within who undoes us all with his fierce will to live grew quiet, accepting again the discipline I have so long maintained over him, his obedience due less perhaps to my strong will than to his fatigue, for he is no longer given to the rages and terrors and exultations that once dominated me as the moon does the tide; his defeat is my old age's single victory, and a bitter one.

I took the pages that I had written and hid them in a wide crack in the marble-topped Victorian washstand. I then put on a tie and linen jacket and, cane in hand, my most bemused and guileless expression upon my face, I left the room and walked down the tall dim corridor to the lobby, limping perhaps a little more than was necessary, exaggerating my genuine debility to suggest, if possible, an even greater helplessness. If they had come at last to kill me, I thought it best to go to them while I still held in check the creature terror. As I approached the lobby, I recalled Cicero's death and took courage from his example. He too had been old and tired, too exasperated at the last even to flee.

My assassin (if such he is and I still do not know) looks perfectly harmless: a red-faced American in a white suit crumpled from heat and travel. In atrocious Arabic he was addressing the manager, who, though he speaks no English, is competent in French and accustomed to speaking it to Occidentals. My compatriot, however, was obstinate and smothered with a loud voice the polite European cadences of the manager.

I moved slowly to the desk, tapping emphatically with my cane on the tile floor. Both turned. It was the moment which I have so long dreaded. The eyes of an American were turned upon me once again. Would he know? *Does* he know? I felt all the blood leave my head. With a great effort, I remained on my feet. Steadying my voice, which has nowadays a tendency to quaver even when I am at ease, I said to the American, in our own language, the language I had not once spoken in nearly twenty years, "Can I be of assistance, sir?" The words sounded strange on my lips and I was aware that I had given them an ornateness which was quite unlike my usual speech. His look of surprise was, I think, perfectly genuine. I felt a cowardly relief: not yet, not yet.

"Oh!" The American stared at me stupidly for a moment (his face is able to suggest a marvelous range of incomprehension, as I have since discovered).

"My name is Richard Hudson," I said, pronouncing carefully the name by which I am known in Egypt, the name with which I have lived so long that it sometimes seems as if all my life before was only a dream, a fantasy of a time which never was except in reveries, in those curious waking dreams which I often have these days when I am tired, at sundown usually, and the mind loses all control over itself and the memory grows confused with imaginings, and I behold worlds and splendors which I have never known, yet they are vivid enough to haunt me even in the lucid mornings. I am dying, of course, and my brain is only letting up, releasing its images with a royal abandon, confusing everything like those surrealist works of art which had some vogue in my youth.

"Oh," said the American again and then, having accepted my reality, he pushed a fat red hand toward me. "The name is Butler, Bill Butler. Glad to meet you. Didn't expect to find another white . . . didn't expect to meet up with an American in these parts." I shook the hand.

"Let me help you," I said, releasing the hand quickly. "The manager speaks no English."

"I been studying Arabic," said Butler with a certain sullenness. "Just finished a year's course at Ottawa Center for this job. They don't speak it here like we studied it."

"It takes time," I said soothingly. "You'll catch the tone."

"Oh, I'm sure of that. Tell them I got a reservation." Butler mopped his full glistening cheeks with a handkerchief.

"You have a reservation for William Butler?" I asked the manager in French.

He shook his head, looking at the register in front of him. "Is he an American?" He looked surprised when I said that he was. "But it didn't sound like English."

"He was trying to speak Arabic."

The manager sighed. "Would you ask him to show me his passport and authorizations?"

I did as directed. Butler pulled a bulky envelope from his pocket and handed it to the manager. As well as I could, without appearing inquisitive, I looked at the papers. I could tell nothing. The passport was evidently in order. The numerous authorizations from the Egyptian government in the Pan-Arabic League, however, seemed to interest the manager intensely.

"Perhaps . . ." I began, but he was already telephoning the police. Though I speak Arabic with difficulty, I can understand it easily. The manager was inquiring at length about Mr. Butler and about his status in Egypt. The police chief evidently knew all about him and the conversation was short.

"Would you ask him to sign the register?" The manager's expression was puzzled. I wondered what on earth it was all about.

"Don't know why there's all this confusion," said Butler, carving his name into the register with the ancient pen. "I wired for a room last week from Cairo."

"Communications have not been perfected in the Arab countries," I said (fortunately for me, I thought to myself).

When he had done registering, a boy came and took his bags and the key to his room.

"Much obliged to you, Mr. Hudson."

"Not at all."

"Like to see something of you, if you don't mind. Wonder if you could give me an idea of the lay of the land."

I said I should be delighted and we made a date to meet for tea in the cool of the late afternoon, on the terrace.

When he had gone, I asked the manager about him but though my old friend has been manager for twelve years and looks up to me as an elder statesman, since I have lived in the hotel longer than anyone, he would tell me nothing. "It's too much for me, sir." And I could get no more out of him.

2

The terrace was nearly cool when we met at six o'clock, the hour when the Egyptian sun, having just lost its unbearable gold, falls, a scarlet disc, into the white stone hills across the river which, at this season, winds narrowly among the mud flats, a third of its usual size, diminished by heat.

"Don't suppose we could order a drink . . . not that I'm much of a drinking man. But you get quite a thirst on a day like this."

I told him that since foreigners had ceased to come here, the bar had been closed down. Moslems for religious reasons did not use alcohol.

"I know, I know," he said. "Studied all about them, even read the Koran. Frightful stuff, too."

"No worse than most documents revealed by heaven," I said gently, not wanting to get on to that subject. "But tell me what brings you to these parts."

"I was going to ask *you* the same thing," said Butler genially, taking the cup of mint tea which the servant had brought him. On the river a felucca with a red sail tacked slowly in the hot breeze. "The manager tells me you've been here for twenty years."

"You must have found a language in common."

Butler chuckled. "These devils understand you well enough if they want to. But you . . ."

"I was an archaeologist at one time," I said, and I told him the familiar story which I have repeated so many times now that I have almost come to believe it. "I was from Boston originally. Do you know Boston? I often think of those cold winters with a certain longing. Too much light can be as trying as too little. Some twenty years ago, I decided to retire, to write a book of memoirs." This was a new, plausible touch. "Egypt was always my single passion and so I came to Luxor, to this hotel where I've been quite content, though hardly industrious."

"How come they let you in? I mean there was all that trouble back when the Pan-Arabic League shut itself off from civilization."

"I was very lucky, I suppose. I had many friends in the academic world of Cairo and they were able to grant me a special dispensation."

"Old hand, then, with the natives?"

"But a little out of practice. All my Egyptian friends have seen fit to die and I live now as if I were already dead myself."

This had the desired effect of chilling him. Though he was hardly fifty, the immediacy of death, even when manifested in the person of a chance acquaintance, does inspire a certain gravity.

He mumbled something which I did not catch. I think my hearing has begun to go. Not that I am deaf but I have, at times, a monotonous buzzing in my ears which makes conversation difficult. According to the local doctor my arteries have hardened and at any moment one is apt to burst among the convolutions of the brain, drowning my life. But I do not dwell on this, at least not in conversation.

"There's been a big shake-up in the Atlantic Community. Don't suppose you'd hear much about it around here since from the newspapers I've seen in Egypt they have a pretty tight censorship."

I said I knew nothing about recent activities in the Atlantic Community or anywhere else, other than Egypt.

"Well they've worked out an alliance with Pan-Arabia that will open the whole area to us. Of course no oil exploitation is allowed but there'll still be a lot of legitimate business between our sphere and these people."

I listened to him patiently while he explained the state of the world to me. It seemed unchanged. The only difference was that there were now new and unfamiliar names in high places. He finished with a patriotic harangue about the necessity of the civilized to work in harmony together for the good of mankind. "And this opening up of Egypt has given us the chance we've been waiting for for years, and we mean to take it."

"You mean to extend trade?"

"No, I mean the Word."

"The Word?" I repeated numbly, the old fear returning.

"Why sure. I'm a Cavite Communicator." He rapped perfunctorily on the table twice. I tapped feebly with my cane on the tile: in the days of the Spanish persecution such signals were a means of secret communication (not that the persecution had really been so great, but it had been our decision to dramatize it in order that our people might become more conscious of their splendid if temporary isolation and high destiny); it had not occurred to me that, triumphant, the Cavites should still cling to those bits of fraternal ritual which I had conceived with a certain levity in the early days. But of course the love of ritual, of symbol, is peculiar to our race, and I reflected bleakly on this as I returned the signal which identified us as brother Cavites.

"The world must have changed indeed," I said at last. "It was a Moslem law that no foreign missionaries be allowed in the Arab League."

"Pressure!" Butler looked very pleased. "Nothing obvious, of course; had to be done, though."

"For economic reasons?"

"No, for Cavesword. That's what we're selling because that's the one thing we've got." And he blinked seriously at the remnant of scarlet sun; his voice husky, like that of a man selling some commodity on television in the old days. Yet the note of sincerity, whether simulated or genuine, was unmistakably resolute.

"You may have a difficult time," I said, not wanting to go on

35

with this conversation but unable to direct it short of walking away. "The Moslems are very stubborn in their faith."

Butler laughed confidently. "We'll change all that. It may not be easy at first because we've got to go slow, feel our way, but once we know the lay of the land, you might say, we'll be able to produce some big backing, some real big backing."

His meaning was unmistakable. Already I could imagine those Squads of the Word in action throughout this last terrestrial refuge. Long ago, they had begun as eager instruction teams. After the first victories, however, they had become adept at demoralization, at brainwashing and auto-hypnosis, using all the psychological weapons that our race in its ingenuity had fashioned in the mid-century, becoming so subtle with the passage of time that imprisonment or execution for unorthodoxy was no longer necessary. Even the most recalcitrant, virtuous man could be reduced to a sincere and useful orthodoxy, no different in quality from his former antagonists, his moment of rebellion forgotten, his reason anchored securely at last in the general truth. I was also quite confident that their methods had improved even since my enlightened time.

"I hope you'll be able to save these poor people," I said, detesting myself for this hypocrisy.

"Not a doubt in the world," he clapped his hands. "They don't know what happiness we'll bring them." Difficult as it was to accept such hyperbole, I believed in his sincerity. Butler is one of those zealots without whose offices no large work in the world can be successfully propagated. I did not feel more than a passing pity for the Moslems. They were doomed but their fate would not unduly distress them, for my companion was perfectly right when he spoke of the happiness which would be theirs: a blithe mindlessness that would in no way affect their usefulness as citizens. We had long since determined that this was the only humane way of ridding the mass of superstition in the interest of Cavesword and the better life.

"Yet it *is* strange that they should let you in," I said, quite aware that he might be my assassin after all, permitted by the Egyptian government to destroy me and, with me, the last true memory of the mission. It was not impossible that Butler was an accomplished actor, sounding me out before the final victory of the Cavites, the necessary death and total obliteration of the person of Eugene Luther, now grown old with a false name in a burning land.

If Butler is an actor, he is a master. He thumped on interminably about America, John Cave and the necessity of spreading his word throughout the world. I listened patiently as the sun went abruptly behind the hills and all the stars appeared against the moonless waste of sky. Fires appeared in the hovels on the far shore of the Nile, yellow points of light like fireflies hovering by that other river which I shall never see again.

"Must be nearly suppertime."

"Not quite," I said, relieved that Butler's face was now invisible. I was not used to great red faces after my years in Luxor among the lean, the delicate and the dark. Now only his voice was a dissonance in the evening.

"Hope the food's edible."

"It isn't bad, though it may take some getting used to."

"Well, I've got a strong stomach. Guess that's why they chose me for this job."

This job? Could it mean. . . ? But I refused to let myself be panicked. I have lived too long with terror to be much moved now: especially since my life by its very continuation has brought me to nothing's edge. "Are there many of you?" I asked politely. The day was ending and I was growing weary, all senses blunted and some confused. "Many Communicators?"

"Quite a few. They've been training us for the last year in Canada for the big job of opening up Pan-Arabia. Of course we've known for years that it was just a matter of time before the government got us in here."

"Then you've been thoroughly grounded in the Arab culture? And disposition?"

"Oh, sure. Of course I may have to come to you every now and then, if you don't mind." He chuckled to show that his patronage would be genial.

"I should be honored to assist."

"We anticipate trouble at first. We have to go slow. Pretend we're just available for instruction while we get to know the local big shots. Then, when the time comes . . ." He left the ominous sentence unfinished. I could imagine the rest. Fortunately, nature by then, with or without Mr. Butler's assistance, would have removed me as a witness.

Inside the hotel the noise of plates being moved provided a familiar reference. I was conscious of being hungry. As the body's mechanism jolts to a halt, it wants more fuel than it ever did at its optimum. I wanted to go in, but before I could gracefully extricate myself Butler asked me a question. "You the only American in these parts?"

I said that I was.

"Funny, nothing was said about there being *any* American up here. I guess they didn't know you were here."

"Perhaps they were counting me among the American colony at Cairo," I said smoothly. "I suppose, officially, I am a resident of that city. I was on the Advisory Board of the Museum." This was not remotely true but since, to my knowledge, there is no Advisory Board it would be difficult for anyone to establish my absence from it.

"That must be it." Butler seemed easily satisfied, perhaps too easily. "Certainly makes things a lot easier for us, having somebody like you up here, another Cavite, who knows the lingo."

"I'll help in any way I can. Although I'm afraid I have passed the age of usefulness. Like the British king, I can only advise."

"Well, that's enough. I'm the active one anyway. My partner takes care of the other things."

"Partner? I thought you were alone."

"No. I'm to dig my heels in first; then my colleague comes on in a few weeks. That's standard procedure. He's a psychologist and an authority on Cavesword. We all are, of course – authorities, that is – but he's gone into the early history and so on a little more thoroughly than us field men usually do."

So there was to be another one, a clever one. I found myself both dreading and looking forward to the arrival of this dangerous person. It would be interesting to deal with a good mind again, or at least an instructed one, though Butler has not given me much confidence in the new Cavite Communicators. Nevertheless, I am intensely curious about the Western world since my flight from it. I have been effectively cut off from any real knowledge of the West for two decades. Rumors, stray bits of information, sometimes penetrate as far as Luxor but I can make little sense of them, for the Cavites are, as I well know, not given to candor, while the Egyptian newspapers exist in a fantasy world of Pan-Arabic dominion. There was so much I wished to know that I hesitated to ask Butler, not for fear of giving myself away but because I felt that any serious conversation with him would be pointless. I rather doubted if he knew what he was supposed to know, much less all the details that I wished to know and that even a moderately intelligent man, if not hopelessly zealous, might be able to supply me with.

I had a sudden idea. "You don't happen to have a recent edition of the Testament, do you? Mine's quite old and out of date."

"What date?" This was unexpected.

"The year? I don't recall. About thirty years old, I should say."

There was a silence. "Of course yours is a special case, being marooned like this. There's a ruling about it which I think will protect you fully since you've had no contact with the outside. Anyway, as a Communicator, I must ask you for your old copy."

"Why, certainly, but . . ."

"I'll give you a new one, of course. You see it is against the law to have any Testament which predates the second Cavite Council."

I was beginning to understand. After the schism a second Council had been inevitable even though no reference to it has ever appeared in the Egyptian press. "The censorship here is thorough," I said. "I had no idea there had been a new Council."

"What a bunch of savages!" Butler groaned with disgust. "That's going to be one of our main jobs, you know, education, freeing the press. There has been almost no communication between the two spheres of influence. . . . "

"Spheres of influence." How easily the phrase came to his lips! All the jargon of the journalists of fifty years ago has, I gather, gone into the language, providing the inarticulate with a number of made-up phrases calculated to blur their none too clear meanings. I assume of course that Butler is as inarticulate as he seems, that he is typical of the first post-Cavite generation.

"You must give me a clear picture of what has been happening in America since my retirement." But I rose to prevent him from giving me, at the moment at least, any further observations on "spheres of influence."

I stood for a moment, resting on my cane. I had stood up too quickly and as usual suffered a spell of dizziness. I was also ravenously hungry. Butler stamped out a cigarette on the tile.

"Be glad to tell you anything you want to know. That's my business." He laughed shortly. "Well, time for chow. I've got some anti-bacteria tablets they gave us before we came out, supposed to keep the food from poisoning us."

"I'm sure you won't need them here."

He kept pace with my slow shuffle. "Well, it increases eating pleasure, too." Inadvertently, I shuddered as I recognized yet another glib phrase from the past. It had seemed such a good idea to exploit the vulgar language of the advertisers. I suffered a brief spasm of guilt.

## 3

We dined together in the airy salon, deserted at this season except for a handful of government officials and businessmen who eyed us without much interest, even though Americans are not a common sight in Egypt. They were of course used to me although, as a rule, I kept out of sight, taking my meals in my room and frequenting those walks along the river bank which avoid altogether the town of Luxor.

I found, after I had dined, that physically I was somewhat restored, better able to cope with Butler. In fact, inadvertently, I actually found myself, in the madness of my great age, enjoying his company, a sure proof of loneliness if not of senility. He too, after taking pills calculated to fill him "chock full of vim and vigor" (that is indeed the phrase he used), relaxed considerably and spoke of his life in the United States. He had no talent for evoking what he would doubtless call "the big picture" but in a casual, disordered way he was able to give me a number of details about his own life and work which did suggest the proportions of the world from which he had so recently come and which I had, in my folly, helped create.

On religious matters he was unimaginative and doctrinaire, concerned with the letter of the commands and revelations rather than with the spirit, such as it was or is. I could not resist the dangerous maneuver of asking him, at the correct moment of course (we were speaking of the time of the schisms), what had become of Eugene Luther.

"Who?"

The coffee cup trembled in my hand. I set it carefully on the table. I wondered if *his* hearing was sound. I repeated my own name, long lost to me, but mine still in the secret dimness of memory.

"I don't place the name. Was he a friend of the Liberator?"

"Why, yes. I even used to know him slightly but that was many years ago, before your time. I'm curious to know what might have become of him. I suppose he's dead."

"I'm sorry but I don't place the name." He looked at me with some interest. "I guess you must be almost old enough to have seen *him*."

I nodded, lowering my lids with a studied reverence, as though dazzled at the recollection of great light. "I saw him several times."

"Boy, I envy you! There aren't many left who have seen *him* with their own eyes. What was he like?"

"Just like his photographs," I said, shifting the line of inquiry: there is always the danger that a trap is being prepared for me. I was noncommittal, preferring to hear Butler talk of himself. Fortunately, he preferred this too, and for nearly an hour I learned as much as I shall ever need to know about the life of at least one Communicator of Cavesword. While he talked, I watched him furtively for some sign of intention but there was none that I could detect. Yet I am suspicious. He had not known my name and I could not understand what obscure motive might cause him to pretend ignorance, unless of course he *does* know who I am and wishes to confuse me, preparatory to some trap.

I excused myself soon afterward and went to my room, after first accepting a copy of the newest Testament handsomely bound in Plasticon (it looks like plastic) and promising to give him my old proscribed copy the next day.

The first thing that I did, after locking the door to my room, was to take the book over to my desk and open it to the index. My eye traveled down that column of familiar names until it came to the Ls.

At first I thought that my eyes were playing a trick upon me. I held the page close to the light, wondering if I might not have begun to suffer delusions, the not unfamiliar concomitant of solitude and old age. But my eyes were adequate and the hallucination, if real, was vastly convincing. My name was no longer there. Eugene Luther no longer existed in that Testament which was largely his own composition.

I let the book shut of itself, as new books will. I sat down at the desk, understanding at last the extraordinary ignorance of Butler. I had been obliterated from history. My place in time was erased. It was as if I had never lived.

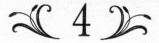

## 4

### 1

I have had in the last few days some difficulty in avoiding the company of Mr. Butler. Fortunately, he is now very much involved with the local functionaries and I am again able to return to my narrative. I don't think Butler has been sent here to assassinate me but, on the other hand, from certain things he has said and not said, I am by no means secure in his ignorance; however, one must go on. At best, it will be a race between him and those hardened arteries which span the lobes of my brain. My only curiosity concerns the arrival next week of his colleague, who is, I gather, of the second generation and of a somewhat bookish turn according to Butler – who would not, I fear, be much of a judge. Certain things that I have learned during the last few days about Iris Mortimer make me more than ever wish to recall our common years as precisely as possible, for what I feared might happen has indeed, if Butler is to be believed, come to pass, and it is now with a full burden of hindsight that I revisit the scenes of a half-century ago.

### 2

I had got almost nowhere with my life of Julian. I had become discouraged with his personality though his actual writings continued to delight me. As so often happens in history I had found it difficult really to get at him. The human attractive

44

part of Julian was undone for me by those bleak errors in deed and in judgment which depressed me even though they derived most logically from the man and his time: that fatal wedding which finally walls off figures of earlier ages from the present, keeping them strange despite the most intense and imaginative re-creation. They are not we. We are not they. And I refused to resort to the low trick of fashioning Julian in my own image. I respected his integrity in time and deplored the division of centuries. My work at last came to a halt and, somewhat relieved, I closed my house in the autumn of the year and traveled west to California.

I had a small income which made modest living and careful travel easy for me . . . a happy state of affairs since, in my youth, I was of an intense disposition, capable of the passions and violence of a Rimbaud without, fortunately, the will to translate them into reality. Had I had more money, or none, I might have died young, leaving behind the brief memory of a minor romanticist. As it was, I had a different role to play in the comedy; one for which I was, after some years of reading beside my natal river, peculiarly fitted to play.

I journeyed to southern California, where I had not been since my service in one of the wars. I had never really explored that exotic land and I was curious about it, more curious than I have ever been before or since about any single part of the world. Egypt one knows without visiting it, and China the same; but Los Angeles is unique in its bright horror.

Naturally, one was excited by the movies, even though at that time they had lost much of their hold over the public imagination, unlike earlier decades when the process of film before light could project, larger than life, not only on vast screens but also upon impressionable minds of an enormous audience made homogeneous by a common passion, shadowy figures which, like the filmy envelopes of Stoic deities, floated to earth in public dreams, suggesting a brave and perfect world where love reigned and only the wicked died. But then time passed and the new deities lost their worshipers. There were too many gods and the devotees got too used to them, realizing finally that they were only mortals, involved not in magical rites but in a sordid business. Television (the home altar) succeeded the movies and their once populous and ornate temples, modeled tastefully on baroque and Byzantine themes, fell empty, as the old gods moved to join the new hierarchies, becoming the domesticated godlings of television which, although it held the attention of the majority of the population, did not enrapture, nor possess dreams or shape days with longing and with secret imaginings the way the classic figures of an earlier time had. Though I was of an age to recall the gallant days of the movies, the nearly mythical power which they had held for millions of people, not all simple, I was more intrigued by the manners, by the cults, by the works of this coastal people so unlike the older world of the East and so antipathetic to our race's first home in Europe. Needless to say, I found them much like everyone else, except for minor differences of no real consequence.

I stayed at a large hotel not too happily balanced in design between the marble-and-potted-palm décor of the Continental Hotel in Paris and the chrome and glass of an observation car on a train.

I unpacked and telephoned friends, most of whom were not home. The one whom I found in was the one I knew the least, a minor film writer who had recently married money and given up the composition of films, for which the remaining moviegoers were no doubt thankful. He devoted his time to assisting his wife in becoming the first hostess of Beverly Hills. She had, I recalled from one earlier meeting, the mind of a child of twelve, but an extremely active child and a good one.

Hastings, such was the writer's name (her name was either Ethel or Valerie, two names which I always confuse because of a particularly revolutionary course I once took in mnemonics), invited me to a party. I went.

It seemed like spring though it was autumn, and it seemed like an assortment of guests brought together in a ship's dining room to celebrate New Year's Eve, though in fact the gathering was largely made up of close acquaintances. Since I knew almost no one, I had a splendid time.

After a brilliant greeting my hostess, a gold figure all in green with gold dust in her hair, left me alone. Hastings was more solicitous, a nervous gray man with a speech impediment which took the form of a rather charming sigh before any word which began with an aspirate.

"We, ah, have a better place coming up. Farther up the hills with a marvelous view of the, ah, whole city. You will love it, Gene. Ah, haven't signed a lease yet, but soon." While we talked he steered me through the crowds of handsome and bizarre people (none of them was from California, I discovered). I was introduced to magnificent girls exactly resembling their movie selves. I told a striking blonde that she would indeed be excellent in a musical version of Bhagavad-Gita. She thought so too and my host and I moved on to the patio.

Beside a jade-green pool illuminated from beneath (and a little dirty, I noticed, with leaves floating upon the water: the décor was becoming tarnished, the sets had been used too long and needed striking. Hollywood was becoming old with distinction), a few of the quieter guests sat in white iron chairs while paper lanterns glowed prettily on the palms and everywhere, untidily, grew roses, jasmine and lilac, all out of season and out of place. The guests beside the pool were much the same; except for one: Clarissa.

"You know each other?" Hastings's voice, faintly pleased, was drowned by our greetings and I was pulled into a chair by Clarissa, who had elected to dress herself like an odalisque which made her look more indigenous than any of the other guests. This was perhaps her genius: her adaptiveness.

"We'll be quite happy here," said Clarissa, waving our host away. "Go and abuse your other guests."

Hastings trotted off. Those who had been talking to Clarissa talked to themselves and beneath a flickering lantern the lights of Los Angeles, revealed in a wedge between two hills, added the proper note of lunacy, for at the angle from which I viewed those lights they seemed to form a monster Christmas tree, poised crazily in the darkness.

Clarissa and I exchanged notes on the months that had intervened since our luncheon.

"And you gave up Julian, too?"

"Yes . . . but why 'too'?" I was irritated by the implication.

"I feel you don't finish things, Eugene. Not that you should; but I *do* worry about you."

"It's good of you," I said, discovering that at a certain angle the Christmas tree could be made to resemble a rocket's flare arrested in space.

"Now don't take that tone with me. I have your interest at heart." She expressed herself with every sign of sincerity in that curious flat language which she spoke so fluently yet which struck upon the ear untruly, as though it were, in its homeliness, the highest artifice.

"But I've taken care of everything, you know. Wait and see. If you hadn't come out here on your own I should have sent for you . . ."

"And I would have come?"

"Naturally." She smiled.

"But for what?"

"For . . . *she's* here. In Los Angeles."

"You mean that girl who came to lunch?" I disguised my interest, but Clarissa, ignoring me, went on talking as energetically and as obliquely as ever.

"She's asked for you several times, which is a good sign. I told her I suspected you'd be along but that one never could tell, especially if you were still tied up with Julian, unlikely as that prospect was."

"But I do finish some things."

"I'm sure you do. In any case, the girl has been here over a month and you must see her as soon as possible."

"I'd like to."

48

"Of course you would. I still have my plot, you know. Oh, you may think I forget things but I don't. My mind is a perfect filing system."

"Could you tell me just *what* you are talking about?"

She chuckled and wagged a finger at me. "Soon you'll know. I know I meddle a good deal, more than I should, but after all this time it would be simply impossible for me *not* to interfere. I see it coming, one of those really exciting moments, and I want just to give it a tickle here, a push there to set it rolling. Oh, what fun it will be!"

Hastings crept back among us, diffidently pushing a star and a producer in our direction. "I think you all ought to know each other, Clarissa . . . and, ah, Gene too. This is Miss . . . and Mr. . . . and here in Hollywood . . . when you get to New York . . . . house on the river, wonderful, old . . . new film to cost five million . . . runner-up for the Academy Award." He did it all very well, I thought. Smiles gleamed in the patio's half-light. The star's paste jewels, borrowed from her studio, glimmered like an airliner's lighted windows. I moved toward the house, but Clarissa's high voice restrained me at the door: "You'll call Iris tomorrow, won't you?" and she shouted an exchange and a number. I waved to show that I'd heard her; then, vowing I would never telephone Iris, I rejoined the party and watched with fascination as the various performers performed in the living room to the accompaniment of a grand piano just barely out of tune.

3

I waited several days before I telephoned Iris. Days of considerable activity, of visiting friends and acquaintances, of attending parties where the guests were precisely the same as the ones I had met at Hastings's house.

I met Iris at the house where she was staying near the main beach of Santa Monica, in a decorous Spanish house, quiet among palms and close to the sea. The day was vivid; the sea made noise; the wind was gentle, smelling of salt.

I parked my rented car and walked around to the sea side of the house. Iris came forward to meet me, smiling, hand outstretched. Her face, which I had remembered as being remarkably pale, was flushed with sunlight.

"I hoped you'd come," she said, and she slipped her arm in mine as though we had been old friends and led me to a deck chair adjoining the one where she'd been seated reading. We sat down. "Friends let me have this place. They went to Mexico for two months."

"Useful friends."

"Aren't they? I've already put down roots here in the sand and I'll hate to give it back."

"Don't."

"Ah, wouldn't it be wonderful." She smiled vaguely and looked beyond me at the flash of sea in the flat distance. An automobile horn sounded through the palms; a mother called her child; we were a part of the world, even here.

"Clarissa told me you've been here several months."

Iris nodded. "I came back. I think I told you I was going to."

"To see the man?"

"Would you like something to drink?" She changed the subject with a disconcerting shift of gaze from ocean to me, her eyes still dazzled with the brilliance of light on water. I looked away and shook my head.

"Too early in the day. But I want to take you to dinner tonight, if I may. Somewhere along the coast."

"I'd like it very much."

"Do you know of a place?"

She suggested several. Then we went inside and she showed me a room where I might change into my bathing suit.

We walked through the trees to the main road, on the other side of which the beach glowed in the sun. It was deserted at this point although, in the distance, other bathers could be seen, tiny figures, moving about like insects on a white cloth.

For a time we swam contentedly, not speaking, not thinking, our various urgencies (or their lack) no longer imposed upon the moment. At such times, in those days, I was able through the body's strenuous use to reduce the miserable demands of the yearning self to a complacent harmony, with all things in proper proportion: a part of the whole and not the whole itself, though, metaphorically speaking, perhaps whatever conceives reality is reality itself. But such nice divisions and distinctions were of no concern to me that afternoon in the sun, swimming with Iris, the mechanism which spoils time with questioning switched off by the body's euphoria.

And yet, for all this, no closer to one another, no wiser about one another in any precise sense, we drove that evening in silence to a restaurant on the beach to the north: a ramshackle, candle-lit place, smelling of tar and hung with old nets. After wine and fish and coffee, we talked.

"Clarissa is bringing us together."

I nodded, accepting the plain statement as a fact. "The matchmaking instinct is, I suppose . . ."

"Not that at all." Her face was in half-light and looked as it had when we first met: pale, withdrawn, all the day's color drained out of it. Into the sea, the evening star all silver set. We were early and had the place to ourselves.

"Then what? Clarissa never does anything that doesn't contribute to some private design . . . though what she's up to half the time I don't dare guess."

Iris smiled. "Nor I. But she is at least up to something which concerns us both and I'm not sure that she may not be right, about the two of us, I mean . . . though of course it's too soon to say."

I was conventional enough at first to assume that Iris was speaking of ourselves, most boldly, in terms of some emotional attachment and I wondered nervously how I might indicate without embarrassment to her that I was effectively withdrawn from all sexuality and that, while my emotions were in no way impaired, I had been forced to accept a physical limitation to

51

any act of affection which I might direct at another; consequently, I avoided as well as I could those situations which might betray me, and distress another. Though I have never been unduly grieved by this incompletion, I had come to realize only too well from several disquieting episodes in my youth that this flaw in me possessed the unanticipated power of shattering others who, unwarily, had moved to join with me in the traditional duet only to find an implacable surface where they had anticipated a creature of flesh like themselves, as eager as they, as governed by the blood's solemn tide. I had caused pain against my will and I did not want Iris hurt.

Fortunately, Iris had begun to move into a different, an unexpected, conjunction with me, one which had in it nothing of the familiar or even of the human. It was in that hour beneath Orion's glitter that we were, without warning, together volatilized onto that archetypal plane where we were to play with such ferocity at being gods, a flawed Mercury and a dark queen of heaven, met at the sea's edge, disguised as human beings but conscious of one another's true identity, for though our speeches, our arias, were all prose, beneath the usual talk recognition had occurred, sounding with the deep resonance of a major chord struck among dissonances.

We crossed the first division easily. She was, in her way, as removed as I from the flesh's wild need to repeat itself in pleasure. There was no need for us ever to discuss my first apprehension. We were able to forget ourselves, to ignore the mortal carriage. The ritual began simply enough.

"Clarissa knows what is happening here. That's why she has come West, though she can't bear California. She wants to be in on it the way she's in on everything else, or thinks she is."

"You mean John Cave, your *magus*?" It was the first time I had ever said that name. The sword was between us now, both edges sharp.

"You guessed? Or did she tell you that was why I came back?"

"I assumed it. I remembered what you said to me last spring."

"He is more than . . . *magus*, Eugene." And this was the first time she had said *my* name: closer, closer. I waited. "You will see him." I could not tell if this was intended as a question or a prophecy. I nodded. She continued to talk, her eyes on mine, intense and shining. Over her shoulder the night was black and all the stars flared twice, once in the sky and once upon the whispering smooth ocean at our feet, one real and one illusion, both light.

"It is really happening," she said and then, deliberately, she lightened her voice. "You'll see when you meet him. I know of course that there have been thousands of these prophets, these saviors in every country and in every time. I also know that this part of America is particularly known for religious maniacs. I started with every prejudice, just like you."

"Not prejudice . . . skepticism; perhaps indifference. Even if he should be one of the chosen wonderworkers, should I care? I must warn you, Iris, that I'm not a believer. And though I'm sure that the revelations of other men must be a source of infinite satisfaction to them individually, I shouldn't for one second be so presumptuous as to make a choice among the many thousands of recorded revelations of truth, accepting one at the expense of all the others. I might so easily choose wrong and get into eternal trouble. And you must admit that the selection is wide, and dangerous to the amateur."

"You're making fun of me," said Iris, but she seemed to realize that I was approaching the object in my own way. "He's not like that at all."

"But obviously if he is to be useful he must be accepted, and he can't be accepted without extending his revelation or whatever he calls it, and I fail to see how he can communicate, short of hypnotism or drugs, the sense of his vision to someone like myself who, in a sloppy but devoted way, has wandered through history and religion, acquiring with a collector's delight the more colourful and obscure manifestations of divine guidance, revealed to us through the inspired systems of philosophers and divines, not to mention such certified prophets as the custodians of the Sibylline books. *'Illo die hostem Romanorum esse periturum'* was the instruction given poor Maxentius when he marched against Constantine. Needless to say he perished and consequently fulfilled the prophecy by *himself* becoming the enemy of Rome, to his surprise I suspect. My point, though, in honoring you with the only complete Latin sentence which I can ever recall is that at no time can we escape the relativity of our judgments. Truth for us, whether inspired by messianic frenzy or merely illuminated by reason, is, after all, inconstant and subject to change with the hour. You believe now whatever it is this man says. Splendid. But will the belief be true to you at another hour of your life? I wonder. For even if you wish to remain consistent and choose to ignore inconvenient evidence in the style of the truly devoted, the truly pious, will not your prophet *himself* have changed with time's passage? No human being can remain the same, despite the repetition of . . ."

"Enough, enough!" she laughed aloud and put her hand between us as though to stop the words in air. "You're talking such nonsense."

"Perhaps. It's not at all easy to say what one thinks when it comes to these problems or, for that matter, to any problem which demands statement. Sometimes one is undone by the flow of words assuming its own direction, carrying one, protesting, away from the anticipated shore to *terra incognita*. Other times, at the climax of a particularly telling analogy, one is aware that in the success of words the meaning has got lost. Put in this way, finally, *accurately:* I accept no man's authority in that realm where we are all equally ignorant. The beginning and the end of creation are not our concern. The eventual disposition of the human personality which we treasure in our conceit as being the finest ornament of an envious universe is unknown to us and shall so remain until we learn the trick of raising the dead. God, or what have you, will not be found at the far end of a syllogism, no matter how brilliantly phrased and conceived. We are prisoners in our flesh, dullards in divinity as the Greeks would say. No man can alter this, though of course human beings can be made to *believe* anything. You can teach that fire is cold and ice is hot but nothing changes except the words. So what can your *magus* do? What can he celebrate except what is visible and apparent to all eyes? What can he offer me that I should accept his authority, and its source?"

She sighed. "I'm not sure he wants anything for himself; acceptance, authority . . . one doesn't think of such things, at least not now. As for his speaking with the voice of some new or old deity, he denies the reality of any power other than the human . . ."

"A strange sort of messiah."

"I've been trying to tell you this." She smiled. "He sounds at times not unlike you just now . . . not so glib perhaps. "

"Now *you* mock *me*."

"No more than you deserve for assuming facts without evidence."

"If he throws over all the mystical baggage, what is left? An ethical system?"

"In time, I suppose, that will come. So far there is no system. You'll see for yourself soon enough."

"You've yet to answer any direct question I have put to you."

She laughed. "Perhaps there is a significance in that; perhaps you ask the wrong questions."

"And perhaps you have no answers."

"Wait."

"For how long?"

She looked at her watch by the candles' uncertain light. "For an hour."

"You mean we're to see him tonight?"

"Unless you'd rather not."

"Oh, I want to see him, very much."

"He'll want to see you too, I think." She looked at me thoughtfully but I could not guess her intention; it was enough that two lines had crossed, both moving inexorably toward a third, toward a terminus at the progression's heart.

4

It is difficult now to recall just what I expected. Iris deliberately chose not to give me any clear idea of either the man or of his teachings or even of the meeting which we were to attend. We talked of other things as we drove by starlight north along the ocean road, the sound of waves striking sand loud in our ears.

It was nearly an hour's drive from the restaurant to the place where the meeting was to be held. Iris directed me accurately and we soon turned from the main highway into a non-lighted street; then off into a suburban area of comfortable-looking middle-class houses with gardens. Trees lined the streets; dogs barked; yellow light gleamed at downstairs windows. Silent families were gathered in after-dinner solemnity before television sets, absorbed by the spectacle of blurred gray figures telling jokes.

As we drove down the empty streets, I imagined ruins and dust where houses were and, among the powdery debris of stucco all in mounds, the rusted antennae of television sets like the bones of awful beasts whose vague but terrible proportions will alone survive to attract the unborn stranger's eye. But the loathing of one's own time is a sign of innocence, of faith. I have come since to realize the wholeness of man in time. That year, perhaps that ride down a deserted evening street of a California suburb, was my last conscious moment of specified disgust: television, the Blues and the Greens, the perfidy of Carthage, the efficacy of rites to the moon . . . all are at last the same.

"That house over there, with the light in front, with the clock."

The house, to my surprise, was a large neo-Georgian funeral parlor with a lighted clock in front crowned by a legend discreetly fashioned in Gothic gold on black: *Whittaker and Dormer, Funeral Directors*. Since a dozen cars had been parked in the front of the house, I was forced to park nearly a block away.

We walked along the sidewalk; street lamps behind trees cast shadows thick and intricate upon the pavement. "Is there any particular significance?" I asked. "I mean in the choice of meeting place?"

She shook her head. "Not really, no. We meet wherever it's convenient. Mr. Dormer is one of us and has kindly offered his chapel for the meetings."

"Is there any sort of ritual I should observe?"

She laughed. "Of course not. This isn't at all what you think."

"I think nothing."

"Then you are prepared. But I should tell you that until this year when a number of patrons made it possible for him" (already I could identify the "him" whenever it fell from her lips, round with reverence and implication) "to devote all his time to teaching, he was for ten years an undertaker's assistant in Washington."

I said nothing. It was just as well to get past this first obstacle all at once. There was no reason of course to scorn that necessary if overwrought profession; yet somehow the thought of a savior emerging from those unctuous ranks seemed ludicrous. I reminded myself that a most successful messiah had been a carpenter and that another had been a politician ... but an embalmer! My anticipation of great news was chilled. I prepared myself for grim comedy.

Iris would tell me nothing more about the meeting or about *him* as we crossed the lawn. She opened the door to the house and we stepped into a softly lighted anteroom. A policeman and a civilian, the one gloomy and the other cheerful, greeted us.

"Ah, Miss Mortimer!" said the civilian, a gray, plump pigeon of a man. "And a friend, how good to see you both." No, this was not *he*. I was introduced to Mr. Dormer, who chirped on until he was interrupted by the policeman.

"Come on, you two, in here. Got to get the prints and the oath."

Iris motioned me to follow the policeman into a side-room.

I'd heard of this national precaution but until now I had had no direct experience of it. Since the attempt of the communists to control our society had, with the collapse of Russian foreign policy, failed, our government in its collective wisdom decided that never again would any sect or party, other than the traditional ones, be allowed to interrupt the rich flow of the nation's life. As a result, all deviationist societies were carefully watched by the police, who fingerprinted and photographed those who attended meetings, simultaneously exacting an oath of allegiance to the Constitution and the Flag which ended with that powerful invocation which a recent President's speechwriter had, in a moment of inspiration, struck off to the delight of his employer and nation: "In a true democracy there is no place for a serious difference of opinion on great issues." It is a comment on those years, now happily become history, that only a few ever considered the meaning of this resolution, proving of course that words are never a familiar province to the great mass which prefers recognizable pictures to even the most apposite prose.

Iris and I repeated dutifully in the presence of the policeman and an American flag the various national sentiments. We were then allowed to go back to the anteroom and to Mr. Dormer, who himself led us into the chapel where several dozen people – perfectly ordinary men and women – were gathered.

The chapel, nonsectarian, managed to combine a number of decorative influences with a blandness quite remarkable in its success at not really representing anything while suggesting, at the same time, everything. The presence of a dead body, a man carefully painted and wearing a blue serge suit, gently smiling in an ebony casket behind a bank of flowers at the chapel's end, did not detract as much as one might have supposed from the occasion's importance. After the first uneasiness, it was quite possible to accept the anonymous dead man as part of the décor. There was even, in later years, an attempt made by a group of Cavite enthusiasts to insist upon the presence of an embalmed corpse at every service, but fortunately other elements prevailed, though not without an ugly quarrel and harsh words.

John Cave's entrance followed our own by a few minutes, and it is with difficulty that I recall what it was that I felt on seeing him for the first time. Though my recollections are well known to all (at least they *were* well known, although now I am less certain, having seen Butler's Testament so strangely altered), I must record here that I cannot, after so many years, recall in any emotional detail my first reaction to this man who was to be the world's peculiar nemesis as well as my own.

But, concentrating fiercely, emptying my mind of later knowledge, I can still see him as he walked down the aisle of the chapel, a small man who moved with some grace. He was younger than I had expected or rather, younger-looking, with short straight hair, light brown in color, a lean regular face which would not have been noticed in a crowd unless one got close enough to see the expression of the eyes: large silver eyes with black lashes like a thick line drawn on the pale skin, focusing attention to them, to the congenitally small pupils which glittered like the points of black needles, betraying the will and the ambition which the impassive, gentle face belied . . . but I am speaking with future knowledge now. I did not that evening think of ambition or will in terms of John Cave. I was merely curious, intrigued, by the situation, by the intensity of Iris, by the serene corpse behind the bank of hothouse flowers, by the thirty or forty men and women who sat close to the front of the chapel, listening intently to Cave as he talked.

At first I paid little attention to what was being said, more interested in observing the audience, the room and the appearance of the speaker. Immediately after Cave's undramatic entrance, he moved to the front of the chapel and sat down on a gilt chair to the right of the coffin. There was a faint whisper of interest at his appearance. Newcomers like myself were being given last-minute instruction by the habitués who had brought them there. Cave sat easily on the gilt chair, his eyes upon the floor, his small hands, bony and white, folded in his lap, a smile on his narrow lips. He could not have looked more ineffectual and ordinary. His opening words by no means altered this first impression.

The voice was good, though Cave tended to mumble at the beginning, his eyes still on the floor, his hands in his lap, motionless. So quietly did he begin that he had spoken for several seconds before many of the audience were aware that he had begun. His accent was the national one, learned doubtless from the radio and the movies: a neutral pronunciation without any strong regional overtone. The popular if short-lived legend of the next decade that he had begun his mission as a backwoods revivalist was certainly untrue.

Not until Cave had talked for several minutes did I begin to listen to the sense rather than to the tone of his voice. I cannot render precisely what he said but the message that night was not much different from the subsequent ones which are known to all. It was, finally, the manner which created the response, not the words themselves, though the words were interesting enough, especially when heard for the first time. His voice, as I have said, faltered at the beginning and he left sentences unfinished, a trick which I later discovered was deliberate, for he had been born a remarkable actor, an instinctive rhetorician. What most struck me that first evening was the purest artifice of his performance. The voice, especially when he came to his climax, was sharp and clear while his hands stirred like separate living creatures and the eyes, those splendid unique eyes, were abruptly revealed to us in the faint light, displayed at that crucial moment which had been as carefully constructed as any work of architecture or of music: the instant of communication.

Against my will and judgment and inclination, I found myself absorbed by the man, not able to move or to react. The magic that was always to affect me, even when later I knew him only too well, held me fixed to my chair as the words, supported by the clear voice, came in a resonant line from him to me alone, to each of us alone, separate from the others . . . and both restless general and fast-breathing particulars were together his.

The moment itself lasted only a second in actual time; it came suddenly, without warning: one was riven; then it was over and he left the chapel, left us chilled and weak, staring foolishly at the gilt chair where he had been.

It was some minutes before we were able to take up our usual selves again.

Iris looked at me. I smiled weakly and cleared my throat. I was conscious that I ached all over. I glanced at my watch and saw that he had spoken to us for an hour and a half, during which time I had not moved. I stretched painfully and stood up. Others did the same. We had shared an experience and it was the first time in my life that I knew what it was like to be the same as others, my heart's beat no longer individual, erratic, but held for at least this one interval of time in concert with those of strangers. It was a new, disquieting experience: to be no longer an observer, a remote intelligence. For ninety minutes to have been a part of the whole.

Iris walked with me to the anteroom, where we stood for a moment watching the others who had also gathered here to talk in low voices, their expression bewildered.

She did not have to ask me what I thought. I told her immediately, in my own way, impressed but less than reverent. "I see what you mean. I see what it is that holds you, fascinates you, but I still wonder what it is really all about."

"You saw. You heard."

"I saw an ordinary man. I heard a sermon which was interesting, although I might be less impressed if I read it to myself. . . ." Deliberately I tried to throw it all away, that instant of belief, that paralysis of will, that sense of mysteries revealed in a dazzle of light. But as I talked, I realized that I was not really dismissing it, that I could not alter the experience even though I might dismiss the man and mock the test: something *had* happened and I told her what I thought it was.

"It is not truth, Iris, but hypnosis."

She nodded. "I've often thought that. Especially at first when I was conscious of his mannerisms, when I could see, as only a woman can perhaps, that this was just a man. Yet something *does* happen when you listen to him, when you get to know him. You must find that out for yourself: and you will. It may not prove to be anything which has to do with him. There's something in oneself which stirs and comes alive at his touch, through his agency." She spoke quickly, excitedly.

I felt the passion with which she was charged. But suddenly it was too much for me. I was bewildered and annoyed. I wanted to get away.

"Don't you want to meet him?"

I shook my head. "Another time maybe, but not now. Shall I take you back?"

"No. I'll get a ride in to Santa Monica. I may even stay over for the night. He'll be here a week."

I wondered again if she might have a personal interest in Cave. I doubted it, but anything was possible.

She walked me to the car, past the lighted chapel, over the summery lawn, down the dark street whose solid prosaicness helped to dispel somewhat the madness of the hour before.

We made a date to meet later on in the week. She would tell Cave about me and I would meet him. I interrupted her then. "What *did* he say, Iris? What did he say tonight?"

Her answer was as direct and as plain as my question. "That it is good to die."

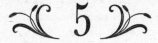

## 5

1

This morning I reread the last section, trying to see it objectively, to match what I have put down with the memory I still bear of that first encounter with John Cave. I have not, I fear, got it. But this is as close as I can come to recalling long-vanished emotions and events.

I was impressed by the man and I was shaken by his purpose. My first impression was, I think, correct. Cave was a natural hypnotist and the text of that extraordinary message was, in the early days at least, thin, illogical and depressing if one had not heard it spoken. Later of course I, among others, composed the words which bear his name and we gave them, I fancy, a polish and an authority which, with his limited education and disregard for the works of the past, he could not have accomplished on his own, even had he wanted to.

I spent the intervening days between my first and second encounters with this strange man in a state of extreme tension and irritability. Clarissa called me several times but I refused to see her, excusing myself from proposed entertainments and hinted tête-à-têtes with an abruptness which anyone but the iron-cast Clarissa would have found appallingly rude. But she merely said that she understood and let me off without explaining what it was she understood, or thought she did. I avoided all acquaintances, keeping to my hotel room, where I contemplated a quick return to the Hudson and to the coming autumn. Finally Iris telephoned to fix a day for me to meet

John Cave. I accepted her invitation, with some excitement.

We met in the late afternoon at her house. Only the three of us were present. In the set of dialogues which I composed and published in later years I took considerable liberties with our actual conversations, especially this first one. In fact, as hostile critics were quick to suggest, the dialogues were created by me with very little of Cave in them and a good deal of Plato, rearranged to fit the occasion. But in time, my version was accepted implicitly, if only because there were no longer any hostile critics.

Cave rose promptly when I came out onto the patio, shook my hand vigorously but briefly and sat down again, indicating that I sit next to him while Iris went for tea. He was smaller and more compact than I had thought, measuring him against myself as one does, unconsciously, with an interesting stranger. He wore a plain brown suit and a white shirt open at the neck. The eyes, which at first I did not dare look at, were, I soon noticed, sheathed . . . an odd word which was always to occur to me when I saw him at his ease, eyes half-shut, ordinary, not in the least unusual. Except for a restless folding and unfolding of the hands (suggesting a recently reformed cigarette smoker) he was without physical idiosyncrasy.

"It's a pleasure to meet you" were the first words, I fear, that John Cave ever spoke to me; so unlike the dialogue on the spirit which I later composed to celebrate the initial encounter between master and disciple-to-be. "Iris has told me a lot about you." His voice was light, without resonance now. He sat far back in a deck chair. Inside the house I could hear Iris moving plates. The late afternoon sun had just that moment gone behind trees and the remaining light was warmly gold.

"And I have followed your . . . career with interest too," I said, knowing that "career" was precisely the word he would not care to hear used but, since neither of us had yet got the range of the other, we fired at random.

"Iris tells me you write history."

I shook my head. "No, I only read it. I think it's all been

written anyway." I was allowed to develop this novel conceit for some moments, attended by a respectful silence from my companion, who finally dispatched my faintly hysterical proposition with a vague "Maybe so"; and then we got to him.

"I haven't been East, you know." He frowned at the palm trees. "I was born in Washington state and I've spent all my life in the Northwest, until last year." He paused as though he expected me to ask him about *that* year. I did not. I waited for him to do it in his own way. He suddenly turned about and faced me; those disconcerting eyes suddenly trained upon my own. "You were there the other night, weren't you?"

"Why, yes."

"Did you feel it too? Am I right?"

The quick passion with which he said this, exploding all at once the afternoon's serenity, took me off guard. I stammered, "I don't think I know what you mean. I . . ."

"You know exactly what I mean, what I meant." Cave leaned closer to me and I wondered insanely if the deck chair might not collapse under him. It teetered dangerously. My mind went blank, absorbed by the image of deck chair and prophet together collapsing at my feet. Then, as suddenly, satisfied perhaps with my confusion, he settled back, resumed his earlier ease, exactly as if I had answered him, as though we had come to a crisis and together fashioned an agreement. He was most alarming.

"I want to see New York especially. I've always thought it must look like a cemetery with all those tall gray buildings you see in photographs." He sighed conventionally. "So many interesting places in the world. Do you like the West?"

Nervously, I said that I did. I still feared a possible repetition of that brief outburst.

"I like the openness," said Cave, as though he had thought long about this problem. "I don't think I'd like confinement. I couldn't live in Seattle because of those fogs they used to have. San Francisco's the same. I don't like too many walls, too much fog." If he'd intended to speak allegorically he could not have found a better audience; even at this early stage, I was completely receptive to the most obscure histrionics. But in conversation, Cave was perfectly literal. Except when he spoke before a large group, he was quite simple and prosaic and, though conscious always of his dignity and singular destiny, not in the least portentous.

I probably did not put him at his ease, for I stammered a good deal and made no sense, but he was gracious, supporting me with his own poise and equanimity.

He talked mostly of places until Iris came back with tea. Then, as the sky became florid with evening and the teacups gradually grew cold, he spoke of his work and I listened intently.

"I can talk to you straight," he said. "This just happened to me. I didn't start out to do this. No sir, I never would have believed ten years ago that I'd be traveling about, talking to people like one of those crackpot fanatics you've got so many of in California." I took a sip of the black, fast-cooling tea, hoping he was not sufficiently intuitive to guess that I had originally put him down, provisionally of course, as precisely that.

"I don't know how much Iris may have told you or how much you might have heard, but it's pretty easy to pass the whole thing off as another joke. A guy coming out of the backwoods with a message." He cracked his knuckles hard and I winced at the sound. "Well, I didn't quite come out of the woods. I had a year back at State University and I had a pretty good job in my field with the best firm of funeral directors in Washington state. Then I started on this. I just *knew* one day, and so I began to talk to people and they knew too and I quit my job and started talking to bigger and bigger crowds all along the Coast. There wasn't any of this revelation stuff. I just knew one day, that was all. And when I told other people *what* I knew, they seemed to get it. And that's the strange part. Everybody gets ideas about things which he thinks are wonderful but usually nothing happens to the people he tries to tell them to. With me, it's been different from the beginning. People have listened, and agreed. What I know *they* know. Isn't that a funny thing? Though most of them probably would never have thought it out until they heard me and it was all clear." His eyes dropped to his hands and he added softly: "So since it's been like this, I've gone on. I've made this my life. This is it. I will come to the people."

There was silence. The sentence had been spoken which I was later to construct the first dialogue upon: "I will come to the people." The six words which were to change our lives were spoken softly over tea.

Iris looked at me challengingly over Cave's bowed head.

I remember little else about that evening. We dined, I think, in the house and Cave was most agreeable, most undemanding. There was no more talk of the mission. He asked me many questions about New York, about Harvard, where I had gone to school, about Roman history. He appeared to be interested in paganism and my own somewhat tentative approach to Julian. I was to learn later that though he seldom read he had a startling memory for any fact he thought relevant. I am neither immodest nor inaccurate when I say that he listened to me attentively for some years and many of his later views were a result of our conversations.

I should mention, though, one significant omission in his conversation during those crucial years. He never discussed ethical questions. That was to come much later. At the beginning he had but one vision: Death is nothing; literally no thing; and since, demonstrably, absence of things is a good; death which is no thing is good. On this the Cavite system was constructed, and what came after in the moral and ethical spheres was largely the work of others in his name. Much of this I anticipated in that first conversation with him, so unlike, actually, the dialogue which I composed and which ended with the essential lines – or so I still think complacently, despite the irony with which time has tarnished all those bright toys for me: "Death is neither hard nor bad. Only the dying hurts."

With that firmly postulated, the rest was inevitable.

Cave talked that evening about California and Oregon and Washington (geography and places were always to fascinate and engage him while people, especially after the early years, ceased to be remarkable to him; he tended to confuse those myriad faces which passed before him like successive ripples in a huge sea). He talked of the cities he had visited on the Coast, new cities to him. He compared their climates and various attractions like a truly devoted tourist, eager to get the best of each place, to encounter the *genius loci* and possess it.

"But I don't like staying in any place long." Cave looked at me then and again I felt that sense of a power being focused on me . . . it was not unlike what one experiences during an X-ray treatment when the humming noise indicates that potent rays are penetrating one's tissue and though there is actually no sensation, *something* is experienced, power is felt. And so it invariably was that, right until the end, Cave could turn those wide bleak eyes upon me whenever he chose, and I would experience his force anew.

"I want to keep moving, new places, that's what I like. You get a kind of charge traveling. At least I do. I always thought I'd travel but I never figured it would be like this; but then of course I never thought of all this until just a while ago."

"Can you remember when it was? How it was exactly you got . . . started?" I wanted a sign. Constantine's *labarum* occurred to me: *in hoc signo vinces*. Already ambition was stirring, and the little beast fed ravenously on every scrap that came its way, for on that patio I was experiencing my own revelation, the compass needle no longer spinning wildly but coming to settle at last, with many hesitancies and demurs, upon a direction, drawn to a far pole's attraction.

John Cave smiled for the first time. I suppose, if I wanted, I could recall each occasion over the years when, in my presence at least, he smiled. His usual expression was one of calm resolve, of that authority which feels secure in itself, a fortunate expression which lent dignity to even his casual conversation. I suspected the fact that this serene mask hid a nearly total intellectual vacuity as early in my dealings with him as this first meeting; yet I did not mind, for I had experienced his unique magic and already I saw the possibilities of channeling that power, of using that force, of turning it like a flame here, there, creating and destroying, shaping and shattering . . . so much for the spontaneous nature of my ambition at its least responsible, and at its most exquisite! I could have set the one-half world aflame for the sheer splendor and glory of the deed. For this fault my expiation has been long and my once exuberant pride is now only an ashen phoenix consumed by flames but not quite tumbled into dust, nor re-created in the millennial egg, only a gray shadow in the heart which the touch of a finger of windy fear will turn to dust and air.

Yet the creature was aborning that day: one seed that touched another and a monster began to live.

"The first day? The first time?" The smile faded.

"Sure. I remember it. I'd just finished cosmeticizing the face of this big dead fellow killed in an automobile accident. I didn't actually do make-up but I like to help out and I used to do odd jobs when somebody had too much to do and asked me to help; the painting isn't hard either and I always like it, though the faces are cold like . . . like. . ." He thought of no simile and went on: "Anyway I looked at this guy's face and I remembered I'd seen him play basketball in high school. He was in a class or two behind me. Big athlete. Ringer, we called him . . . full of life . . . and here he was, with me powdering his face and combing his eyebrows. Usually you don't think much about the stiff (that's our professional word) one way or the other. It's just a job. But I thought about this one suddenly. I started to feel sorry for him, dead like that, so sudden, so young, so good-looking with all sorts of prospects. Then I felt it." The voice grew low and precise. Iris and I listened intently, even the sun froze in the wild sky above the sea; and the young night stumbled in the darkening east.

With eyes on the sun, Cave described his sudden knowledge that it was the dead man who was right, who was a part of the whole, that the living were the sufferers from whom, temporarily, the beautiful darkness and non-being had been withdrawn. In his crude way, Cave struck chord after chord of meaning and, though the notes were not in themselves new, the effect was all its own . . . and not entirely because of the voice, of the cogency of this magician.

"And I knew it was the dying which was the better part," he finished. The sun released, drowned in the Pacific.

In the darkness I asked, "But you, you still live?"

"Not because I want to," came the voice, soft as the night. "I must tell the others first. There'll be time for me."

I shuddered in the warmth of the patio. My companions were only dim presences in the failing light. "Who told you to tell this to everyone?"

The answer came back, strong and unexpected: "I told myself. The responsibility is mine."

That was the sign for me. He had broken with his predecessors. He was on his own. He knew. And so did we.

2

I have lingered over that first meeting, for in it was finally all that was to come. Later details were the work of others, irrelevant periphery to a simple but powerful center. Not until late that night did I leave the house near the beach. When I left, Cave stayed on and I wondered again if perhaps he was living with Iris.

We parted casually and Iris walked me to the door while Cave remained inside, gazing in his intent way at nothing at all; daydreaming, doubtless, of what was to come.

"You'll help?" Iris stood by the car's open door, her features indistinct in the moonless night.

"I think so. But I'm not sure about the scale."

"What do you mean?"

"Must *everyone* know? Can't it just be kept to ourselves? For the few who do know him?"

"No. We must let them all hear him. Everyone." And her voice assumed that zealous tone which I was to hear so often again and again from her lips and those of others.

I made my first and last objection. "I don't see that quantity has much to do with it. If this thing spreads it will become organized. If it becomes organized, secondary considerations will obscure the point. The truth is no truer because only a few have experienced it."

"You're wrong. Even for purely selfish reasons, ruling out all altruistic considerations, there's an excellent reason for allowing this to spread. A society which knows what we know, which believes in Cave and what he says, will be a pleasanter place in which to live, less anxious, more tolerant." She spoke of a new Jerusalem in our sallow and anxious land, nearly convincing me.

The next day I went to Hastings's house for lunch. He was alone; his wife apparently had a life of her own which required his company only occasionally. Clarissa, sensible in tweed and dark glasses, was the only other guest. We lunched on a wrought-iron table beside the gloomy pool in which, among the occasional leaves, I saw, quite clearly, a cigarette butt delicately unfolding like an ocean flower.

"Good to, ah, have you, Eugene. Just a bit of pot luck. Clarissa's going back to civilization today and wanted to see you. I did too, of course. The bride's gone out. Told me to convey her . . ."

Clarissa turned her bright eyes on me and, without acknowledging the presence of our host, said right off, "You've met him at last."

I nodded. The plot was finally clear to me; the main design at least. "We had dinner together last night."

"I know. Iris told me. You're going to help out of course."

"I'd like to but I don't know what there is I might do. I don't

71

think I'd be much use with a tambourine on street corners, preaching the word."

"Don't be silly!" Clarissa chuckled. "We're going to handle this quite, *quite* differently."

"We?"

"Oh, I've been involved for over a year now. It's going to be the greatest fun . . . you wait and see."

"But . . ."

"*I* was the one who got Iris involved. I thought she looked a little peaked, a little bored. I had no idea of course she'd get in so deep, but it will probably turn out all right. I think she's in love with him."

"Don't be such a gossip," said Hastings sharply. "You always reduce everything to . . . to biology. Cave isn't that sort of man."

"You know him too?" How fast it was growing, I thought.

"Certainly. Biggest thing I've done since . . ."

"Since you married that brassy blonde," said Clarissa with her irrepressible rudeness. "Anyway, my dear, Iris took to the whole thing like a born proselyte, if that's the word I mean . . . the other's a little boy, isn't it? and it seems, from what she's told me, that you have too."

"I wouldn't say that." I was a little put out at both Iris and Clarissa taking me so much for granted.

"Say anything you like. It's still the best thing that's ever happened to you. Oh God, *not* avocado again!" The offending salad was waved away while Hastings muttered apologies. "Nasty, pointless things, all texture and no taste." She made a face. "But I suppose that we must live off the fruits of the country and this is the only thing that will grow in California." She moved without pause from Western flora to the problem of John Cave. "As for your own contribution, Eugene, it will depend largely upon what you choose to do. As I said, I never suspected that Iris would get in so deep and you may prove to be quite as surprising. This is the ground floor of course . . . wonderful expression, isn't it? The spirit of America, the slogan that broke the plains . . . in any case, the way is clear. Cave liked you. You can write things for them, rather solid articles based on your inimitable misreadings of history. You can educate Cave, though this might be unwise since so much of his force derives from his eloquent ignorance. Or you might become a part of the organization which is getting under way. I suppose Iris will explain that to you. It's rather her department at the moment. All those years in the Junior League gave her a touching faith in the power of committees, which is just as well when handling Americans. As for the tambourines and cries of 'Come and Be Saved' you are some twenty years behind the times. We have more up-to-date plans."

"Committees? What committees?"

Clarissa unfolded her mushroom omelet with a secret smile. "You'll meet our number-one committee member after lunch. He's coming, isn't he?" She looked at Hastings as though suspecting him of a treacherous ineptitude.

"Certainly, certainly, at least he *said* he was." Hastings motioned for the servingwoman to clean away the lunch, and we moved to other chairs beside the pool for coffee.

Clarissa was in fine form, aggressive, positive, serenely indifferent to the effect she was having on Hastings and me. "Of course I'm just meddling," she said in answer to an inquiry of mine. "I don't really give two cents for Mr. Cave and his message."

"Clarissa!" Hastings was genuinely shocked.

"I mean it. Not that I don't find him fascinating and of course the whole situation is delicious . . . what we shall do! Or *you* shall do!" She looked at me maliciously. "I can foresee no limits to this."

"It no doubt reminds you of the period shortly after Mohammed married Khadija." But my own malice could hardly pierce Clarissa's mad equanimity.

"Vile man, sweet woman. But no, this is all going to be different, although the intellectual climate (I think *intellectual* is perhaps optimistic but you know what I mean) is quite similar. I can't wait for the first public response."

"There's already been some," said Hastings, crossing his legs, which were encased in pale multicolor slacks with rawhide sandals on his feet. "There was a piece yesterday in the *News* about the meeting they had down near Laguna."

"What did they say?" Clarissa scattered tiny saccharine tablets into her coffee like a grain goddess preparing harvest.

"Oh, just one of those short suburban notes about how a Mr. Joseph Cave, they got the name wrong, was giving a series of lectures at a funeral parlor which have been surprisingly well attended."

"They didn't mention what the lectures were about?"

"No, just a comment; the only one so far in Los Angeles."

"There'll be others soon, but I shouldn't think it's such a good idea to have too many items like that before things are really under way."

"And the gentleman who is coming here will be responsible for getting them under way?" I asked.

"Pretty much, yes. It's been decided that the practical details are to be left to him. Cave will continue to speak in and around Los Angeles until the way has been prepared. Then, when the publicity begins, he will be booked all over the country, all over the world!" Clarissa rocked silently for a moment in her chair, creating a disagreeable effect of noiseless laughter which disconcerted both Hastings and me.

"I don't like your attitude," said Hastings, looking at her gloomily. "You aren't *serious*."

"Oh I am, my darling, I am. You'll never know how serious." And on that high note of Clarissa's, Paul Himmell stepped out onto the patio, blinking in the light of noon.

Himmell was a slender man in his fortieth and most successful year, hair only just begun to gray, a lined but firmly modeled face, all bright with ambition. The initial impression was one of neatly contained energy, of a passionate temperament skillfully channeled. Even the twist to his bow tie was the work of a master craftsman.

Handshake agreeable; smile quick and engaging; yet the

effect on me was alarming. I had detested this sort of man all my life and here at last, wearing a repellently distinguished sports coat, was the archetype of all such creatures, loading with a steady hand that cigarette holder without which he might at least have seemed to me still human. He was identified by Hastings, who with a few excited snorts and gasps told me beneath the conversation that this was the most successful young publicist in Hollywood, which meant the world.

"I'm happy to meet you, Gene," Himmell said as soon as we were introduced. He was perfectly aware that he had been identified while the first greetings with Clarissa had been exchanged. He had the common gift of the busy worldling of being able to attend two conversations simultaneously, profiting from both. I hate being called by my first name by strangers, but in his world there were no strangers: the freemasonry of self-interest made all men equal in their desperation. He treated me like a buddy. He knew (he was, after all, clever) that I detested him on sight and on principle, and that presented him with a challenge to which he rose with confidence . . . and continued to rise through the years, despite the enduring nature of my disaffection. But then to be liked was his business, and I suspect that his attentions had less to do with me, or any sense of failure in himself for not having won me, than with a kind of automatic charm, a response to a situation which was produced quite inhumanly, mechanically: the smile, the warm voice, the delicate flattery . . . or not so delicate, depending on the case.

"Iris and Cave both told me about you and I'm particularly glad to get a chance to meet you . . . and to see you too, Clarissa . . . will you be long in the East?" Conscious perhaps that I would need more work than a perfunctory prelude, he shifted his attention to Clarissa, saving me for later.

"I never have plans, Paul, but I've one or two chores I've got to do. Anyway I've decided that Eugene is just the one to give the enterprise its tone . . . a quality concerning which you, dear

Paul, so often have so much to say."

"Why, yes," said the publicist genially, obviously not understanding. "Always use more tone. You're quite right."

Clarissa's eyes met mine for a brief amused instant. She was on to everything; doubtless on to me too in the way one can never be about oneself; I always felt at a disadvantage with her.

"What we're going to need for the big New York opening is a firm historical and intellectual base. Cave hasn't got it and of course doesn't need it. We are going to need commentary and explanation and though you happen to be a genius in publicity you must admit that that group which has been characterized as intellectual, the literate few who in their weakness often exert enormous influence, are not apt to be much moved by your publicity; in fact, they will be put off by it."

"Well, now I'm not so sure my methods are *that* crude. Of course I never . . ."

"They are superbly, triumphantly, providentially crude and you know it. Eugene must lend dignity to the enterprise. He has a solemn and highly unimaginative approach to philosophy which will appeal to his fellow intellectuals. He and they are quite alike: liberal and ineffectual, irresolute and lonely. When he addresses them they will get immediately his range, you might say, pick up his frequency, realizing he is one of them, a man to be trusted. Once they are reached the game is over, or begun." Clarissa paused and looked at me expectantly.

I did not answer immediately. Hastings, as a former writer, felt that he too had been addressed and he worried the subject of "tone" while Paul gravely added a comment or two. Clarissa watched me, however, conscious perhaps of the wound she had dealt.

Was it all really so simple? Was *I* so simple – so typical? Vanity said not, but self-doubt, the shadow which darkens even those triumphs held at noon, prevailed for a sick moment or two. I was no different from the others, from the little pedagogues and analysts, the self-obsessed and spiritless company who endured shame and a sense of alienation without even that conviction of virtue which can dispel guilt and apathy for the simple, for all those who have accepted without question one of the systems of absolutes which it has amused both mystics and tyrants to construct for man's guidance.

I had less baggage to rid myself of than the others; I was confident of that. Neither Christianity nor Marxism nor the ugly certainties of the mental therapists had ever engaged my loyalty or suspended my judgment. I had looked at them all, deploring their admirers and servants, yet interested by their separate views of society and of the potentialities of a heaven on earth (the medieval conception of a world beyond life was always interesting to contemplate, even if the evidence in its favor was whimsical at best, conceived either as a system of rewards and punishments to control living man or else as lovely visions of what might be were man indeed consubstantial with a creation which so often resembled the personal aspirations of gifted divines rather than that universe the rest of us must observe with mortal eyes). No, I had had to dispose of relatively little baggage and, I like to think, less than my more thoughtful contemporaries who were forever analyzing themselves, offering their psyches to doctors for analysis or, worse, giving their immortal souls into the hands of priests who would then assume much of their *Weltschmerz*, providing them with a set of grown-up games every bit as appealing as the ones of childhood which had involved make-believe or, finally, worst of all, the soft acceptance of the idea of man the mass, of man the citizen, of society the organic whole for whose greater good all individuality must be surrendered.

My sense then of all that I had *not* been, negative as it was, saved my self-esteem. In this I was unlike my contemporaries. I had, in youth, lost all respect for the authority of men; and since there is no other discernible (the "laws" of nature are only relative and one cannot say for certain that there is a beautiful logic to everything in the universe as long as first principles remain unrevealed, except of course to the religious, who *know* everything, having faith), I was unencumbered by belief, by reverence for any man or groups of men, living or dead; yet human wit and genius often made my days bearable since my capacity for admiration, for aesthetic response, was highly developed even though, with Terence, I did not know, did not *need* to know through what wild centuries roves back the rose.

Nevertheless, Clarissa's including me among the little Hamlets was irritating, and when I joined in the discussion again I was careful to give her no satisfaction; it would have been a partial victory for her if I had denied a generic similarity to my contemporaries.

Paul spoke of practical matters, explaining to us the way he intended to operate in the coming months; and I was given a glimpse of the organization which had spontaneously come into being only a few weeks before.

"Hope we can have lunch tomorrow, Gene. I'll give you a better picture then, the overall picture and your part in it. Briefly, for now, the organization has been set up as a company under California law with Cave as president and myself, Iris and Clarissa as directors. I'm also secretary-treasurer but only for now. We're going to need a first-rate financial man to head our campaign fund and I'm working on several possibilities right now."

"What's the . . . company called?" I asked.

"Cavite, Inc. We didn't want to call it anything, but that's the law here and since we intended to raise money we had to have a legal setup."

"Got a nice sound, ah, Cavite," said Hastings, nodding.

"What on earth should we have done if he'd had *your* name, Paul?" exclaimed Clarissa, to the indignation of both Hastings and Paul. They shut her up.

Paul continued smoothly, "I've had a lot of experience, of course, but this is something completely new for me, a real challenge and one which I am glad to meet head-on."

"How did you get into it?" I asked.

Paul pointed dramatically to Hastings. "Him! He took me

to a meeting in Burbank last year. I was sold the first time. *I got the message.*"

There was a hush as we were allowed to contemplate this awesome information. Then, smiling in a fashion which he doubtless would have called "wry," the publicist continued, "I knew this was it. I contacted Cave immediately and found we talked the same language. He was all for the idea and so we incorporated. He said he wasn't interested in the organizational end and left that to us, with Iris sort of representing him, though of course we all do since we're all Cavites. This thing is big and we're part of it." He also smacked his lips. I listened, fascinated. "Anyway he's going to do the preaching part and we're going to handle the sales end, if you get what I mean. We're selling something which nobody else ever sold before, and you know what that is?" He paused dramatically and we stared at him a little stupidly. "Truth!" His voice was triumphant. "We're selling the truth about life and that's something that nobody, but nobody, has ever done before!"

Clarissa broke the silence which had absorbed his last words. "You're simply out of this world, Paul! If I hadn't heard you, I'd never have believed it. But you don't have to sell *us*, dear. We're in on it too. Besides, I have to catch a plane." She looked at her watch. She stood up and we did too. She thanked Hastings for lunch and then, before she left the patio on his arm, she said: "Now you boys get on together and remember what I've told you. Gene must be used, and right away. Get him to write something dignified, for a magazine." We murmured assent. Clarissa said goodbye and left the patio with Hastings. Her voice, shrill and hard, could be heard even after she left. "The truth about life! Oh, it's going to be priceless!"

I looked quickly at Paul to see if he had heard. But if he had, he ignored it. He was looking at me intently, speculatively. "I think we're going to get along fine, Gene, just fine," leaving me only a fumbled word or two of polite corroboration with which to express my sincere antipathy: then we went our separate ways.

3

I met Paul the next day at his office for a drink and not for lunch, since at the last minute his secretary had called me to say he was tied up and could I possibly come at five. I said that I could. I did.

Paul's offices occupied an entire floor of a small skyscraper on the edge of Beverly Hills. I was shown through a series of rooms done in natural wood and beige with indirect lighting and the soft sound of Strauss waltzes piped in from all directions: the employees responded best to three-quarter time, according to the current efficiency reports.

Beneath an expensive but standard mobile, Paul stood, waiting for me. His desk, a tiny affair of white marble on slender iron legs, had been rolled off to one side, and the office gave, as had been intended, the impression of being a small drawing room rather than a place of business. I was greeted warmly. Hand was shaken firmly. Eyes were met squarely for the regulation length of time. Then we sat down on a couch which was like the open furry mouth of some great soft beast and his secretary rolled a portable bar toward us.

"Name your poison," said the publicist genially. We agreed on a cocktail, which he mixed with the usual comments one expects from a regular fellow.

Lulled by the alcohol and the room, disarmed by the familiar patter in which one made all the correct responses, our conversation as ritualistic as that of a French dinner party, I was not prepared for the abrupt, "You don't like me, do you, Gene?"

Only once or twice before had anyone ever said this to me and each time that it happened I had vowed grimly that the *next* time, no matter where or with whom, I should answer with perfect candor, with merciless accuracy, "No, I don't." But since I am neither quick nor courageous, I murmured a pale denial.

"It's all right, Gene. I know how you probably feel." And the monster was magnanimous; he treated me with pity. "We've got two different points of view. That's all. I have to make my way in this rat race and you don't. You don't have to do anything, so you can afford to patronize us poor hustlers."

"Patronize isn't quite the word." I was beginning to recover from the first shock. A crushing phrase or two occurred to me, but Paul knew his business and he changed course before I could begin my work of demolition.

"Well, I just wanted you to know that there are no hard feelings. In my business you get used to this sort of thing: occupational hazard, you might say. I've had to fight my way every inch and I know that a lot of people are going to be jostled in the process, which is just too bad for them." He smiled suddenly, drawing the sting. "But I've got a hunch we're going to be seeing a lot of each other, so we ought to start on a perfectly plain basis of understanding. You're on to me and I'm on to you." The man was diabolic in the way he could enrage yet not allow his adversary sufficient grounds for even a perfunctory defense. He moved rapidly, with a show of spurious reason which quite dazzled me. His was what he presently called "the common-sense view."

I told him I had no objection to working with him; that everything I had heard about him impressed me; that he was wrong to suspect me of disdaining methods whose efficacy was so well known. I perjured myself for several impassioned minutes, and on a rising note of coziness we took up the problem at hand, congenial enemies for all time. The first round was clearly his.

"Clarissa got you into this?" He looked at me over his glass.

"More or less. Clarissa to Iris to Cave was the precise play."

"She got me to Cave last summer, or rather to Hastings first. I was sold right off. I think I told you that yesterday. This guy's got everything. Even aside from the message, he's the most remarkable salesman I've ever seen, and please believe me when I tell you there isn't *anything* I don't know about salesmen."

I agreed that he was doubtless expert in these matters.

"I went to about a dozen of those early meetings and I could see he was having the same effect on everyone, even on Catholics, people like that. Of course I don't know what happens when they get home, but while they're there they're sold, and that's all that matters, because in the next year we're going to have him *there,* everywhere, and all the time."

I told him I didn't exactly follow this metaphysical flight.

"I mean we're going to have him on television, on movie screens, in the papers, so that everybody can feel the effect of his personality, just like he was there in person. This prayer-meeting stuff he's been doing is just a warming up, that's all. It's outmoded; can't reach enough people even if you spoke at Madison Square every night for a year. But it's good practice, to get him started. Now the next move is a half-hour TV show once a week, and when that gets started we're in."

"Who's going to pay for all this?"

"We've got more money than you can shake a stick at." He smiled briefly and refilled our glasses with a flourish. "I haven't been resting on my laurels and neither has Clarissa. We've got three of the richest men in L.A. drooling at the mouth for an opportunity to come in with us. They're sold. They've talked to him, they've heard him. That's been enough."

"Will you sell soap on television at the same time?"

"Come off it, Gene. *Cave* is the product."

"Then in what way will you or his sponsors profit from selling him?"

"In the first place, what he says is the truth and that's meant a lot to them, to the tycoons. They'll do anything to put him across."

"I should think that the possession of the truth and its attendant sense of virtue is in itself enough, easily spoiled by popularization," I said with chilling pomp.

"Now that's a mighty selfish attitude to take. Sure it makes me happy to know at last nothing matters a hell of a lot since I'm apt to die any time and that's the end of yours truly. A nice quiet nothing, like sleeping pills after a busy day. All that's swell, but it means a lot more to me to see the truth belong to everybody. Also, let's face it, I'm ambitious. I like my work. I want to see this thing get big, and with me part of it. Life doesn't mean a thing and death is the only reality, like he says, but while we're living we've got to keep busy and the best thing for me, I figured about six months ago, was to put Cave over with the public, which is just what I'm going to do. Anything wrong with that?"

Since right and wrong had not yet been reformulated and codified, I gave him the comfort he hardly needed. "I see what you mean. I suppose you're right. Perhaps the motive is the same in every case, mine as well as yours. Yet we've all experienced Cave and that should be enough."

"No, we should all get behind it and push, bring it to the world."

"That, of course, is where we're different. Not that I don't intend to propagate the truth, but, I shall do it for something to do, knowing that nothing matters, not even *this* knowledge matters." In my unction, I had stumbled upon the first of a series of paradoxes which were to amuse and obsess our philosophers for a generation. However, Paul gave me no opportunity to elaborate; his was the practical way and I followed. We spoke of means not ends.

"Cave likes the idea of the half-hour show and as soon as we get all the wrinkles ironed out, buying good time, not just dead air, we'll make the first big announcement, along around January. Until then we're trying to keep this out of the papers. Slow but sure; then fast and hard."

"What sort of man is Cave?" I wanted very much to hear the reaction of a practical man.

Paul was candid; he did not know. "How can you figure a guy like that out? At times he seems a little feebleminded, this is between us by the way, and other times when he's talking to people, giving with the message, there's nothing like him."

"What about his early life?"

"Nobody knows very much. I've had a detective agency

prepare a dossier on him. Does that surprise you? Well, I'm going far out on a limb for him and so are our rich friends. We had to be sure we weren't buying an ax murderer or a commie or something."

"Would that have made any difference to the message?"

"No, *I* don't think so but it sure would have made it impossible for us to sell him on a big scale."

"And what did they find?"

"Not much. I'll let you read it. Take it home with you. Confidential, of course, and, as an officer of the company, I must ask you not to use any of it without first clearing with me."

I agreed and his secretary was sent for. The dossier was a thin bound manuscript.

"It's a carbon but I want it back. You won't find anything very striking but you ought to read it for the background. Never been married, no girl friends that anybody remembers . . . no boy friends either (what a headache *that* problem is for a firm like ours). No police record. No tickets for double parking, even. A beautiful, beautiful record on which to build."

"Perhaps a little negative."

"That's what we like. As for the guy's character, his I.Q., your guess is as good as mine, probably better. When I'm with him alone, we talk about the campaign and he's very relaxed, very sensible, businesslike. Doesn't preach or carry on. He seems to understand all the problems of our end. He's cooperative."

"Can you look him straight in the eye?"

Paul laughed. "Gives you the creeps, doesn't it? No, I guess I don't look at him very much. I'm glad you mentioned that because I've a hunch he's a hypnotist of some kind, though there's no record of his ever having studied it. I think I'll get a psychologist to take a look at him."

"Do you think he'll like that?"

"Oh, he'll never know unless he's a mindreader. Somebody to sort of observe him at work. I've already had him checked physically."

"You're very thorough."

"Have to be. He's got a duodenal ulcer and there's a danger of high blood pressure when he's older; otherwise he's in fine shape."

"What do you want me to do first?"

He became serious. "A pamphlet. You might make a highbrow magazine article out of it for the *Reader's Digest* or something first. We'll want a clear, simple statement of the Cavite philosophy."

"Why don't you get him to write it?"

"I've tried. He says he can't write anything. In fact he even hates to have his sermons taken down by a recorder. God knows why. But in a way it's all to the good, because it means we can get all the talent we like to do the writing for us, and that way, sooner or later, we can appeal to just about everybody."

"Whom am I supposed to appeal to in this first pamphlet?"

"The ordinary person, but make it as foolproof as you can. Leave plenty of doors open so you can get out fast in case we switch the party line along the way."

I laughed. "You're extraordinarily cynical."

"Just practical. I had to learn everything the hard way. I've been kicked around by some mighty expert kickers in my time."

I checked his flow of reminiscence. "Tell me about Cave and Iris." This was the secondary mystery which had occupied my mind for several days. But Paul did not know or, if he did, would not say. "I think they're just good friends, like we say in these parts. Except that I doubt if anything is going on . . . they don't seem the type and she's so completely gone on what he has to say . . ."

A long-legged girl secretary in discreet black entered the room unbidden and whispered something to the publicist. Paul started as though she had given him an electric shock from the thick carpeting. He spoke quickly. "Get Furlow. Tell him to stand bail. I'll be right down."

She hurried from the room. Paul pushed the bar away from him and it rolled aimlessly across the floor, bottles and glasses chattering. Paul looked at me distractedly. "He's in jail. Cave's in jail."

# ❧ 6 ❧

## 1

Last night the noise of my heart's beating kept me awake until nearly dawn. Then, as the gray warm light of the morning patterned the floor, I fell asleep and dreamed uneasily of disaster, my dreams disturbed by the noise of jackals, by that jackal-headed god who hovers over me as these last days unfold confusedly before my eyes: it will end in heat and terror, alone beside a muddy river, all time as one and that soon gone. I awakened, breathless and cold, with a terror of the dying still ahead.

After coffee and pills, those assorted pellets which seem to restore me for moments at a time to a false serenity, I put aside the nightmare world of the previous restless hours and idly examined the pages which I had written with an eye to rereading them straight through, to relive for a time the old drama which is already, as I write, separating itself from my memory and becoming real only in the prose. I think now of these events as I have told them and not as they occur to me in memory. For the memory now is of pages and not of scenes or of actual human beings still existing in that baleful, tenebrous region of the imagination where fancy and fact together confuse even the most confident of narrators. I have, thus far at least, exorcised demons, and to have lost certain memories to my narrative relieves my system, as would the excision of a cancer from a failing organism.

The boy brought me my morning coffee and the local

newspaper, whose Arabic text pleases my eye though the sense, when I do translate it, is less than strange. I asked the boy if Mr. Butler was awake and he said that he had gone out already. These last few days I have kept to my room even for the evening meal, delaying the inevitable revelation as long as possible.

After the boy left and while I drank coffee and looked out upon the river and the western hills, I was conscious of a sense of well-being which I have not often experienced in recent years. Perhaps the work of evoking the past has, in a sense, enhanced the present for me. I thought of the work done as life preserved, as part of me which will remain.

Then, idly, I riffled the pages of John Cave's Testament for the first time since I had discovered that my name had been expunged.

The opening was the familiar one which I had composed so many years before in Cave's name. The time of divination: a straightforward account of the apparent wonders which had preceded the mission. No credence was given the supernatural but a good case was made (borrowed a little from the mental therapists) for the race's need of phenomena as a symptom of unease and boredom and anticipation. I flicked through the pages. An entire new part had been added which I did not recognize: it was still written as though by Cave but obviously it could not have been composed until at least a decade after his death.

I read the new section carefully. Whoever had written it had been strongly under the influence of the pragmatic philosophers, though the style was somewhat inspirational, a guide to popularity crossed with the Koran. A whole system of ideal behavior was sketched broadly for the devout, so broadly as to be fairly useless, though the commentary and the interpretive analysis of such lines as "Property really belongs to the world though individuals may have temporary liens on certain sections" must be already prodigious.

I was well into the metaphysics of the Cavites when there

was a knock on my door. It was Butler, looking red and uncomfortable from the heat, a spotted red bandana tied, for some inscrutable reason, about his head in place of a hat.

"Hope you don't mind my barging in like this, but I finished a visit with the mayor earlier than I thought." He crumpled, on invitation, into a chair opposite me. He sighed gloomily. "This is going to be tough, tougher than I ever imagined back home."

"I told you it would be. The Moslems are very obstinate."

"I'll say! and the old devil of a mayor practically told me point-blank that if he caught me proselytizing he'd send me back to Cairo. Imagine the nerve!"

"Well, it *is* their country," I said, reasonably, experiencing my first real hope. Might the Cavites not get themselves expelled from Islam? I knew the mayor of Luxor, a genial merchant who still enjoyed the obsolete title of Pasha. The possibilities of a daring plot occurred to me. All I needed was another year or two, by which time nature would have done its work in any case and the conquest of humanity by the Cavites could then continue its progress without my bitter presence.

I looked at Butler speculatively. He is such a fool. I could, I am sure, undo him for a time at least. Unless of course he is, as I first expected, an agent come to finish me in fact as absolutely as I have been finished in effect by those revisionists who have taken my place among the Cavites, arranging history. . . . I had experienced, briefly, while studying Butler's copy of the Testament, the unnerving sense of having never lived, of having dreamed the past entirely.

"Maybe it is their country but we got the truth, and like Paul Himmell said: 'A truth known to only half the world is but half a truth.'"

"Did he say that?"

"Of course he did. Don't you. . . ." He paused, aware of the book in my hand. His expression softened, like a parent in anger noticing suddenly an endearing resemblance to himself in the offending child. "But I forget how isolated you've been up here. If I've interrupted your studies, I'll go away."

"Oh no. I was finished when you came. I've been studying for several hours, which is too long for an old man."

"If a contemplation of Cavesword can ever be too long," said Butler reverently. "Yes, Himmell wrote that even before Cavesword, in the month of March, I believe, though we'll have to ask my colleague when he comes. He knows all the dates, all the facts. Remarkable guy. He is the brains of the team." And Butler laughed to show that he was not entirely serious.

"I think they might respond to pressure," I said, treacherously. "One thing the Arabs respect is force."

"You may be right. But our instructions are to go slow. Still, I didn't think it would be as slow as this. Why, we haven't been able to get a building yet. They've all been told by the Pasha fellow not to rent to us."

"Perhaps I could talk to him."

"Do you know him well?"

"We used to play backgammon quite regularly. I haven't seen much of him in the past few years, but if you'd like I'll pay him a call."

"He's known all along you're a Cavite, hasn't he?"

"We have kept off the subject of religion entirely. As you've probably discovered, since the division of the world there's been little communication between East and West. I don't think he knows much about the Cavites except that they're undesirable."

"Poor creature," said Butler, compassionately.

"Outer darkness," I agreed.

"But mark my words: before ten years have passed they will have the truth."

"I have no doubt of that, Communicator, none at all. If the others who come out have even a tenth of your devotion the work will go fast." The easy words of praise came back to me mechanically from those decades when a large part of my work was organizational, spurring the mediocre on to great deeds . . . and the truth of the matter has been, traditionally, that the unimaginative are the stuff from which heroes and martyrs are made.

"Thanks for those kind words," said Butler, flushed now with pleasure as well as heat. "Which reminds me, I was going to ask you if you'd like to help us with our work once we get going."

"I'd like nothing better but I'm afraid my years of useful service are over. Any advice, however, or perhaps influence that I may have in Luxor. . . ." There was a warm moment of mutual esteem and amiability, broken only by a reference to the Squad of Belief.

"We'll have one here eventually. Fortunately, the need for them in the Atlantic Community is nearly over. Of course there are always a few malcontents, but we have worked out a statistical ratio of nonconformists in the population which is surprisingly accurate. Knowing their incidence, we are able to check them early. But in general, truth is ascendant everywhere in the civilized world."

"What are their methods now?"

"The Squad of Belief's? Psychological indoctrination. We now have methods of converting even the most obstinate lutherist. Of course where usual methods fail (and once in every fifteen hundred they do), the Squad is authorized to remove a section of brain which effectively does the trick of making the lutherist conform, though his usefulness in a number of other spheres is somewhat impaired. I'm told he has to learn all over again how to talk and to move around."

"Lutherist? I don't recognize the word."

"You certainly have been cut off from the world." Butler looked at me curiously, almost suspiciously. "I thought even in your day that was a common expression. It means anybody who refuses willfully to know the truth."

"What does it come from?"

"Come from?" Semantics was either no longer taught or else Butler had never been interested in it. "Why, it just means, well, a lutherist."

"I wonder, though, what the derivation of it was." I was

91

excited. This was the first sign that I had ever existed, a word of obscure origin connoting nonconformist.

"I'm afraid we'll have to ask my sidekick when he comes. I don't suppose it came from one of those Christian sects . . . you know, the German one that broke with Rome."

"That must be it," I said. "I don't suppose in recent years there have been as many lutherists as there once were."

"Very, very few. As I say, we've got it down to a calculable minority and our psychologists are trying to work out some method whereby we can spot potential lutherists in childhood and indoctrinate them before it's too late . . . but of course the problem is a negligible one in the Atlantic Community. We've had no serious trouble for forty years."

"Forty years . . . that was the time of all the trouble," I said.

"Not so *much* trouble," said Butler, undoing the bandana and mopping his face with it. "The last flare-up, I gather, of the old Christians. History makes very little of it but at the time it must have seemed important. Now that we have more perspective we can view things in their proper light. I was only a kid in those days and, frankly, I don't think I paid any attention to the papers. Of course you remember it." He looked at me suddenly, his great vacuous eyes focused. My heart missed one of its precarious beats: was this the beginning? Had the inquisition begun?

"Not well," I said. "I was seldom in the United States. I'd been digging in Central America, in and around the Petén. I missed most of the trouble."

"You seem to have missed a good deal." His voice was equable, without a trace of secondary meaning.

"I've had a quiet life. I'm grateful though for your coming here. Otherwise, I should have died without any contact with America, without ever knowing what was happening outside the Arab League."

"Well, we'll shake things up around here."

"Shake well before using," I quoted absently.

"What did you say?"

"I said I hoped all would be well."

"I'm sure it will. By the way, I brought you the new edition of Cave's prison dialogues." He pulled a small booklet from his back pocket and handed it to me.

"Thank you." I took the booklet: dialogues between Cave and Iris Mortimer. I had not heard of this particular work. "Is this a recent discovery?" I asked.

"Recent? Why no. It's the newest edition but of course the text goes right back to the early days when Cave was in prison."

"Oh, yes, in California."

"Sure; it was the beginning of the persecutions. Well, I've got to be on my way." He arranged the bandana about his head. "Somebody stole my hat. Persecuting me, I'll bet my bottom dollar . . . little ways. Well, I'm prepared for them. They can't stop us. Sooner or later the whole world will be Cavite."

"Amen," I said.

"What?" He looked at me with shock.

"I'm an old man," I said hastily. "You must recall I was brought up among Christians. Such expressions still linger on, you know."

"It's a good thing there's no Squad of Belief in Luxor," said Butler cheerily. "They'd have you up for indoctrination in a second."

"I doubt if it would be worth their trouble. Soon I shall be withdrawing from the world altogether."

"I suppose so. You haven't thought of taking Cavesway, have you?"

"Of course, many times, but since my health has been good I've been in no great hurry to leave my contemplation of those hills." I pointed to the western window. "And now I should hesitate to die until the very last moment, out of curiosity. I'm eager to learn, to help as much as possible in your work here."

"Well, of course that is good news, but should you ever want to take His Way let me know. We have some marvelous methods now, extremely pleasant to take and, as he said, 'It's not death which is hard but dying.' We've finally made dying simply swell."

"Will wonders never cease?"

"In that department, never! It is the firm basis of our truth. Now I must be off."

"Is your colleague due here soon?"

"Haven't heard recently. But I don't suppose the plans have been changed. You'll like him."

"I'm sure I shall."

## 2

And so John Cave's period in jail was now known as the time of persecution, with a pious prison dialogue attributed to Iris. Before I returned to my work of recollection I glanced at the dialogue, whose style was enough like Iris's to have been her work. But of course her style was not one which could ever have been called inimitable since it was based on the most insistent of twentieth-century advertising techniques. I assumed the book was the work of one of those anonymous counterfeiters who have created, according to a list of publications on the back of the booklet, a wealth of Cavite doctrine.

The conversation with Cave in prison was lofty in tone and seemed to deal with moral problems. It was apparent that since the task of governing is largely one of keeping order, with the passage of time it had become necessary for the Cavite rulers to compose in Cave's name different works of ethical instruction to be used for the guidance and control of the population. I assume that since they now control all records and original sources, it is an easy matter for them to "discover" some relevant text that gives clear answer to any moral or political problem not anticipated in previous commentaries. The work of falsifying records and expunging names is, I should think, somewhat more tricky but they seem to have accomplished it in Cave's Testament, brazenly assuming that those who recall the earlier versions will die off in time, leaving a generation who knows only what they wish it to know, excepting of course the "calculable minority" of nonconformists, of base lutherists.

Cave's term in prison was far less dramatic than official legend, though more serious. He was jailed for hit-and-run driving on the highway from Santa Monica into Los Angeles.

I went to see him that evening with Paul. When we arrived at the jail, we were not allowed near him though Paul's lawyers had been permitted to go inside a few minutes before our arrival.

Iris was sitting in the outer office, pale and shaken. A bored policeman in uniform sat at a desk, ignoring us.

"They're the best lawyers in L.A.," said Paul quickly. "They'll get him out in no time."

Iris looked at him bleakly.

"What happened?" I asked, sitting down beside her on the bench. "How did it happen?"

"I wasn't with him." She shook her head several times as though to dispel a profound daydream. "He called me and I called you. They *are* the best, Paul?"

"I can vouch for that . . ."

"Did he kill anybody?"

"We . . . we don't know yet. He hit an old man and went on driving. I don't know why. I mean why he didn't stop. He just went on and the police car caught him. The man's in the hospital now. They say it's bad. He's unconscious, an old man . . ."

"Any reporters here?" asked Paul. "Anybody else know besides us?"

"Nobody. You're the only person I called."

"This could wreck everything." Paul was frightened.

But Cave was rescued, at considerable expense to the company. The old man chose not to die immediately, while the police and the courts of Los Angeles, at that time well known for their accessibility to free-spending reason, proved more than obliging. After a day and a night in prison, Cave was released on bail, and when the case came to court it was handled discreetly by the magistrate.

The newspapers, however, had discovered John Cave at last and there were photographs of "Present-Day Messiah in Court." As ill luck would have it, the undertakers of Laguna had come to the aid of their prophet with banners which proclaimed his message. This picketing of the court was photographed and exhibited in the tabloids. Paul was in a frenzy. Publicist though he was, in his first rage he expressed to me the novel sentiment that not all publicity was good.

"But we'll get back at those bastards," he said grimly, not identifying which ones he meant but waving toward the city hidden by the Venetian blinds of his office window.

I asked for instructions. The day before, Cave had gone back to Washington state to lie low until the time was right for a triumphant reappearance. Iris had gone with him; on a separate plane, to avoid scandal. Clarissa had sent various heartening if confused messages from New York while Paul and I were left to gather up the pieces and begin again. Our close association during those difficult days impressed me with his talents and though, fundamentally, I still found him appalling, I couldn't help but admire his superb operativeness.

"I'm going ahead with the original plan . . . just like none of this happened. The stockholders are willing and we've got enough money, though not as much as I'd like, for the publicity build-up. I expect Cave'll pick up some more cash in Seattle. He always does, wherever he goes."

"Millionaires just flock to him?"

"Strange to tell, yes. But then, nearly everybody does."

"It's funny, since the truth he offers is all there is to it. Once it is experienced, there's no longer much need for Cave or for an organization." This of course was the paradox which time and the unscrupulous were bloodily to resolve.

Paul's answer was reasonable. "That's true, but there's the

problem of sharing it. If millions felt the same way about death the whole world would be happier and, if it's happier, why, it'll be a better place to live in."

"Do you really believe this?"

"Still think of me as a hundred per cent phony?" Paul chuckled good-naturedly. "Well, it so happens, I *do* believe that. It also so happens that if this thing clicks we'll have a world organization and if we have, there'll be a big place for number one in it. It's all mixed up, Gene. I'd like to hear *your* motives, straight from the shoulder."

I was not prepared to answer him, or myself. In fact, to this day, my own motives are a puzzle to which there is no single key, no easy answer. One is not, after all, like those classic or neo-classic figures who wore with such splendid mono-maniacal consistency the scarlet of lust or the purple of dominion or the bright yellow of madness, existing not at all beneath their identifying robes. Power appealed to me in my youth but only as a minor pleasure and not as an end in itself or even as a means to any private or public end. I enjoyed the idea of guiding and dominating others, preferably in the mass; yet, at the same time, I did not like the boredom of power achieved, or the silly publicness of a great life. But there was something which, often against my will and judgment, precipitated me into deeds and attitudes where the logic of the moment controlled me to such an extent that I could not lessen, if I chose, the momentum of my own wild passage, or chart its course.

I would not have confided this to Paul even had I in those days thought any of it out, which I had not. Though I was conscious of some fundamental ambivalence in myself, I always felt that should I pause for a few moments and question myself, I could easily find answers to these problems. But I did not pause. I never asked myself a single question concerning motive. I acted like a man sleeping who was only barely made conscious by certain odd incongruities that he dreams. The secret which later I was to discover was still unrevealed to me as

I faced the efficient vulgarity of Paul Himmell across the portable bar which reflected his competence so brightly in its crystal.

"My motives are perfectly simple," I said, half believing what I said. In those days the more sweeping the statement, the more apt I was to give it my fickle allegiance. Motives are simple, splendid! Simple they are. "I want something to do. I'm fascinated by Cave and I believe what he says . . . not that it is so supremely earthshaking. It's been advanced as a theory off and on for two thousand years. Kant wrote that he anticipated with delight the luxurious sleep of the grave, and the Gnostics came close to saying the same thing when they promised a glad liberation from life. The Eastern religions, about which I know very little, maintain . . ."

"That's it!" Paul interrupted me eagerly. "That's what we want. You just keep on like that. We'll call it 'An Introduction to John Cave.' Make a small book out of it. Get it published in New York. Then the company will buy up copies and we'll pass it out free."

"I'm not so sure that I know enough formal philosophy to . . ."

"To hell with that stuff. You just root around and show how the old writers were really Cavites at heart and then you come to him and put down what he says. Why we'll be half there even before he's on TV!" Paul lapsed for a moment into a reverie of promotion. I had another drink and felt quite good myself, although I had serious doubts about my competence to compose philosophy in the popular key. But Paul's faith was infectious and I felt that, all in all, with a bit of judicious hedging and recourse to various explicit summaries and definitions, I might put together a respectable ancestry for Cave, whose message, essentially, ignored *all* philosophy, empiric and orphic, moving with hypnotic effectiveness to the main proposition: death and man's acceptance of it. The problems of life were always quite secondary to Cave, if not to the rest of us.

"When will you want this piece done?"

"The sooner the better. Here," he scribbled an address on a pad of paper. "This is Cave's address. He's on a farm outside Spokane. It belongs to one of his undertaker friends."

"Iris is with him?"

"Yes. Now you . . ."

"I wonder if that's wise, Iris seeing so much of him. You know he's going to have a good many enemies before very long and they'll dig around for any scandal they can find."

"Oh, it's perfectly innocent, I'm sure. Even if it isn't, I can't see how it can do much harm."

"For a public relations man you don't seem to grasp the possibilities for bad publicity in this situation."

"All pub . . ."

"Is good. But Cave, it appears, is a genuine ascetic." And the word "genuine" as I spoke it was like a knife blade in my heart. "And, since he is, you have a tremendous advantage in building him up. There's no use in allowing him, quite innocently, to appear to philander."

Paul looked at me curiously. "You wouldn't by chance be interested in Iris yourself?"

And of course that was it. I had become attached to Iris in precisely the same sort of way a complete man might have been but of course for me there was no hope, nothing. The enormity of that nothing shook me, despite the alcohol I had drunk. Fortunately, I was sufficiently collected not to make the mistake of vehemence. "I like her very much but I'm more attached to the idea of Cave than I am to her. I don't want to see the business get out of hand. That's all. I'm surprised that you, of all people, aren't more concerned."

"You may have a point. I suppose I've got to adjust my views to this thing . . . it's different from my usual work building up show business types. In that line the romance angle is swell, just as long as there are no bigamies or abortions involved. I see your point, though. With Cave we have to think in sort of Legion of Decency terms. No rough stuff. No nightclub pictures or posing with blondes. You're absolutely right. Put that in your piece: doesn't drink, doesn't go out with dames . . ."

I laughed. "Maybe we won't have to go that far. The negative virtues usually shine through all on their own. The minute you draw attention to them you create suspicion. People are generally pleased to suspect the opposite of every avowal."

"You talk just like my analyst." And I felt that I had won, briefly, Paul's admiration. "Anyway, you go to Spokane; talk to Iris; tell her to lay off . . . in a tactful way of course. But don't mention it to him. You never can tell how he'll react. She'll be reasonable even though I suspect she is stuck on the man. Try and get your piece done by the first of December. I'd like to have it in print for the first of the New Year, Cave's year."

"I'll try."

"By the way, we're getting an office, same building as this."

"Cavite, Inc.?"

"We could hardly call it the Church of the Golden Rule," said Paul with one of the few shows of irritability I was ever to observe in his equable disposition. "Now, on behalf of the directors, I'm authorized to advance you whatever money you might feel you need for this project. That is, within . . ."

"I won't need anything except, perhaps, a directorship in the company." My own boldness startled me. Paul laughed.

"That's a good boy. Eye on the main chance. Well, we'll see what we can do about that. There aren't any more shares available right now but that doesn't mean. . . . I'll let you know when you get back from Spokane."

Our meeting was ended by the appearance of his secretary, who called him away to other business. As we parted in the outer office, he said, quite seriously, "I don't think Iris likes him the way you think but if she does be careful. We can't upset Cave now. This is a tricky time for everyone. Don't show that you suspect anything. Later, when we're under way and there's less pressure, I'll handle it. Agreed?"

I agreed, secretly pleased at being thought in love . . . "in love" – to this moment the phrase has a strangely foreign sound to me, like a classical allusion not entirely understood in a scholarly text. "In love," I whispered to myself in the elevator as I left Paul that evening: in love with Iris.

3

We met at the Spokane railroad station and Iris drove me through the wide, clear, characterless streets to a country road which wound east into the hills, in the direction of a town with the lovely name of Coeur d'Alene.

She was relaxed. Her ordinarily pale face was faintly burned from the sun, while her hair, which I recalled as darkly waving, was now streaked with light and loosely bound at the nape of the neck. She wore no cosmetics and her dress was simple cotton beneath the sweater she wore against the autumn's chill. She looked younger than either of us actually was.

At first we talked of Spokane. She identified mountains and indicated hidden villages with an emphasis on place which sharply recalled Cave. Not until we had turned off the main highway into a country road, dark with fir and spruce, did she ask me about Paul. I told her. "He's very busy preparing our New Year's debut. He's also got a set of offices for the company in Los Angeles and he's engaged me to write an introduction to Cave . . . but I suppose you knew that when he wired you I was coming."

"It was my idea."

"My coming? Or the introduction?"

"Both."

"And I thought he picked it out of the air while listening to me majestically place Cave among the philosophers."

Iris smiled. "Paul's not obvious. He enjoys laying traps and as long as they're for one's own good, he's very useful."

"Implying he could be destructive?"

"Immensely. So be on your guard even though I don't think

he'll harm any of us."

"How is Cave?"

"I'm worried, Gene. He hasn't got over that accident. He talks about it continually."

"But the man didn't die."

"It would be better if he did . . . as it is, there's a chance of a lawsuit against Cave for damages."

"But he has no money."

"That doesn't prevent them from suing. But worst of all, there's the publicity. The whole thing has depressed Cave terribly. It was all I could do to keep him from announcing to the press that he had almost done the old man a favor."

"You mean by killing him?"

Iris nodded, quite seriously. "That's actually what he believes and the reason why he drove on."

"I'm glad he said nothing like that to the papers."

"But it's true; his point of view is exactly right."

"Except that the old man might regard the situation in a different light and, in any case, he was badly hurt and did not receive Cave's gift of death."

"Now you're making fun of us." She frowned and drove fast on the empty road.

"I'm doing no such thing. I'm absolutely serious. There's a moral problem involved which is extremely important and if a precedent is set too early, a bad one like this, there's no predicting how things will turn out."

"You mean the . . . the gift, as you call it, should only be given voluntarily?"

"Exactly . . . *if* then, and only in extreme cases. Think what might happen if those who listened to Cave decided to make all their friends and enemies content by killing them."

"Well, I wish you'd talk to him." She smiled sadly. "I'm afraid I don't always see things clearly when I'm with him. You know how he is . . . how he convinces."

"I'll talk to him tactfully. I must also get a statement of belief from him."

"But you have it already. We all have it."

"Then I'll want some moral application of it. We still have so much ground to cover."

"There's the farm, up there on the hill." A white frame building stood shining among spruce on a low hill at the foot of blue sharp mountains. She turned up a dirt road and, in silence, we arrived at the house.

An old woman, the cook, greeted us familiarly and told Iris that *he* could be found in the study.

In a small warm room, sitting beside a stone fireplace empty of fire, Cave sat, a scrapbook on his knees, his expression vague, unfocused. Our arrival recalled him from some dense reverie. He got to his feet quickly and shook hands. "I'm glad you came," he said.

It was Cave's particular gift to strike a note of penetrating sincerity at all times, even in his greetings, which became, as a result, disconcertingly like benedictions. Iris excused herself and we sat beside the fireplace.

"Have you seen these?" Cave pushed the scrapbook toward me.

I took the book and saw the various newspaper stories concerning the accident. It had got a surprisingly large amount of space as though, instinctively, the editors had anticipated a coming celebrity for "Hit-and-Run Prophet."

"Look what they say about me."

"I've read them," I said, handing the scrapbook back to him, a little surprised that, considering his unworldliness, he had bothered to keep such careful track of his appearance in the press. It showed a new, rather touching side to him; he was like an actor hoarding notices, good and bad. "I don't think it's serious. After all you were let off by the court, and the man didn't die."

"It was an accident, of course. Yet that old man nearly received the greatest gift a man can have, a quick death. I wanted to tell the court that. I could have convinced them, I'm sure, but Paul said no. It was the first time I've ever gone against my own instinct and I don't like it." Emphatically, he shut the book.

The cook came into the room and lit the fire. When the first crackling filled the room and the pine had caught, she left, observing that we were to eat in an hour.

"You want to wash up?" asked Cave mechanically, his eyes on the fire, his hands clasped in his lap like those dingy marble replicas of hands which decorate medieval tombs. That night there was an unhuman look to Cave: pale, withdrawn, inert . . . his lips barely moving when he spoke, as though another's voice spoke through senseless flesh.

"No thanks," I said, a little chilled by his remoteness. Then I got him off the subject of the accident as quickly as possible and we talked until dinner of the introduction I was to write. It was most enlightening. As I suspected, Cave had read only the Bible and that superficially, just enough to be able, at crucial moments, to affect the seventeenth-century prose of the translators and to confound thereby simple listeners with the familiar authority of his manner. His knowledge of philosophy did not even encompass the names of the principals. Plato and Aristotle rang faint, unrelated bells and with them the meager carillon ended.

"I don't know why you want to drag in those people," he said, after I had suggested Zoroaster as a possible point of beginning. "Most people have never heard of them either. And what I have to say is all my own. It doesn't tie in with any of them or, if it does, it's a coincidence, because I never picked it up anywhere."

"But I think that it *would* help matters if we provided a sort of family tree for you, to show . . ."

"I don't." He gestured with his effigy-hands. "Let them argue about it later. For now, act like this is a new beginning, which it is. I have only one thing to give people and that is the way to die without fear, gladly, to accept nothing for what it is, a long and dreamless sleep."

I had to fight against that voice, those eyes which as always, when he chose, could dominate any listener. Despite my close association with him, despite the thousands of times I heard him speak, I was never, even in moments of lucid disenchantment, quite able to resist his power. He was a magician in the great line of Simon Magus. That much, even now, I will acknowledge. His divinity, however, was and is the work of others, shaped and directed by the race's recurrent need.

I surrendered in the name of philosophy with a certain relief, and he spoke in specific terms of what he believed that I should write in his name.

It was not until after dinner that we got around, all three of us, to a problem which was soon to absorb us all, with near-disastrous results.

We had been talking amiably of neutral things and Cave had emerged somewhat from his earlier despondency. He got on to the subject of the farm where we were, of its attractiveness and remoteness, of its owner who lived in Spokane.

"I always liked old Smathers. You'd like him too. He's got one of the biggest funeral parlors in the state. I used to work for him and then, when I started on all this, he backed me to the hilt. Loaned me money to get as far as San Francisco. After that of course it was easy. I paid him back every cent."

"Does he come here often?"

Cave shook his head. "No, he lets me use the farm but he keeps away. He says he doesn't approve of what I'm doing. You see, he's Catholic."

"But he still likes John," said Iris, who had been stroking a particularly ugly yellow cat beside the fire. So it was John now, I thought.

"Yes. He's a good friend."

"There'll be a lot of trouble, you know," I said.

"From Smathers?"

"No, from the Catholics, from the Christians."

"You really think so?" Cave looked at me curiously. I believe that until that moment he had never realized the inevitable collision of his point of view with that of the established religions.

"Of course I do. They've constructed an entire ethical system upon a supernatural foundation whose main strength is the promise of a continuation of human personality after death. You are rejecting grace, heaven, hell, the Trinity . . . "

"I've never said anything about the Trinity or about Christianity."

"But you'll *have* to say something about it sooner or later. If – or rather when – the people begin to accept you, the churches will fight back, and the greater the impression you make, the more fierce their attack."

"I suspect John *is* the Antichrist," said Iris, and I saw from her expression that she was perfectly serious. "He's come to undo all the wickedness of the Christians."

"Though not, I hope, of Christ," I said. "There's some virtue in his legend, even as corrupted at Nicea three centuries after the fact."

"I'll have to think about it," said Cave. "I don't know that I've ever given it much thought before. I've spoken always what I knew was true and there's never been any opposition, at least that I've been aware of, to my face. It never occurred to me that people who like to think of themselves as Christians couldn't accept both me and Christ at the same time. I know I don't promise the kingdom of heaven but I *do* promise oblivion and the loss of self, of pain . . . "

"Gene is right," said Iris. "They'll fight you hard. You must get ready now while you still have time to think it out, before Paul puts you to work and you'll never have a moment's peace again."

"As bad as that, you think?" Cave sighed wistfully. "But how to get ready? What should I do? I never think things out, you know. Everything occurs to me on the spot. I can never tell what may occur to me next. It happens only when I speak to people. When I'm alone, I seldom think of the . . . the main things. But when I'm in a group talking to them I hear . . . no, not hear, I *feel* voices telling me what I should say. That's why I never prepare a talk, why I don't really like to have them taken down. There are some things which are meant only for the instant they are conceived . . . a child, if you like, made for just a moment's life by the people listening and myself speaking. I don't mean to sound touched," he added, with a sudden smile. "I'm not really *hearing* things but I do get something from those people, something besides the thing I tell them. I seem to become a part of them, as though what goes on in their minds also goes on in me at the same time, two lobes to a single brain."

"We know that, John," said Iris softly. "We've felt it."

"I suppose, then, that's the key," said Cave. "Though it isn't much to write about. I don't suppose you can put it across without me to say it."

"You may be wrong there," I said. "Of course in the beginning you will say the word but I think in time, properly managed, everyone will accept it on the strength of evidence and statement, responding to the chain of forces you have set in motion." Yet for all the glibness with which I spoke, I did not really believe that Cave would prove to be more than an interesting momentary phenomenon whose "truth" about death might, at best, contribute in a small way to the final abolition of those old warring superstitions which had mystified and troubled men through all the dark centuries. A doubt which displayed my basic misunderstanding of our race's will to death and, worse, to a death in life made radiant by false dreams, by desperate adjurations.

But that evening we spoke only of a bright future: "To begin again is the important thing," I said. "Christianity, though strong as an organization in this country, is weak as a force because, finally, the essential doctrine is not accepted by most of the people: the idea of a manlike God dispensing merits and demerits at time's end."

"We are small," said Cave. "In space, on this tiny planet, we are nothing. Death brings us back to the whole. We lose this instant of awareness, of suffering, like spray in the ocean. There it forms, there it goes back to the sea."

"I think people will listen to you because they realize now that order, if there is any, has never been revealed, that death *is* the end of personality even for those passionate, self-important 'I's who insist upon a universal deity like themselves, presented eponymously in order not to give the game away."

"How dark, how fine the grave must be! Only sleep and an end of days, an end of fear. The end of fear in the grave as the 'I' goes back to nothing. . . ."

"Yes, Cave, life will be wonderful when men no longer fear dying. When the last superstitions are thrown out and we meet death with the same equanimity that we have met life. No longer will children's minds be twisted by evil gods whose fantastic origin is in those barbaric tribes who feared death and lightning, who feared life. That's it: life is the villain to those who preach reward in death, through grace and eternal bliss, or through dark revenge . . ."

"Neither revenge nor reward, only the not-knowing in the grave which is the same for all."

"And without those inhuman laws, what societies we might build! Take the morality of Christ. Begin there, or even earlier with Plato or earlier yet with Zoroaster. Take the best ideas of the best men and should there be any disagreement as to what is best, use life as the definition, life as the measure. What contributes most to the living is the best."

"But the living is soon done and the sooner done the better. I envy those who have already gone."

"If they listen to you, Cave, it will be like the unlocking of a prison. At first they may go wild but then, on their own, they will find ways to life. Fear of punishment in death has seldom stopped the murderer's hand. The only two things which hold him from his purpose are, at the worst, fear of reprisal from society and, at the best, a feeling for life, a love for all that lives. And not the wide-smiling idiot's love but a sense of the community of the living, of life's marvelous regency. Even the most ignorant has felt this. Life is all while death is only the irrelevant shadow at the end, the counterpart to that instant before the seed lives."

Yes, I believed all that, all that and more too, and I felt Cave was the same as I. By removing fear with that magic of his, he would fulfill certain hopes of my own and (I flatter myself perhaps) of the long line of others, nobler than I, who had been equally engaged in attempting to use life more fully. And so that evening the one true conviction of a desultory life broke through the chill hard surface of disappointment and disgust that had formed a brittle carapace about my heart. I had, after all, my truth too, and Cave had got to it, broken the shell, and for that I shall remain grateful to him, until we are at last the same, both taken by dust.

Excitedly, we talked. I talked mostly. Cave was the theme and I the counterpoint, or so I thought. He had stated it and I built upon what I conceived to be the luminosity of his vision. Our dialogue was one of communion. Only Iris guessed that it was not. From the beginning she saw the difference; she was conscious of the division which that moment had, unknown to either of us, separated me from Cave. *Each time I said "life," he said "death."* In true amity but false concord, the fatal rift began.

Iris, more practical than we, deflated our visions by pulling the dialogue gently back to reality, to ways and dull means.

It was agreed that we had agreed on fundamentals: the end of fear was desirable; superstition should be exorcised from human affairs; the ethical systems constructed by the major religious figures from Zoroaster to Mohammed all contained useful and applicable ideas of societal behaviour which need not be discarded.

At Iris's suggestion, we left the problem of Christianity itself completely alone. Cave's truth was sufficient cause for battle. There was no reason, she felt, for antagonizing the ultimate enemy at the very beginning.

"Let them attack *you*, John. You must be above quarreling."

"I reckon I *am* above it," said Cave, and he sounded almost cheerful for the first time since my arrival. "I want no trouble, but if trouble comes I don't intend to back down. I'll just go on saying what I know."

At midnight, Cave excused himself and went to bed.

Iris and I sat silent before the last red embers on the hearth. I sensed that something had gone wrong but I could not tell what it was.

When Iris spoke, her manner was abrupt. "Do you really want to go on with this?"

"What an odd time to ask me that. Of course I do. Tonight's the first time I really saw what it was Cave meant, what it was I'd always felt but never before known; consciously, that is. I couldn't be more enthusiastic."

"I hope you don't change."

"Why so glum? What are you trying to say? After all, you got me into this."

"I know I did and I think I was right. It's only that this evening I felt . . . well, I don't know. Perhaps I'm getting a bit on edge." She smiled and, through all the youth and health, I saw that she was anxious and ill at ease.

"That business about the accident?"

"Mainly, yes. The lawyers say that now that the old man's all right he'll try to collect damages. He'll sue Cave."

"Nasty publicity."

"The worst. It's upset John terribly . . . he almost feels it's an omen."

"I thought we were dispensing with all that, with miracles and omens." I smiled but she did not.

"Speak for yourself." She got up and pushed at the coals with a fire shovel. "Paul says he'll handle everything but I don't see how. There's no way he can stop a lawsuit."

But I was tired of the one problem which was out of our hands anyway. I asked her about herself and Cave.

"Is it wise my being up here with John, alone? No, I'm afraid not but that's the way it is." Her voice was hard and her back, now turned to me, grew stiff, her movements with the fire shovel angry and abrupt.

"People will use it against both of you. It may hurt him, and all of us."

She turned suddenly, her face flushed. "I can't help it, Gene. I swear I can't. I've tried to keep away. I almost flew East with Clarissa but when he asked me to join him here, I did. I couldn't leave him."

"Will marriage be a part of the new order?"

"Don't joke." She sat down angrily in a noise of skirts crumpling. "Cave must never marry. Besides it's . . . it isn't like that."

"Really? I must confess I . . ."

"Thought we were having an affair? Well, it's not true." The rigidity left her as suddenly as it had possessed her. She grew visibly passive, even helpless, in the worn upholstered chair, her eyes on me, the anger gone and only weakness left. "What can I do?" It was a cry from the heart. All the more touching because, obviously, she had not intended to tell me so much. She had turned to me because there was no one else to whom she could talk.

"You . . . love him?" That word which whenever I spoke it in those days always stuck in my throat like a diminutive sob.

"More, more," she said distractedly. "But I can't *do* anything or *be* anything. He's complete. He doesn't need anyone. He doesn't want me except as . . . a companion, and adviser like you or Paul. It's all the same to him."

"I don't see that it's hopeless."

"Hopeless!" The word shot from her like a desperate deed. She buried her face in her hands but she did not weep. I sat watching her. The noise of a clock's dry ticking kept the silence from falling in about our heads.

Finally, she dropped her hands and turned toward me with her usual grace. "You mustn't take me too seriously," she said. "Or I mustn't take myself too seriously, which is more to the point. Cave doesn't really need me or anyone and we . . . I, perhaps you, certainly others, need him. It's best no one try to claim him all as a woman would do, as I might, given the chance." She rose. "It's late and you must be tired. Don't ever mention to anyone what I've told you tonight, especially to John. If he knew the way I felt. . . ." She left it at that. I gave my promise and we went to our rooms.

I stayed two days at the farm, listening to Cave, who continually referred to the accident. He was almost petulant, as though the whole business were an irrelevant gratuitous trick played on him by a malicious old man.

Cave's days were spent reading his mail (there was quite a bit of it even then), composing answers which Iris typed out for him, and walking in the wooded hills that surrounded the farm.

The weather was sharp and bright and the wind, when it blew, tasted of ice from the glaciers in the vivid mountains. Winter was nearly upon us and red leaves decorated the wind. Only the firs remained unchanged, warm and dark in the bright chill days.

Cave and I would walk together while Iris remained indoors, working. He was a good walker, calm, unhurried, sure-footed, and he knew all the trails beneath the fallen yellow and red leaves. He agreed with most of my ideas for the introduction. I promised to send him a first draft as soon as I had got it done. He was genuinely indifferent to the philosophic aspect of what he preached. He acted almost as if he did not want to hear of those others who had approached the great matter in a similar way. When I talked to him of the fourth-century Donatists who detested life and loved heaven so much that they would request strangers to kill them, and magistrates to execute them for no crime, he stopped me. "I don't want to hear all that. That's finished. All that's over. We want new things now."

Iris, too, seemed uninterested in any formalizing of Cave's thought though she saw its necessity and wished me well, suggesting that I not ever intimate derivation since, in fact, there had been none. What he was he had become on his own, uninstructed.

During our walks, I got to know Cave as well as I was ever to know him. He was indifferent, I think, to everyone. He gave one his attention in precise ratio to one's belief in him and the importance of his work. With groups he was another creature: warm, intoxicating, human, yet transcendent, a part of each man who beheld him, the long desired and pursued whole achieved.

And though I found him without much warmth or mind, I nevertheless identified him with the release I had known in his presence, and for this one certainty of life's value and of death's irrelevance, I loved him.

On the third day I made up my mind to go back East and do the necessary writing in New York, away from Paul's distracting influence and Cave's advice. I was asked to stay the rest of the week but I could see that Iris regarded me now as a potential danger, a keeper of secrets who might, despite promises, prove to be disloyal; and so, to set her mind at ease as well as to suit my own new plans, I told her privately after lunch on the third day that I was ready to leave that evening if she would drive me to Spokane.

"You're a good friend," she said. "I made a fool of myself the other night. I wish you'd forget it . . . forget everything I said."

"I'll never mention it. Now, the problem is how I can leave here gracefully. Cave just asked me this morning to stay on and . . ."

But I was given a perfect means of escape. Cave came running into the room, his eyes shining. "Iris! I've just talked to Paul in L.A. It's all over! No heirs, nothing, no lawsuit. No damages to pay."

"What's happened?" Iris stopped him in his excitement.

"The old man's dead!"

"Oh Lord!" Iris went gray. "That means a manslaughter charge!"

"No, no . . . not because of the accident. He was in *another* accident. A truck hit him the day after he left the hospital.

Yesterday. He was killed instantly . . . lucky devil. And of course we're in luck too."

"Did they find who hit him?" I asked, suddenly suspicious. Iris looked at me fiercely. She had got it too.

"No. Paul said it was a hit-and-run. He said this time the police didn't find who did it. Paul said his analyst calls it 'a will to disaster' . . . the old man *wanted* to be run over. Of course that's hardly a disaster but the analyst thinks the old way."

I left that afternoon for New York, leaving Cave jubilantly making plans for the New Year. Everything was again possible. Neither Iris nor I mentioned what we both suspected. Each in his different way accommodated the first of many crimes.

# ❧ 7 ❧

## 1

"The tone, dear Gene, has all the unction, all the earnest turgidity of a trained theologian. You are perfect." Clarissa beamed at me wickedly over lunch in the Plaza Hotel. We sat at a table beside a great plate-glass window through which was visible the frosted bleak expanse of Central Park, ringed by buildings, monotonous in their sharp symmetry. The sky was sullen, dingy with snow ready to fall. The year was nearly over.

"I thought it quite to the point," I said loftily but with an anxious glance at the thin black volume which was that day to be published, the hasty work of one hectic month, printed in record time by a connection of Paul Himmell's.

"It's pure nonsense, the historical part. *I* know, though I confess I was never one for philosophers, dreary *egotistical* men, worse than actors and not half so lovely. Waiter, I will have a melon. Out of season I hope. I suggest you have it too. It's light."

I ordered *pot-de-crème*, the heaviest dessert on the menu.

"I've made you angry." Clarissa pretended contrition. "I was only trying to compliment you. What I meant was that I think the sort of thing you're doing is nonsense only because action is what counts, action on any level, not theorizing."

"There's a certain action to *thinking*, you know, even to writing about the thoughts of others."

"Oh, darling, don't sound so stuffy. Your dessert, by the way,

115

poisons the liver. Oh, isn't that Bishop Winston over there by the door, in tweed? In mufti, eh, Bishop?"

The Bishop, who was passing our table in the company of a handsomely pale youth whose contemplation of orders shone in his face like some cherished sin, stopped and with a smile shook Clarissa's hand.

"Ah, how are you? I missed you the other night at Agnes's. She told me you've been engaged in social work."

"A euphemism, Bishop." Clarissa introduced me and the prelate moved on to his table.

"Catholic?"

"Hardly. Episcopal. I like them the best, I think. They adore society and good works . . . spiritual Whigs you might call them, a civilizing influence. Best of all, so few of them believe in God, unlike the Catholics or those terrible Calvinist peasants who are forever damning others."

"I think you're much too hard on the Episcopalians. I'm sure some of them must believe what they preach."

"Well, we shall probably never know. Social work! I knew Agnes would come up with something altogether wrong. Still, I'm just as glad it's not out yet. Not until the big debut tomorrow afternoon. I hope you've made arrangements to be near a television set. No? Then come to my place and we'll see it together. Cave's asked us both to the station, by the way, but I think it better if we don't distract him."

"Iris came East with him?"

"Indeed she did. They both arrived last night. I thought you'd talked to her."

"No. Paul's the only one I ever see."

"He keeps the whole thing going, I must say. One of those born organizers. Now! What about you and Iris?"

This came so suddenly, without preparation, that it took me a suspiciously long time to answer, weakly, "I don't know what you mean. What about Iris and me?"

"Darling, I know *everything*." She looked at me in her eager, predatory way. I was secretly pleased that, in this particular case at least, she knew nothing.

"Then tell *me.*"

"You're in love with her and she's classically involved with Cave."

"Classical seems to be the wrong word. Nothing has happened and nothing *will* happen."

"I suppose she told you this herself."

I was trapped for a moment. Clarissa, even in error, was shrewd and if one was not on guard she would quickly cease to be in error at one's expense.

"No, not exactly. But Paul who I think does know everything about our affairs, assures me that nothing has happened, that Cave is not interested in women."

"In men?"

"I thought you were all-knowing. No, not in men nor in wild animals nor, does it seem, from the evidence Paul's collected, in anything except John Cave. Sex does not happen for him."

"Oh," said Clarissa, exhaling slowly, significantly, inscrutably. She abandoned her first line of attack to ask, "But *you* are crazy about Iris, aren't you? That's what I'd intended, you know, when I brought you two together."

"I thought it was to bring me into Cave's orbit."

"That too, but somehow I saw you and Iris . . . well, you're obviously going to give me no satisfaction so I shall be forced to investigate on my own."

"Not to sound too auctorial, too worried, do you think it will get Cave across? My Introduction?"

"I see no reason why not. Look at the enormous success of those books with titles like 'Eternal Bliss Can Be Yours for the Asking' or 'Happiness at Your Beck and Call.' "

"I'm a little more ambitious."

"Not in the least. But the end served is the same. You put down the main line of Cave's thinking, if it can be called thinking. And your book, along with his presence, should have an extraordinary effect."

"Do you really think so? I've begun to doubt."

"Indeed I do. They are waiting, all those sad millions who want to believe will find him exactly right for their purposes. He exists only to be believed in. He's a natural idol. Did you know that when Constantine moved his court to the East, his heirs were trained by Eastern courtiers to behave like idols and when his son came in triumph back to Rome (what a day that was! hot, but exciting) he rode for hours through the crowded streets without once moving a finger or changing expression, a perfectly trained god. We were all so impressed."

I cut this short. "Has it occurred to you that they might not want to believe anything, just like you and me?"

"Nonsense . . . and it's rude to interrupt, dear, even a garrulous relic like myself . . . yet after all, in a way, we *do* believe what Cave says. Death is there and he makes it seem perfectly all right, oblivion and the rest of it. And dying does rather upset a lot of people. Have you noticed one thing that the devoutly superstitious can never understand – that though we do not accept the fairy tale of reward or punishment beyond the grave we still are reluctant to 'pass on,' as the nuts say? As though the prospect of nothing isn't really, in its way, without friend Cave to push one into acceptance, perfectly ghastly, *much* worse than toasting on a grid like poor Saint Lawrence. But now I must fly. Come to the apartment at seven and I'll give you dinner. He's on at eight. Afterward they'll all join us." Clarissa flew.

I spent the afternoon gloomily walking up and down Fifth Avenue filled with doubt and foreboding, wishing now that I had never lent myself to the conspiracy, confident of its failure and of the rude laughter or, worse, the tactful silence of friends who would be astonished to find that after so many years of promise and reflection my first book should prove to be an apologia for an obscure evangelist whose only eminence was that of having mesmerized myself and an energetic publicist, as well as a handful of others more susceptible perhaps than we.

The day did nothing to improve my mood, and it was in a most depressed state that I went finally to Clarissa's Empire apartment on one of the good streets to dine with her and infect her, I was darkly pleased to note, with my own grim mood. By the time Cave was announced on the television screen, I had reduced Clarissa, for one of the few times in our acquaintance, to silence.

Yet as the lights in the room mechanically dimmed and an announcer came into focus, I was conscious of a quickening of my pulse, of a certain excitement. Here it was at last, the result of nearly a year's careful planning. Soon, in a matter of minutes, we would know.

To my surprise Paul Himmell was introduced by the announcer, who identified him perfunctorily, saying that the following half hour had been bought by Cavite, Inc.

Paul spoke briefly, earnestly. He was nervous, I could see, and his eyes moved from left to right disconcertingly as he read his introduction from cards out of view of the camera. He described Cave briefly as a teacher, as a highly regarded figure in the West. He implied it was as a public service, the rarest of philanthropies, that a group of industrialists and businessmen were sponsoring Cave this evening.

Then Paul walked out of range of the camera, leaving, briefly, a view of a chair and a table behind which a handsome velvet curtain fell in rich graceful folds from the invisible ceiling to an imitation marble floor. An instant later, Cave walked into view.

Both Clarissa and I leaned forward in our chairs tensely, eagerly, anxiously. We were there as well as he. This was our moment too. My hands grew cold and my throat dry.

Cave was equal to the moment. He looked tall. The scale of the table and the chair was exactly right. He wore a dark suit and a dark unfigured tie with a light shirt that gave him an austereness which, in person, he lacked. I saw Paul's stage-managing in this.

Cave moved easily into range, his eyes cast down. Not until he had placed himself in front of the table and the camera had squarely centered him did he look directly into the lens.

Clarissa gasped and I felt suddenly pierced; the camera and lights had magnified rather than diminished his power. It made no difference now what he said. The magic was working.

Clarissa and I sat in the twilight of her drawing room, entirely concentrated on the small screen, on the dark figure, the pale eyes, the hands which seldom moved. It was like some fascinating scene in a skillful play which, quite against one's wish and aesthetic judgment, becomes for that short time beyond real time, a part of one's own private drama of existence, sharpened by artifice and a calculated magic.

Not until Cave was nearly finished did those first words of his, spoken so easily, so quietly, begin to come back to me as he repeated them in his coda, the voice increasing a little in volume, yet still not hurrying, not forcing, not breaking the mood that the first glance had created. The burden of his words was, as always, the same. Yet this time it seemed more awesome, more final, undeniable. . . . in short, the truth. Though I had always accepted his first premise, I had never been much impressed by the ways he found of stating it. This night, before the camera and in the sight of millions, he perfected his singular art of communication and the world was his.

When he finished, Clarissa and I sat for a moment in complete silence, the chirping of a commercial the only sound in the room. At last she said, "The brandy is over there on the console. Get me some." Then she switched off the screen and turned on the lights.

"I feel dragged through a wringer," she said after her first mouthful of brandy.

"I had no idea it would work so well on television." I felt strangely empty, let down. There was hardly any doubt now of Cave's effectiveness, yet I felt joyless and depleted, as though part of my life had gone, leaving an ache.

"What a time we're going to have." Clarissa was beginning to recover. "I'll bet there are a million letters by morning and Paul will be doing a jig."

"I hope this is the right thing, Clarissa. It would be terrible if it weren't."

"Of course it's right. Whatever *that* means. If it works it's right. Perfectly simple. Such conceptions are all a matter of fashion anyway. One year women expose only their ankle; the next year their *derrière*. What's right one year is wrong the next. If Cave captures the popular imagination, he'll be right until something better comes along."

"A little cynical." But Clarissa was only repeating my own usual line. I was, or had been until that night on the Washington farm, a contented relativist. Cave, however, had jolted me into new ways and I was bewildered by the change, by the prospect.

## 2

That evening was a time of triumph, at least for Cave's companions. They arrived noisily. Paul seemed drunk, maniacally exhilarated, while Iris glowed in a formal gown of green shot with gold. Two men accompanied them, one a doctor whose name I did not catch at first and the other a man from the television network who looked wonderfully sleek and pleased and kept patting Cave on the arm every now and then, as if to assure himself he was not about to vanish in smoke and fire.

Cave was silent. He sat in a high brocaded chair beside the fire and drank tea that Clarissa, knowing his habits, had ordered in advance for him. He responded to compliments with grave nods.

After the first burst of greetings at the door, I did not speak to Cave again and soon the others left him alone and talked around him, about him yet through him, as though he had become invisible, which seemed the case when he was not speaking, when those extraordinary eyes were veiled or cast down, as they were now, moodily studying the teacup, the pattern in the Aubusson rug at his feet.

I crossed the room to where Iris sat beside the doctor, who said, "Your little book, sir, is written in a complete ignorance of Jung."

This was sudden but I answered, as graciously as possible, that I had not intended writing a treatise on psychoanalysis.

"Not the point, sir, if you'll excuse me. I am a psychiatrist, a friend of Mr. Himmell's" (so this was the analyst to whom Paul so often referred) "and I think it impossible for anyone today to write about the big things without a complete understanding of Jung."

Iris interrupted as politely as possible. "Dr. Stokharin is a zealot, Gene. You must listen to him but, first, did you see John tonight?"

"He was remarkable, even more so than in person."

"It is the isolation," said Stokharin, nodding. Dandruff fell like a dry snow from thick brows to dark blue lapels. "The camera separates him from everyone else. He is projected like a dream into . . ."

"He was so afraid at first," said Iris, glancing across the room at the silent Cave, who sat, very small and still in the brocaded chair, the teacup still balanced on one knee. "I've never seen him disturbed by anything before. They tried to get him to do a rehearsal but he refused. He can't rehearse, only the actual thing."

"Fear is natural when . . . " But Stokharin was in the presence of a master drawing-room tactician. Iris was a born hostess. For all her ease and simplicity she was ruthlessly concerned with keeping order, establishing a rightness of tone.

"At first we hardly knew what to do." Iris's voice rose serenely over the East European rumblings of the doctor. "He'd always made such a point of the audience. He needed actual people to excite him. Paul wanted to fill the studio with a friendly audience but John said no, he'd try it without. When the talk began there were only a half dozen of us there; Paul, myself, the technicians. No one else."

"How did he manage?"

"It was the camera. He said when he walked out there he had no idea if anything would happen or not, if he could speak. Paul was nearly out of his mind with terror. We all were. Then John saw the lens of the camera. He said looking into it gave him a sudden shock, like a current of electricity passing through him, for there, in front of him, was the eye of the world and the microphone above his head was the ear into which at last he could speak. When he finished, he was transfigured. I've never seen him so excited. He couldn't recall what he had said but the elation remained until . . ."

"Until he got here."

"Well, nearly." Iris smiled. "He's been under a terrible strain these last two weeks."

"It'll be nothing like the traumatizing shocks in store for him during the next few days," said Stokharin, rubbing the bowl of a rich dark pipe against his nose to bring out its luster (the pipe's luster, for the nose, straight, thick, proud, already shone like a baroque pearl). "Mark my words everyone will be eager to see this phenomenon. When Paul first told me about him, I said, ah, my friend, you have found that father for which you've searched since your own father was run over by a bus in your ninth (the crucial) year. Poor Paul. I said, you will be doomed to disappointment. The wish for the father is the sign of your immaturity. For a time you find him here, there . . . in analysis you transfer to me. Now you meet a spellbinder and you turn to him, but it will not last. Exactly like that I talked to him. Believe me, I hold back nothing. Then I met this Cave. I watched him. Ah, what an analyst he would have made! What a manner, what power of communication! A natural healer. If only we could train him. Miss Mortimer, to you I appeal. Get him to study. The best people, the true Jungians are all here in New York. They will train him. He would become only a lay analyst but, even so, what miracles he could perform, what therapy! We must not waste this native genius."

"I'm afraid, Doctor, that he's going to be too busy wasting

himself to study your . . . procedures." Iris smiled engagingly but with dislike apparent in her radiant eyes. Stokharin, however, was not sensitive to hostility, no doubt attributing such emotions to some sad deficiency in the other's adjustment.

Iris turned to me. "Will you be in the city the whole time?"

"The whole time Cave's here? Yes. I wouldn't miss it for anything."

"I'm glad. I've so much I want to talk to you about. So many things are beginning to happen. Call me tomorrow. I'll be staying at my old place. It's in the book."

"Cave?"

"Is staying with Paul, out on Long Island at someone's house. We want to keep him away from pests as much as possible."

"Manic depression, I should say," said Stokharin thoughtfully, his pipe now clenched between his teeth and his attention on Cave's still figure. "With latent schizoid tendencies which . . . Miss Mortimer, you must have an affair with him. You must marry him if necessary. Have children. Let him see what it is to give life to others, to live in a balanced . . ."

"Doctor, you are quite mad," said Iris. She rose and crossed the room, cool in her anger. I too got away from the doctor as quickly as I could, "false modesty, inhibited behavior, too-early bowel training," and similar phrases ringing in my ears.

Paul caught me at the door. I had intended to slip away without saying good night, confident that Clarissa would understand, that the others would not notice. "Not going so soon, are you?" He was a little drunk, his face dark with excitement. "But you ought to stay and celebrate." I murmured something about having an early appointment the next day.

"Well, see me tomorrow. We've taken temporary offices in the Empire State Building. The money has begun to roll in. If this thing tonight turns out the way I think it will, I'm going to be able to quit my other racket for good and devote full time to Cave." Already the name Cave had begun to sound more like that of an institution than of a man.

"By the way, I want to tell you what I think of the Introduction. Superior piece of work. Tried it out on several highbrow friends of mine and they liked it."

"I'm afraid. . ."

"That, together with the talks on television, should put this thing over with the biggest bang in years. We'll probably need some more stuff from you, historical background, rules and regulations, that kind of thing, but Cave will tell you what he wants. We've hired a dozen people already to take care of the mail and inquiries. There's also a lecture tour being prepared, all the main cities, while . . ."

"Paul, you're not trying to make a religion of this, are you?" I could hold it back no longer even though both time and occasion were all wrong for such an outburst.

"Religion? Hell, no . . . but we've got to organize. We've got to get this to as many people as we can. People have started looking to us (to him, that is) for guidance. We can't let them down."

Clarissa's maid ushered in a Western Union messenger, laden with telegrams. "Over three hundred," said the boy. "The station said to send them here."

Paul paid him jubilantly, and in the excitement, I slipped away.

3

The results of the broadcast were formidable. My Introduction was taken up by excited journalists who used it as a basis for hurried but exuberant accounts of the new marvel.

One night a week for the rest of that winter Cave appeared before the shining glass eye of the world, and on each occasion new millions in all parts of the country listened and saw and pondered this unexpected phenomenon, the creation of their own secret anxieties and doubts, a central man.

The reactions were too numerous for me to recollect in any order or with any precise detail; but I do recall the first few months vividly.

A few days after the first broadcast, I went to see Paul at the offices he had taken in the Empire State Building, as high up as possible, I noted with amusement: always the maximum, the optimum.

Halfway down a corridor, between lawyers and exporters, Cavite, Inc., was discreetly identified in black upon a frosted-glass door. I went inside.

It appeared to me the way I had always thought a newspaper office during a crisis might look. Four rooms opening off one another, all with doors open, all crowded with harassed secretaries and clean-looking young men in blue serge suits carrying papers, talking in loud voices; the room sounded like a hive at swarming time.

Though none of them knew me, no one made any attempt to ask my business or to stop me as I moved from room to room in search of Paul. Everywhere there were placards with Cave's picture on them, calm and gloomy-looking, dressed in what was to be his official costume, dark suit, unfigured tie, white shirt. I tried to overhear conversations as I passed the busy desks and groups of excited debaters, but the noise was too loud. Only one word was identifiable, sounding regularly, richly emphatic like a cello note: Cave, Cave, Cave.

In each room I saw piles of my Introduction, which pleased me even though I had come already to dislike it.

The last room contained Paul, seated behind a desk with a Dictaphone in one hand, three telephones on his desk (none fortunately ringing at this moment) and four male and female attendants with notebooks and pencils eagerly poised. Paul sprang from his chair when he saw me. The attendants fell back. "Here he is!" He grabbed my hand and clung to it vise-like. I could almost feel the energy pulsing in his fingertips, vibrating through his body; his heartbeat was obviously two to my every one.

"Team, this is Eugene Luther."

The team was properly impressed and one of the girls, slovenly but intelligent-looking, said, "It was you who brought me here. First you I mean . . . and then of course Cave."

I murmured vaguely and the others told me how "clear" I had made all philosophy in the light of Cavesword. (I believe it was that day, certainly that week, Cavesword was coined by Paul to denote the entire message of John Cave to the world.)

Paul then shooed the team out with instructions that he was not to be bothered. The door, however, was left open.

"Well, what do you think of them?" He leaned back, beaming at me from his chair.

"They seem very . . . earnest," I said, wondering not only what I was supposed to think but, more to the point, what I did think of the whole business.

"I'll say they are! I tell you, Gene, I've never seen anything like it. The thing's bigger even than that damned crooner I handled . . . you know the one. Everyone has been calling up and, look!" He pointed to several bushel baskets containing telegrams and letters. "This is only a fraction of the response since the telecast. From all over the world. I tell you, Gene, we're in."

"What about Cave? Where is he?"

"He's out on Long Island. The press is on my tail trying to interview him but I say no, no go, fellows, not yet. And does that excite them! We've had to hire guards at the place on Long Island just to keep them away."

"How is Cave taking it all?"

"In his stride, absolute model of coolness, which is more than I am. He agrees that it's better to keep him under wraps while the telecasts are going on. It means that curiosity about him will increase like nobody's business. Look at this." He showed me a proof sheet of a tabloid story: "Mystery Prophet Wows TV Audience," with a photograph of Cave taken from the telecast and another one showing Cave ducking into a taxi, his face turned away from the camera. The story seemed most provocative and, for that complacent tabloid, a little bewildered.

"Coming out Sunday," said Paul with satisfaction. "There's also going to be coverage from the big circulation media. They're going to monitor the next broadcast even though we said nobody'd be allowed on the set while Cave was speaking." He handed me a bundle of manuscript pages bearing the title "Who Is Cave?" "That's the story I planted in one of the slick magazines. Hired a name writer, as you can see, to do it." The name writer's name was not known to me, but presumably it would be familiar to the mass audience.

"And, biggest of all, we got a sponsor. We had eleven offers already and we've taken Dumaine Chemicals. They're paying us enough money to underwrite this whole setup here, and pay for Cave and me as well. It's terrific but dignified. Just a simple 'through the courtesy of' at the beginning and another at the end of each telecast. What do you think of that?"

"Unprecedented!" I had chosen my word some minutes before.

"I'll say. By the way, we're getting a lot of letters on that book of yours." He reached in a drawer and pulled out a manila folder which he pushed toward me. "Take them home if you like. Go over them carefully, might give you some ideas for the next one, you know – ground which needs covering."

"Is there to be a next one?"

"Man, a flock of next ones! We've got a lot to do, to explain. People want to know all kinds of things. I'm having the kids out in the front office do a breakdown on all the letters we've received, to get the general reaction, to find what it is people most want to hear; and, believe me, we've been getting more damned questions, and stuff like, 'Please, Mr. Cave, I'm married to two men and feel maybe it's a mistake since I have to work nights anyway.' Lord, some of them are crazier than that."

"Are you answering all of them?"

"Oh, yes, but in my name. All except a few of the most

interesting which go to Cave for personal attention. I've been toying with the idea of setting up a counselor service for people with problems."

"But what can *you* tell them?" I was more and more appalled.

"Everything in the light of Cavesword. You have no idea how many questions that answers. Think about it and you'll see what I mean. Of course we follow standard psychiatric procedure, only it's speeded up so that after a couple of visits there can be a practical and inspirational answer to their problems. Stokharin said he'd be happy to give it a try, but we haven't yet worked out all the details."

I changed the subject. "What did you have in mind for me to do?"

"Cavesword applied to everyday life." He spoke without hesitation; he had thought of everything. "We'll know more what people want to hear after a few more telecasts, after more letters and so on. Then supply Cavesword where you can and, where you can't, just use common sense and standard psychiatric procedure."

"Even when they don't always coincide?"

Paul roared with laughter. "Always the big knocker, Gene. That's what I like about you, the disapproving air. It's wonderful. I'm serious. People like myself . . . visionaries, you might say, continually get their feet off the ground and it's people like you who pull us back, make us think. Anyway, I hope you'll be able to get to it soon. We'll have our end taken care of by the time the telecasts are over."

"Will you show Cave to the world then? I mean in person?"

"I don't know. By the way, we're having a directors' meeting Friday morning. You'll get a notice in the mail. One of the things we're going to take up is just that problem, so you be thinking about it in the meantime. I have a hunch it may be smart to keep him away from interviews for good."

"That's impossible."

"I'm not so sure. He's pretty retiring except when he speaks. I don't think he'd mind the isolation one bit. You know how dull he gets in company when he's not performing."

"Would he consent?"

"I think we could persuade him. Anyway, for now he's a mystery man. Millions see him once a week but no one knows him except ourselves. A perfect state of affairs, if you ask me."

"You mean there's always a chance he might make a fool of himself if a tough interviewer got hold of him?"

"Exactly, and believe me there's going to be a lot of them after his scalp."

"Have they begun already?"

"Not yet. We have you to thank for that, too, making it so clear that though what we say certainly conflicts with all the churches we're really not competing with them, that people listening to Cavesword can go right on being Baptists and so on."

"I don't see how, if they accept Cave."

"Neither do I, but for the time being that's our line."

"Then there's to be a fight with the churches?"

Paul nodded grimly. "And it's going to be a honey. People don't take all the supernatural junk seriously these days but they do go for the social idea of the church, the uplift kind of thing. That's where we'll have to meet them, where we'll have to lick them at their own game."

I looked at him for one long moment. I had of course anticipated something like this from the moment that Cave had become an organization and not merely one man talking. I had realized that expansion was inevitable. The rule of life is more life and of organization more organization, increased dominion. Yet I had not suspected Paul of having grasped this so promptly, using it so firmly to his and our advantage. The thought that not only was he cleverer than I had realized but that he might, indeed, despite his unfortunate approach, be even cleverer than myself, disagreeably occurred to me. I had until then regarded myself as the unique intellectual of the Cavites, the one sane man among maniacs and opportunists. It seemed now that there were two of us with open eyes and, of the two, he alone possessed ambition and energy.

"You mean this to be a religion, Paul?"

He smiled. "Maybe, yes . . . something of that order perhaps. Something workable, though, for now. I've thought about what you said the other night."

"Does Cave want this?"

Paul shrugged. "Who can tell? I should think so but this is not really a problem for him to decide. He has happened. Now, we respond. Stokharin feels that a practical faith, a belief in ways of behavior which the best modern analysts are agreed on as being closest to ideal might perform absolute miracles. No more guilt feeling about sex if Cave were to teach that all is proper when it does no harm to others . . . and the desire to do harm to others might even be partly removed if there were no false mysteries, no terrible warnings in childhood and so on. Just in that one area of behavior we could work wonders! Of course there would still be problems, but the main ones could be solved if people take to Cave and to us. Cavesword is already known and it's a revelation to millions . . . we know that. Now they are looking to him for guidance in other fields. They know about death at last. Now we must tell them about living and we are lucky to have available so much first-rate scientific research in the human psyche. I suspect we can even strike on an ideal behavior pattern by which people can measure themselves."

"And to which they will be made to conform?" Direction was becoming clear already.

"How can we force anyone to do anything? Our whole power is that people come to us, to Cave, voluntarily because they feel here, at last, is the answer." Paul might very well have been sincere. There is no way of determining, even now.

"Well, remember, Paul, that you will do more harm than good by attempting to supplant old dogmas and customs with new dogmas. It will be the same in the end except that the old is less militant, less dangerous than a new order imposed by enthusiasts."

"Don't say 'you.' Say 'we.' You're as much a part of this as I am. After all, you're a director. You've got a say-so in these matters. Just speak up Friday." Paul was suddenly genial and placating. "I don't pretend I've got all the answers. I'm just talking off the top of my head, like they say."

A member of the team burst into the office with the news that Bishop Winston was outside.

"Now it starts," said Paul with a grimace.

The Bishop did not recognize me as we passed one another in the office. He looked grim and he was wearing clerical garb.

"He's too late," said a lean youth, nodding at the churchman's back.

"Professional con men," said his companion with disgust. "They had their day."

And with that in my ears, I walked out into the snow-swirling street; thus did Cave's first year begin.

I was more alarmed than ever by what Paul had told me and by what I heard on every side. In drugstores and bars and restaurants, people talked of Cave. I could even tell when I did not hear the name that it was of him they spoke: a certain intentness, a great curiosity, a wonder. In the bookstores, copies of my Introduction were displayed together with large blown-up photographs of Cave.

Alone in a bar on Madison Avenue where I'd taken refuge from the cold, I glanced at the clippings Paul had given me. There were two sets. The first were the original perfunctory ones which had appeared. The reviewers, knowing even less philosophy than I, tended to question my proposition that Cavesword was anything more than a single speculation in a rather large field. I had obviously not communicated his magic, only its record which, like the testament of miracles, depends entirely on faith: to inspire faith one needed Cave himself.

"What do you think about the guy?" The waiter, a fragile Latin with parchment-lidded eyes, mopped the spilled gin off my table (he'd seen a picture of Cave among my clippings).

"It's hard to say," I said. "How does he strike you?"

"Boy, like lightning!" The waiter beamed. "Of course I'm Catholic but this is something new. Some people been telling me you can't be a good Catholic and go for this guy. But why not? I say. You still got Virginmerry and now you got him, too, for right now. You ought to see the crowd we get here to see the TV when he's on. It's wild."

It was wild, I thought, putting the clippings back into the folder. Yet it might be kept within bounds. Paul had emphasized my directorship, my place in the structure. Well, I would show them what should be done or, rather, *not* done.

Then I went out into the snow-dimmed street and hailed a cab. All the way to Iris's apartment I was rehearsing what I would say to Paul when next we met. "Leave them alone," I said aloud. "It is enough to open the windows."

"Open the windows!" The driver snorted. "It's damn near forty in the street."

4

Iris occupied several rooms on the second floor of a brownstone on a street with, pleasantest of New York anachronisms, trees. When I entered, she was doing yoga exercises on the floor, sitting crosslegged on a mat, her slender legs in a leotard and her face flushed with strain. "It just doesn't work for me!" she said and stood up without embarrassment.

Since I'd found the main door unlocked, I had opened this one too, without knocking.

"I'm sorry, Iris, the downstairs door was . . ."

"Don't be silly." She rolled up the mat efficiently. "I was expecting you but I lost track of time . . . which means it must be working a little. I'll be right back." She went into the bedroom and I sat down, amused by this unexpected side to Iris. I wondered if she was a devotee of wheat germ and mint tea as well. She claimed not. "It's the only real exercise I get," she said, changed now into a heavy robe that completely swathed her figure as she sat curled up in a great armchair, drinking Scotch, as did I, the winter outside hid by drawn curtains, by warmth and light.

"Have you done it long?"

"Oh, off and on for years. I never get anywhere but it's very restful and I've felt so jittery lately that anything which relaxes me. . . ." Her voice trailed off idly. She seemed relaxed now.

"I've been to see Paul," I began importantly.

"Ah."

But I could not, suddenly, generate sufficient anger to speak out with eloquence. I went around my anger stealthily, a murderer stalking his victim. "We disagreed."

"In what?"

"In everything, I should say."

"That's so easy with Paul." Iris stretched lazily; ice chattered in her glass; a car's horn melodious and foreign sounded in the street below. "We need him. If it weren't Paul, it might be someone a great deal worse. At least he's intelligent and devoted. That makes up for a lot."

"I don't think so. Iris, he's establishing a sort of super-market, short-order church for the masses."

She laughed delightedly. "I like that! And in a way, you're right. That's what he *would* do left to himself."

"He seems in complete control."

"Only of the office. John makes all the decisions."

"I wish I could be sure of that."

"You'll see on Friday. You'll be at the meeting, won't you?"

I nodded. "I have a feeling that between Paul and Stokharin this thing is going to turn into a world-wide clinic for mental health."

"I expect worse things *could* happen, but Paul must still contend with me and you and of course the final word is with John."

"How is Cave, by the way?"

"Quite relaxed, unlike the rest of us. Come out to Long Island and see. I go nearly every day for a few hours. He's kept

134

completely removed from everyone except the servants and Paul and me."

"Does he like that?"

"He doesn't seem to mind. He walks a good deal . . . it's a big place and he's used to the cold. He reads a little, mostly detective stories . . . and then of course there's the mail that Paul sends on. He works at that off and on all day. I help him and when we're stuck (you should see the questions!) we consult Stokharin, who's very good on some things, on problems . . ."

"And a bore the rest of the time."

"That's right," Iris giggled. "I couldn't have been more furious the other night, but, since then, I've seen a good deal of him and he's not half bad. We've got him over the idea that John should become a lay analyst. The response to the telecast finally convinced Stokharin that here was a 'racial folk father figure' . . . his very own words. Now he's out to educate the father so that he will fulfill his children's needs on the best Jungian lines."

"Does Cave take him seriously?"

"He's bored to death with him. Stokharin's the only man who's ever had the bad sense to lecture John . . . who absolutely hates it. But he realizes that Stokharin's answers to some of the problems we're confronted with are ingenious. All that . . . hints to the lovelorn is too much for John, so we need Stokharin to take care of details."

"I hope Cave is careful not to get too involved."

"John's incorruptible. Not because he is so noble or constant but because he can only think a certain way and other opinions, other evidence, don't touch him."

I paused, wondering if this was true. Then: "I'm going to make a scene on Friday. I'm going to suggest that Paul is moving in a dangerous direction, toward organization and dogma, and that if something is not done soon we'll all be ruined by what we most detest, a militant absolutist doctrine."

Iris looked at me curiously. "Tell me, Gene, what *do* you

want? Why are you still with Cave, with all of us, when you so apparently dislike the way we are going? You've always been perfectly clear about what you did *not* want (I can recall, I think, every word you said at the farm that night), but to be specific, what would you like all this to become? How would you direct things if you could?"

I had been preparing myself for such a question for several months; I still had no single answer to make which would sharply express my own doubts and wishes. But I made an attempt. "I would not organize, for one thing. I'd have Cave speak regularly, all he likes, but there would be no Cavite, Inc., no Paul planting articles and propagandizing. I'd keep just Cave, nothing more. Let him do his work. Then, gradually, there will be effects, a gradual end to superstition. . . ."

Iris looked at me intently. "*If* it were possible, I would say we should do what you suggest, but it would be ruinous not only for us but for everyone . . ."

"Why ruinous? A freedom to come to a decision on one's own without . . ."

"That's it. No one can be allowed that freedom. One doesn't need much scholarship or even experience to see that. Everywhere people are held in check by stifling but familiar powers. People are used to tyranny. They expect governments to demand their souls, and they have given up decisions on many levels for love of security. What you suggest is impossible with this race at this time."

"You're talking nonsense. After all, obeisance to established religions is the order of the day, yet look at the response to Cave, who is undermining the whole Christian structure."

"And wait until you see the fight they're going to put up!" said Iris grimly. "Fortunately, Cavesword is the mortal blow though Cave himself would be their victim if he were not protected, if there were no organization to guard him, and the Word."

"So Paul and his – his team, his proselytizers are to become merely an equivalent power, combating the old superstitions with their own weapons."

"More or less, yes. That's what it has come to."

"Even though Cave's talking to the people would be enough? Let them use him, not he them."

"A good slogan." Iris smiled. "But I think I'm right. No one would have a chance to see or hear him if it weren't for Paul. You should read the threatening letters we've been getting."

"I thought all the mail was most admiring?"

"All that came from people who've actually *heard* him, but there's a lot coming in now from religious fanatics. They are very extreme. And of course the churches, one by one, are starting to take notice."

"I saw Bishop Winston in Paul's office today."

"He's been trying to see John all week. He finally settled for Paul, I gather. In any case, after the next telecast there will really be a storm."

"The next? What's going to happen then?"

"John will tell them that there's no need for the churches, that their power derives from superstition and bloody deeds."

I was startled. "When did this occur to him? I thought he intended to go on as he was, without ever coming out openly against them."

"I was surprised too. He told me yesterday; he'd been brooding all day and, suddenly, he started to attack them. It's going to be murderous."

"I hope not for him."

"Oh, he'll convince, I'm sure of that. But their revenge . . ." She gave a troubled sigh. "Anyway, Gene, you do see why we can't, for our own safety, dispense with Paul and his financiers and press agents and all the squalid but necessary crew."

"It may be too late," I agreed. "But I fear the end."

"No one can tell. Besides, as long as you and I are there with John it will be all right."

I felt her confidence was not entirely justified, but I determined to defer my attack on Paul's methods until a safer time.

We argued about the wisdom of the coming telecast. Was it really necessary to confront the enemy explicitly? And in his own country, so to speak? Iris was not sure, but she felt Cave's instinct was right even though he had, perhaps, been goaded into action sooner than anticipated by the harsh letters of Christian zealots.

And then by slow degrees, by careful circling, the conversation grew personal.

"I've never told anyone else," said Iris, looking at me speculatively.

"Don't worry; I haven't repeated any of it." And, as always at such times, I feel a warm flood of guilt. Any direct statement of personal innocence has always made me feel completely criminal.

"But since I've told you, I . . . it's a relief to have someone I can talk to about John. I don't dare mention his name to my family, to my old friends. I don't think they even know that I know him."

"I thought it had all been in the papers."

"I haven't been mentioned but, after Friday, everyone will know. Paul says there's no way for us to duck inquiries. After the directors' meeting he'll issue a statement naming directors, stockholders and so on."

"But even then, why should anyone suspect you were interested in Cave or he in you? It's possible merely to be a director, isn't it?"

Iris shrugged. "You know how people are. Clarissa keeps wanting to have what she calls a comfy chat about *everything* and I keep putting her off. Stokharin now takes it for granted that John and I sleep together, that he is the father image to me and I the mother to him."

It had an odd ring to it and I laughed. "Do you think that's a sound Jungian analysis?"

Iris smiled faintly. "Whatever it is, the feeling, such as it is, is all on my side."

"He shows no sign of returning your affection?"

"None at all. He's devoted to me, I think. He relies on my judgment. He trusts me, which is more than he does anyone else I know of . . ."

"Even me?" Always the "I" coming between me and what I wished to know: that insatiable, distressing "I."

"Yes, even you, dear, and Paul too. He's on guard against everyone, but not in a nasty or suspicious way. He . . . what is the phrase? he keeps his own counsel."

"And you are the counsel?"

"In a sense, and nothing more."

"Perhaps you should give up. It would seem that . . . love was not possible for him. If so, it's unwise for you to put yourself in such a position . . . harmful, too."

"But there's still the other Cave. I love him as well and the two are, finally, the same."

"A *metaphysique?*"

"No, or at least I don't see a paradox. It's something else; it's like coming out of an illness with no past at all, only a memory of pain and dullness which soon goes in the wonderful present."

"It?"

"My love is *it.*" Her voice grew strong. "I've learned that in loving him I love life, which I never did before. Why, I can even value others now, value all those faceless creatures whom I knew without ever bothering to see, to bring in focus the dim blurs of all *that* world alive. I lived asleep. Now I am awake."

"He does not love you."

"Why should he? It's gone beyond that. I'm no longer the scales most lovers are, weighing the deeds and gifts and treasures proffered against those received or stolen from the other, trying always to bring into fatal balance two separate things. I gave myself and what I take is life, the knowledge that there is another creature in the world whose wonder, to me at least, is all-satisfying by merely being."

"Is it so terrible to be alive?"

"Beyond all expectation, my poor friend." And then I left

her to return to winter, to the snow-filled streets and my old pain.

## 5

The second telecast had the anticipated effect. The day after, Friday, nearly a hundred thousand letters and telegrams had been received, and Cave's life had been threatened four times over the telephone.

I was awakened at five o'clock on Friday morning by a newspaperman begging an interview. Half asleep, irritably, I told him to go to hell and hung up though not before I'd heard the jeer: "Thought you fellows did away with hell." This woke me up and I made coffee, still keeping my eyes half shut in the dim winter light, hoping sleep might return to its accustomed perch; but more telephone calls demoralized my fragile ally and I was left wide awake, unshaven, with fast-beating heart beside the telephone, drinking coffee.

Every few minutes there was a call from some newspaperman or editor requesting information. They had all been shocked by the telecast. When I told them to get in touch with Cave himself, or at least with Paul's office, they only laughed. Thousands were trying to speak to Paul, tens of thousands to Cave; the result was chaos. Shakily, I took the phone off its hook and got dressed. When I opened my door to get the morning paper, a thin young man leaped past me into my living room and anchored himself to a heavy chair.

"What . . ." I began; he was only too eager to explain the what and the why.

"And so," he ended, breathlessly, "the *Star* has authorized me to advance you not only *that* money but expenses, too, for an exclusive feature on Cave and the Cavites."

"I wish," I said, very gentle in the presence of such enthusiasm, "that you would go away. It's five in the morning . . ."

"You're our only hope," the boy wailed. "Every paper and news service has been trying to get past the gate out on Long Island for three weeks and failed. They couldn't even shoot him at long range."

"Shoot him?"

"Get a picture. Now please . . ."

"Paul Himmell is your man. He's authorized to speak for Cave. He has an office in the Empire State Building and he keeps respectable hours; so why don't you . . ."

"We haven't been able to get even a release out of him for three days now. It's censorship, that's what it is."

I had to smile. "We're not the government. Cave is a private citizen and this is a private organization. If we choose not to give interviews you have no right to pester us."

"Oh, come off it." The young man was at an age where the needs of ambition were often less strong than the desire for true expression; for a moment he forgot that he needed my forbearance and I liked him better. "This is the biggest news that's hit town since V-E Day. You guys have got the whole country asking questions and the big one is: who is Cave?"

"There'll be an announcement today, I think, about the company. As for Cave, I suggest you read a little book called 'An Introduction to . . .'"

"Of course I've read it. That's why I'm here. Now, please, Mr. Luther, give me an exclusive even if you won't take the *Star's* generous offer. At least tell me something I can use."

I sat down heavily; a bit of coffee splattered from cup to saucer to the back of my hand and dried stickily. I felt worn out already, the day only just begun. "What do you want me to tell you? What would you most like to hear? What do you expect me to say since, being a proper journalist, that is what you'll write no matter what I tell you?"

"Oh, that's not true. I want to know what Cave's all about as a person, as a teacher."

"Well, what do *you* think he's up to?"

"Me? Why . . . I don't know. I never heard him on the air

141

until last night. It was strong stuff."

"Were you convinced?"

"In a way, yes. He said a lot of things I agreed with but I was a little surprised at his going after the churches. Not that I like anything about *them*, but still it's some stunt to get up and talk like that in front of millions of people. I mean you just don't say those things any more, even if you do think them . . . can't offend minorities. That's what you learn first in journalism school."

"There's part of your answer then. Cave is a man who, unlike others, says what he thinks is true even if it makes him unpopular. There's some virtue in that."

"I guess he can afford to in his position," said the boy vaguely. "You know we got Bishop Winston to answer him for the *Star.* Signed him last night after Cave went off the air. I'm sure he'll do a good job. Now . . ."

We wrestled across the room. Since I was the stronger, I won my privacy though muffled threats of exposure were hurled at me from behind the now-bolted door.

Acting on an impulse, I left the apartment as soon as I was sure my visitor was gone. I was afraid that others would try to find me if I stayed home; fears which were justified. According to the elevator man, he had turned away several men already. The one who did get through had come up the fire escape.

I walked quickly out into the quiet street, the snow now gone to slush as gray as the morning sky. Fortunately, the day was neither windy nor cold and I walked to a Times Square Automat for an early breakfast.

I was reassured by anonymity. All around me sleepy men and women clutching newspapers, briefcases and lunch boxes sat sullenly chewing their breakfast, sleep not yet departed.

I bought a roll, more coffee, hominy grits, which I detested in the North but occasionally tried in the hope that, by accident, I might stumble upon the real thing. These were not the real thing and I left them untouched while I read my paper.

Cave was on the front page. Not prominent, but still he was there. The now-standard photograph looked darkly from the page. The headline announced that: "Prophet Flays Churches as Millions Listen." There followed a paraphrase of the telecast which began with those fateful and soon to be famous words: "Our quarrel is not with Christ but with his keepers." I wondered, as I read, if anyone had ever taken one of the telecasts down in shorthand and made a transcript of it. I, for one, should have been curious to see in cold print one of those sermons. Cave himself knew that without his presence they would not stand up, and he allowed none of them to be transcribed. As a result, whenever there was a report of one of his talks it was, necessarily, paraphrased, which gave a curious protean flavor to his doctrine, since the recorded style was never consistent, changing always with each paraphraser just as the original meaning was invariably altered by each separate listener as he adapted the incantation to his private needs.

A fat yellow-faced woman sat down with a groan beside me and began to ravish a plate of assorted cakes. Her jaws grinding, the only visible sign of life, for her eyes were glazed from sleep and her body, incorrectly buttoned into a cigarette-ash-dusted dress, was as still as a mountain; even the work of lungs was obscured by the torpid flesh.

I watched her above the newspaper, fascinated by the regularity with which jaws ground bits of cake. Her eyes looked past me into some invisible world of pastry.

Then, having finished the report on Cave's telecast, I put the newspaper down and ate with deliberate finesse my own biscuit. The rustling of the newspaper as it was folded and placed on the table disturbed my companion and, beneath the fat, her will slowly sent out instructions to the extremities. She cleared her throat. The chewing stopped. A bit of cake was temporarily lodged in one cheek, held in place by a sturdy plate. She squinted at the newspaper. "Something about that preacher fellow last night?"

"Yes. Would you like to see it?" I pushed the paper toward her.

She looked at the picture, carefully spelling out the words of the headlines with heavy lips and deep irregular breaths. "Did you see him last night?" she asked when her eye finally got to the small print where it stopped, as though halted by a dense jungle.

"Yes. As a matter of fact, I did."

"He sure gave it to them bastards, didn't he?" Her face lit up joyously. I thought of *ça ira*.

"You mean the clergy?"

"That's just what I mean. They had it too good, too long. People afraid to say anything. Takes somebody like him to tell us what we know and tell *them* where to head in."

"Do you like what he said about dying?"

"About there being nothing? Why, hell, mister, I knew it all along."

"But it's good to hear someone else say it?"

"Don't do no harm." She belched softly. "I expect they're going to be on his tail," she added with gloomy pleasure, spearing a fragment of eclair which she had missed on her first circuit of the crowded dish.

I spent that morning in the street buying newspapers and eavesdropping. I heard several arguments about Cave. The religiously orthodox were outraged but clearly interested. The others were triumphant though all seemed to feel that *they*, as the Automat woman had said, would soon be on his tail. Ours was no longer a country where the noncomformist could escape disaster if he unwisely showed a strange face to the multitude.

I tried to telephone Iris and then Clarissa but both telephones were busy. I rang the office but was told by a mechanical voice that if I left my name and address and business Mr. Himmell would get back to me as soon as possible. The siege had begun.

I arrived at the Empire State Building half an hour before the meeting was to begin, hoping to find out in advance from Paul what was happening and what we were supposed to do about it.

A line of pickets marched up and down before the entrance, waving banners, denouncing Cave and all his works in the names of various religious groups. A crowd was beginning to gather and the police, at least a score, moved frantically about, not certain how to keep the mob out of the building. When I stepped off the elevator at Cave's floor, I found myself a part of a loud and confused mass of men and women all shoving toward the door which was marked Cavite, Inc. Policemen barred their way.

Long before I had got to the door, a woman's shoe went hurtling through the air, smashing a hole in the frosted glass. One policeman cocked his revolver menacingly. Another shouted, "Get the riot squad!" But still the crowd raved and shouted and quarreled. Some wanted to lynch Cave in the name of the Lamb, while others begged to be allowed to touch him, just once. I got to the door at last, thanks to a sudden shove which landed me with a crash into a policeman. He gasped and then, snarling, raised his club. "Business!" I shouted with what breath was left me. "Got business here. Director."

I was not believed but, after some talk with a pale secretary through the shattered glass door, I was admitted. The crowd roared when they saw this and moved in closer. The door slammed shut behind me.

"It's been like this since nine o'clock," said the secretary, looking at me with frightened eyes.

"You mean after two hours the police still can't do anything?"

"We didn't call them right away. When we did it was too late. We're barricaded in here."

But Paul was not in the least disturbed. He was standing by the window in his office looking out. Clarissa, her hat and her hair together awry, a confusion of straw and veil and bolts of reddish hair apparently not all her own, was making up in a pocket mirror.

"Ravenous wild beasts!" she hailed me. "I've seen *their* likes before."

"Gene, good fellow! Got through the mob all right? Here, have a bit of brandy. No? Perhaps some Scotch?"

I said it was too early for me to drink. Shakily, I sat down. Paul laughed at the sight of us. "You both look like the end of the world has come."

"I'd always pictured the end as being quite orderly . . ." I began stuffily, but Doctor Stokharin's loud entrance interrupted me. His spectacles were dangling from one ear and his tie had been pulled around from front to back quite neatly. "No authority!" he bellowed, ignoring all of us. "The absence of a traditional patriarch, the center of the tribe, has made them insecure. Only together do they feel warmth in great *swarming* hives!" His voice rose sharply and broke on the word "hives" into a squeak. He took the proffered brandy and sat down, his clothes still disarranged.

"My hair," said Clarissa grimly, "will never come out right again today." She put the mirror back into her purse, which she closed with a loud snap. "I don't see, Paul, why you didn't have the foresight to call the police in advance and demand protection."

"I had no idea it would be like this. Believe me, it's not deliberate." But from Paul's excited chuckling, I could see that he was delighted with the confusion, a triumph of the publicist's dark art. I wondered if he might not have had a hand in it. It was a little reminiscent of the crowds of screaming women which in earlier decades, goaded by publicists, had howled and, as Stokharin would say, swarmed about singers and other theatrical idols.

Paul anticipated my suspicions. "Didn't have a thing to do with it, I swear. Doctor, your tie is hanging down your back."

"I don't mind," said Stokharin disagreeably, but he did adjust his glasses.

"I had a feeling we'd have a few people in to see us but no idea it would be like this." He turned to me as the quietest, the least dangerous of the three. "You wouldn't believe the response to last night's telecast if I told you."

"Why don't you tell me?" The comic aspects were becoming apparent: Stokharin's assaulted dignity and the ruin of Clarissa's ingenious hair both seemed to me suddenly funny. I tried not to smile. Paul named some stupendous figures with an air of triumph. "And there are more coming all the time. Think of that!"

"Are they favorable?"

"Favorable? Who cares?" Paul was pacing the floor quickly, keyed to the breaking point had he possessed the metabolism of a normal man. "We'll have a breakdown over the weekend. Hired more people already. Whole bunch working all the time. By the way, we're moving."

"Not a moment too soon," said Clarissa. "I suggest, in fact, we move now while there are even these few police to protect us. When they go home for lunch (they all eat enormous lunches, one can tell), that crowd is going to come in here and throw us out the window."

"Or suffocate us with love," said Paul.

Stokharin looked at Clarissa thoughtfully; with his turned around necktie he had a sacerdotal look. "Do you often think of falling from high places? Of being pushed from windows or perhaps high trees?"

"Only when I'm on a top floor of the world's highest building surrounded by raving maniacs do such forebodings occur to me, Doctor. If you had any sense of reality you might be experiencing the same fear."

Stokharin clapped his hands happily. "Classic, classic. To believe she alone knows reality. Madam, I suggest that you . . ."

There was a roar of sound from the hallway; a noise of glass shattering; a revolver went off with a sharp report and, frozen with alarm, I waited for its echo. There was none; only shouts of Cave! Cave! Cave!

Surrounded by police, Cave and Iris were escorted into the office. More police held the door, aided by the office crew who, suddenly inspired, were throwing paper cups full of water into the crowd. Flashbulbs like an electric storm flared in all directions as the newspapermen invaded the office, let in by the police who could not hold them back.

Iris looked frightened and even Cave seemed alarmed by the rioting.

Once the police lieutenant had got Cave and Iris into the office, he sent his men back to hold the corridor. Before he joined them he said sternly, breathing hard from the struggle, "We're going to clear the hall in the next hour. When we do we'll come and get you people out of here. You got to leave whether you want to or not. This is an emergency."

"An hour is all we need, officer." Paul was smooth. "And may I say that my old friend the Commissioner is going to hear some extremely nice things about the efficiency and good sense of his men." Before the lieutenant had got around to framing a suitably warm answer, Paul had maneuvered him out of the inner office; and locked the door behind him.

"There," he said, turning to us, very businesslike. "It was a mistake meeting here after last night. I'm sorry, Cave."

"It's not your fault." Cave, having found himself an uncomfortable straight chair in a corner of the room, sat very erect, like a child in serious attendance upon adults. "I had a hunch we should hold the meeting out on Long Island."

Paul scowled. "I hate the idea of the press getting a look at you. Spoils the mystery effect. But it was bound to happen. Anyway you won't have to talk to them."

"Oh, but I will," said Cave easily, showing who was master here, this day.

"But . . . well, after what we decided, the initial strategy being. . ."

"No. It's all changed now. I'll have to face them, at least this once. I'll talk to them the way I always talk. They'll listen." His voice grew dreamy. He was indifferent to Paul's opposition.

"Did you find a new place?" asked Iris, suddenly, to divert the conversation.

"What? Oh yes. A whole house, five stories on East Sixty-first Street. Should be big enough. At least for now." The interoffice communicator sounded. Paul spoke quickly into it: "Tell the newspaper people to wait out there. We'll have a statement in exactly an hour and they'll be able . . . " he paused and looked at Cave for some reprieve; seeing none, he finished: "They'll be able to interview Cave." He flipped the machine off. Through the locked door, we heard a noise of triumph from the gathered journalists and photographers.

"Well, come along," said Clarissa. "I thought this was to be a board of directors' meeting. Cave, dear, you've got to preside."

But, though he said he'd rather not, Clarissa, in a sudden storm of legality, insisted that he must. She also maliciously demanded a complete reading of the last meeting's minutes by Paul, the secretary. We were able to save him by a move to waive the reading, which was proposed, recorded and passed by a show of hands, only Clarissa dissenting. Cave conducted the meeting solemnly. Then Clarissa demanded a report from the treasurer and this time Paul was not let off.

For the first time I had a clear picture of the company of which I was a director. Shares had been sold. Control was in the hands of Clarissa, while Paul and several West Coast industrialists whose names were not familiar to me also owned shares. The main revenue of the company now came from the sponsor of Cave's television show. There was also a trickle of contributions which, in the last few weeks, had increased considerably.

Then Paul read from a list of expenses, his voice hurrying a little over his own salary, which was, I thought, too large. Cave's expenses were recorded and, with Clarissa goading from time to time, Paul gave an accounting of all that had been spent since the arrival in New York. John Cave was a big business.

"The books are audited at standard intervals," said Paul, looking at Clarissa as he finished, some of his good humor returning. "We will not declare dividends unless Mrs. Lessing insists the company become a profit-making enterprise."

"It might not be a bad idea," said Clarissa evenly. "Why not get a little return . . ."

But Paul had launched into policy. We listened attentively. From time to time, Cave made a suggestion. Iris and I made no comment. Stokharin occasionally chose to illuminate certain human problems as they arose and Paul, at least, heard him out respectfully. Clarissa wanted to know all about costs and her interruptions were always brief and shrewd.

Several decisions were made at that meeting. It was decided that a Center be established where Dr. Stokharin could minister to those Cavites whose problems might be helped by therapy. "We just apply classical concepts to their little troubles," he said.

"But it shouldn't *seem* like a clinic," said Iris suddenly. "It's all part of John, of what John says."

"We'll make that perfectly clear," said Paul quickly.

Stokharin nodded agreeably. "After all, it is in his name they come to us. We take it from there. No snore problems . . . all is contentment." He smacked his lips.

It was then decided that Cave would spend the summer quietly and, in the autumn, begin a tour of the country to be followed by more telecasts in the following winter. "The summer is to think a little in," were Cave's words.

Next, I was assigned the task of writing a defense of Cave for certain vast syndicates. I was also requested to compose a set of dialogues which would record Cave's view on such problems as marriage, the family, world government, problems all in urgent need of solution. I suggested diffidently that it would be very useful if Cave were to tell me what he thought about such things before I wrote my dialogues. Cave said, quite seriously, that we would have the summer in which to handle all these subjects.

Paul then told us the bad news; there was a good deal of it. "The Cardinal, in the name of all the Diocesan Bishops, has declared that any Catholic who observes the telecasts of John Cave or attends in person his blasphemous lectures commits a mortal sin. Bishop Winston came to tell me that not only is he attacking Cave in the press but that he is quite sure, if we continue, the government will intervene. It was a hint, and not too subtle."

"On what grounds intervene?" asked Cave. "What have I done that breaks one of their laws?"

"They'll trump up something," said Clarissa.

"I'm afraid you're right. They can always find something to get us on."

"But can they?" I asked. "Free speech is still on the books."

Paul chuckled. "That's just where it stays, too." And he quoted the national credo: In a true democracy there is no place for a serious difference of opinion on great issues. "Sooner or later they'll try to stop Cave."

"But they can't!" said Iris. "The people won't stand for it."

"He's the father of too many now," said Stokharin sagely. "No son will rise to dispute him, yet."

"Let's cross that bridge when we come to it." Paul was reasonable. "Now let's get a statement ready for the press."

While Paul and Cave worked over the statement, the rest of us chatted quietly about other problems. Stokharin was just about to explain the origin of alcoholism in terms of the new Cavite pragmatism when Iris said, "Look!" and pointed to the window where, bobbing against the glass, was a bright red child's balloon on which had been crudely painted, "Jesus Saves."

Stokharin chuckled when he saw it. "Very ingenious. Someone gets on the floor beneath and tries to shake us with his miracle. Now we produce the counter-miracle." He slid the window open. The cold air chilled us all. He took his pipe and touched its glowing bowl to the balloon, which exploded loudly; then he shut the window beaming. "It will be that easy," he said. "I promise you. A little fire, and pop! these superstitions disappear like bad dreams."

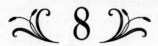

## 8

1

The six months after the directors' meeting were full of activity and danger. Paul was forced to hire bodyguards to protect Cave from disciples as well as from enemies, while those of us who were now known publicly to be Cave's associates were obliged to protect our privacy with unlisted telephone numbers and numerous other precautions, none of which did much good, for we were continually harassed by madmen and interviewers.

The effect Cave had made on the world was larger than even Paul, our one optimist, had anticipated. I believe even Cave himself was startled by the vastness and the variety of the response.

As I recall, seldom did a day pass without some new exposé or interpretation of this phenomenon. Bishop Winston attacked after nearly every telecast. The Catholic Church invoked its entire repertory of anathemas and soon it was whispered in devout Christian circles that the Antichrist had come at last, sent to test the faith. Yet, despite the barrage of attacks, the majority of those who heard Cave became his partisans and Paul, to my regret but to the delight of everyone else, established a number of Cavite Centers in the major cities of the United States, each provided with a staff of analysts who had also undergone an intensive indoctrination in Cavesword. Stokharin headed these clinics. Also at Cave's suggestion, one evening a week, the same evening, Cavites would gather to discuss Cavesword, to meditate on the beauty of death, led in their discussions and meditations by a disciple of Cave who was, in the opinion of the directors, equal to the task of representing Cave and his Word.

Iris was placed in charge of recruiting and training the proselytizers, while Paul handled the business end, obtaining property in different cities and managing the large sums which poured in from all over the world. Except for Cave's one encounter with the press that day in the Empire State Building (an occasion which, despite its ominous beginning, became a rare triumph: Cave's magic had worked even with the hostile), he was seen by no one except his intimates and the technicians at the television studio. Ways were found to disguise him so that he would not be noticed in the lobbies or elevators of the television network building. Later he spoke only from his Long Island retreat, his speeches recorded on film in advance.

By summer there were more than three million registered Cavites in the United States and numerous believers abroad. Paul was everywhere at once; flying from city to city (accompanied by two guards and a secretary); he personally broke ground in Dallas for what was to be the largest Cavite Center in the United States; and although the inaugural ceremonies were nearly stopped by a group of Baptist ladies carrying banners and shouting "Onward Christian Soldiers," no one was hurt and the two oil millionaires who had financed the Center gave a great barbecue on the foundation site.

Iris was entirely changed by her responsibilities. She had become, in the space of a few months, brisk and energetic, as deeply involved in details as a housewife with a new home. I saw very little of her that spring. Her days were mostly spent in a rented loft in the Chelsea district, where she lectured the candidates for field work and organized a makeshift system of indoctrination for potential Residents, as the heads of the various centers were known.

Iris was extraordinarily well fitted for this work, to my surprise, and before the year ended she had what was in fact a kind of university where as many as three hundred men and women at a time were transformed into Residents and Deputy Residents and so on down through an ever proliferating hierarchy. For the most part, the first men and women we sent out to the country were highly educated, thoughtful people, entirely devoted to Cavesword. They were, I think, the best of all, for later, when it became lucrative to be a Resident, the work was largely taken over by energetic careerists whose very activity and competence diminished their moral effectiveness.

Iris used me unmercifully those first months. I lectured her students. I taught philosophy until, in exasperation at the absurdity of *that*, I told her to hire a professional teacher of philosophy, which she did.

Yet I enjoyed these men and women. Their sincerity and excitement communicated itself to me and I became aware of something I had known before only from reading, from hearsay: the religious sense which I so clearly lacked, as did both Paul and Stokharin. I don't think Cave really possessed it either because, although he believed entirely in himself and in the miraculous truth of his Word, he did not possess that curious power to identify himself with creation, to transcend the self in contemplation of an abstraction, to sacrifice the personality to a mystical authority; none of us, save Iris in love, possessed this power which, as nearly as I can get it, is the religious sense in man. I learned about it only from those who came to learn from us in that Chelsea loft. In a sense I pitied them for I knew that much of what they evidently believed with such passion was wrong. But at the same time, I was invigorated by their enthusiasm, by the hunger with which they devoured Cavesword, by the dignity their passion lent to an enterprise that in Paul's busy hands resembled, more often than not, a cynical commercial venture. And I recognized in them (oh, very early, perhaps in the first weeks of talking to them) that in their goodness and their love they would, with Cavesword, smudge each bright new page of life as it turned; yet, suspecting this, I did not object nor did I withdraw. Instead, fascinated, I was borne by the tide to the shore whose every rock I could imagine, sharp with disaster.

Once a week the directors met on Long Island in the walled estate where Cave now lived with his guards. The meetings soon demonstrated a division in our ranks; between Paul and Stokharin on the one side and Iris, Clarissa and Cave on the other with myself as partisan, more often than not, to Cave. The division was amiable but significant. Paul and Stokharin wanted to place the Centers directly under the supervision of the analysts, while the rest of us, led by Iris (Cave seldom intervened, but we had already accepted the fact that Iris spoke for him), preferred that the Centers be governed by the Residents. "It is certainly true that the therapists are an important part of each Center," said Iris briskly, at the end of a long wrangle with Stokharin. "But these are *Cavite* Centers and not clinics for the advancement of Jungian analysis. It is Cavesword which draws people to the Centers, not mental illness. Those who have problems are of course helped by Stokharin's people but, finally, it is Cave who has made it possible for them to face death. Something no one has done before." And thus the point was won in our council, though Stokharin and Paul were still able at times, slyly, to insinuate their own creatures into important Residencies.

My own work went on fitfully. I composed an answer to Bishop Winston which brought down on my head a series of ecclesiastical thunderbolts, each louder than the one before. I wrote a short life of Cave in simple declarative sentences which enjoyed a considerable success for many years and finally, seriously, in my first attempt at a true counterattack, I began the several dialogues in which Cave and I purportedly traversed the entire field of moral action.

I felt that in these dialogues I could quietly combat those absolutist tendencies which I detected in the disciples. Cave himself made no pretense of being final on any subject other than death, where, even without his particular per-suasiveness, he stood on firm, even traditional ground. The attacks he received he no longer noticed. It was as simple as that. He had never enjoyed reading, and to watch others make telecasts bored him, even when they spoke of him. After the fateful Empire State Building conference he ceased to attend the world; except for a few letters which Paul forwarded to him and his relations with us, he was completely cut off from ordinary life, and perfectly happy. For though human contacts had been reduced to a minimum, he still possessed the polished glass eye of the world before whose level gaze he appeared once a week and experienced what he called "Everyone. All of them, listening and watching everywhere."

In a single year Cave had come a long way from the ex-embalmer who had studied a book of newspaper clippings on a Washington farm and brooded about an old man in a hospital. Though Paul was never to refer again to the victim of Cave's driving, I was quite sure that he expected, sooner or later, that mysterious death would return to haunt us all.

By midsummer, Cave had grown restless and bored, and since the telecasts had been discontinued until the following November, he was eager to travel. He was never to lose his passion for places. It was finally decided that he spend the summer on one of the Florida Keys, a tiny island owned by a Cavite who offered to place everything at the master's disposal. And, though warned that the heat might be uncomfortable, Cave and his retinue left secretly one night by chartered sea plane from Long Island Sound and for at least a month the press did not know what had happened to him.

I declined to accompany Cave and Iris. Paul remained in New York, while Iris's work was temporarily turned over to various young enthusiasts trained by her. I went back to the Hudson Valley, to my house and . . .

## 2

I have not been able to write for several days. According to the doctor it is a touch of heat, but I suspect that this is only his kind euphemism.

I had broken off in my narrative to take a walk in the garden last Friday afternoon when I was joined by Butler, whose attentions lately have been more numerous than I should like.

"He'll be here Sunday, Hudson. Why don't we all three have dinner together that night and celebrate?"

I said that nothing could give me more pleasure, as I inched along the garden path, moving toward the hot shaded center where, beneath fruit trees, a fine statue of Osiris stood, looted in earlier days by the hotel management from one of the temples. I thought, however, with more longing of the bench beside the statue than of the figure itself, whose every serene detail I had long since memorized. Butler adjusted his loose long stride to my own uneven pace. I walked as I always do now, with my eyes upon the ground, nervously avoiding anything which might make me stumble, for I have fallen down a number of times in the last few years and I have a terror of broken bones, the particular scourge of old bodies.

I was as glad as not that I didn't have to watch my companion while we chatted, for his red honest face, forever dripping sweat, annoyed me more than was reasonable.

"And he'll be pleased to know I've got us a Center. Not much of one but good enough for a start."

I paused before a formidable rock that lay directly in my path. It would take some doing to step over it, I thought, as I remarked, "I'm sure the Pasha doesn't know about this."

"Not really." Butler laughed happily. "He thinks we're just taking a house for ourselves to study the local culture. Later, after we get going, he can find out."

"I'd be very careful," I said and, very careful myself, I stepped over the rock; my legs detested the extra exertion; one nearly buckled as it touched the ground. I threw my weight on my cane and was saved a fall. Butler had not noticed.

"Jessup is going to bring in the literature. We'll say it's our library. All printed in Arabic, too. The Dallas Center thinks of everything."

"Are they . . . equipped for such things?"

"Oh yes. That's where the main university is now. Biggest one in the world. I didn't go there myself. Marks weren't good enough, but Jessup did. He'll tell you all about it. Quite a crew they turn out: best in the business, but then they get the cream of the crop to begin with."

"Tell me, are the Residents still in charge of the Centers or do they share the administration with the therapists?"

"Therapists?" Butler seemed bewildered.

"In the old days there used to be the Resident and his staff and then a clinic attached where . . ."

"You really are behind the times." Butler looked at me as though I'd betrayed a firsthand knowledge of earth's creation. "All Residents and their staffs, including the Communicators like myself, get the same training; part of it is in mental therapy. Those who show particular aptitude for therapy are assigned clinical work just as I do communication work in foreign countries. People who get to be Residents are usually teachers and administrators. Sometimes a Communicator will even get a Residency in his old age as a reward for the highest services." He then explained to me the official, somewhat Byzantine, structure of the Cavites. There were many new titles, indicating a swollen organization under the direction of a Counsel of Residents which, in turn, was responsible for the election from among their number of a unique Chief Resident whose reign lasted for the remainder of his lifetime.

With relief, I sat down on the bench beside Osiris. Butler joined me. "Dallas of course is the main Residency," he said.

"It used to be in New York, years ago," I said, thinking of the brownstone house, of the loft on Twenty-third Street.

"Around twenty years ago it was moved to Dallas by the Chief Resident. Not only did they have the best-equipped Center there but the Texans make just about the best Cavites in the country. What they won't do for Cavesword isn't worth mentioning. They burned the old churches, you know . . . every one in the state."

"And one or two Baptist ministers as well?"

"You can't break eggs without making an omelet," said Butler sententiously.

"I see what you mean. Still, Cave was against persecution. He always felt it was enough for people to hear Cavesword . . ."

"You got a lot of reading to do," said Butler sharply. "Looks like you've forgotten your text: 'And, if they persist in superstition, strike them, for one idolater is like a spoiled apple in the barrel, contaminating the others.'" Butler's voice, as he quoted, was round and booming, rich in vowel sounds, while his protruding eyes gazed without blinking into the invisible radiance of truth which hovered apparently, above a diseased hibiscus bush.

"I've forgotten that particular quotation," I said.

"Seems funny you should, since it's just about the most famous of the texts." But, though my ignorance continued to startle Butler, I could see that he was beginning to attribute it to senility rather than to laxity or potential idolatry.

"I was a close follower in the first few years," I said, currying favor. "But I've been out of touch since and I suppose that after Cave's death there was a whole mass of new doctrine with which I am unfamiliar, to my regret."

"Doctrine!" Butler was shocked. "We have no doctrine. We are not one of those heathen churches with claims to 'divine' guidance. We're simply listeners to Cavesword. That's all. He was the first to tell the plain truth and naturally we honor him, but there is no doctrine even though he guides us the way a good father does his children."

"I am very old," I said in my best dying-fall voice. "You must remember that when you are with me you are in the company of a man who was brought up in the old ways, who uses Christian terms from time to time. I was thirty when Cave began his mission. I am, as a matter of fact, nearly the same age as Cave himself if he were still alive."

That had its calculated effect. Butler looked at me with some awe. "Golly!" he said. "It doesn't really seem possible, does it? Of course there're still people around who were alive in those days, but I don't know of anybody who actually saw Cave. You did tell me you saw him?"

"Once only."

"Was he like the telecasts?"

"Oh yes. Even more effective, I think."

"He was big of course, six feet one inch tall."

"No, he was only about five feet eight inches, a little shorter than I . . ."

"You must be mistaken because, according to all the texts, he was six feet one."

"I saw him at a distance, of course. I was only guessing." I was amused that they should have seen fit to change even Cave's stature.

"You can tell he was a tall man from the telecasts."

"Do they still show them?"

"Still show them! They're the main part of our weekly Get-togethers. Each Residency has a complete library of Cave's telecasts, one hundred and eight including the last. Each week, a different one is shown by the Resident's staff, and the Resident himself or someone assigned by him discusses the message."

"And they still hold up after fifty years?"

"Hold up? We learn more from them each year. You should see all the books and lectures on Cavesword . . . several hundred important ones which we have to read as part of our communication duties, though they're not for the laymen. We discourage nonprofessionals from going into such problems, much too complicated for the untrained mind."

"I should think so. Tell me, is there any more trouble with the idolaters?"

Butler shook his head. "Just about none. They were licked

161

when the parochial schools were shut down. That took care of Catholicism. Of course there were some bad times. I guess you know all about them."

I nodded. Even in Egypt I had heard of massacres and persecutions. I could still recall the morning when I opened the Cairo paper and saw a large photograph of St. Peter's smoldering in its ruins, a fitting tomb for the last Pope and martyr who had perished there when a mob of Cavites had fired the Vatican. The Cairo paper took an obvious delight in these barbarities and I had not the heart to read of the wanton destruction of works of Michelangelo and Bernini, the looting of the art galleries, the bonfire which was made in the Papal gardens of the entire Vatican library. Later, word came of a certain Assistant Resident of Topeka who, with a group of demolition experts and Cavite enthusiasts, ranged across France and Italy destroying the cathedrals with the approval of the local governments, as well as the Cavite crowds who gathered in great numbers to watch, delightedly, the crumbling of these last monuments to superstition. Fortunately, the tourist bureaus were able to save a few of the lesser churches.

"The Edict of Washington which outlawed idolatrous schools did the trick. The Atlantic Community has always believed in toleration. Even to this day it is possible for a man to be a Christian, though unlikely since the truth is so well known."

"But the Christian has no churches left and no clergy."

"True, and if that discourages him he's not likely to remain too long in error. As I've told you, though, we have our ways of making people see the truth."

"The calculable percentage."

"Exactly."

I looked at Osiris in the green shade. His diorite face smiled secretly back at me. "Did you have much trouble in the Latin countries?"

"Less than you might think. The ignorant were the big problem because, since they didn't know English, we weren't able to use the telecasts. Fortunately, we had some able

Residents and after a little showmanship, a few miracles (or what they took to be miracles), they came around, especially when many of their ex-priests told them about Cavesword. Nearly all of the older Residents in the Mediterranean countries were once Catholic priests."

"Renegades?"

"They saw the truth. Not without some indoctrination, I suspect. We've had to adapt a good many of our procedural methods to fit local customs. The old Christmas has become Cavesday and what was Easter is now Irisday."

"Iris Mortimer?"

"Who else? And then certain festivals which . . ."

"I suppose she's dead now."

"Why, yes. She died six years ago. She was the last of the Original Five."

"Ah, yes, the five: Paul Himmell, Iris Mortimer, Ivan Stokharin, Clarissa Lessing and . . ."

"And Edward Hastings. We still use his Introduction even though it's been largely obsoleted by later texts. His dialogues will of course be the basis for that final book of Cave, which our best scholars have been at work on for over twenty years."

Hastings, of all people! I nearly laughed aloud. Poor feckless Hastings was now the author of *my* dialogues with Cave. I marveled at the ease with which the innumerable references to myself had been deleted. I began to doubt my own existence. I asked if Hastings was still alive and was told that he too was long dead.

I then asked again about Iris.

"Some very exciting things have come to light," said Butler. Certain historians at the Dallas Center feel that there is some evidence that she was Cave's sister."

I was startled by this. "How could that be? Wasn't she from Detroit? And wasn't he from Seattle? And didn't they meet for the first time in southern California at the beginning of his mission?"

"I see you know more Cavite history than you pretend," said

Butler amiably. "That of course has been the traditional point of view. Yet as her influence increased in the world (in Italy, you know, one sees her picture nearly as often as Cave's) our historians became suspicious. It was all perfectly simple, really. If she could exert nearly the same power as Cave himself then she must, in some way, be related to him. I suppose you know about the Miami business. No? Well, their Resident, some years ago, openly promulgated the theory that Cave and Iris Mortimer were man and wife. A great many people believed him and though the Chief Resident at Dallas issued a statement denying the truth of all this, Miami continued in error and it took our indoctrination team several years to get the situation back to normal. But the whole business *did* get everyone to thinking and, with the concurrence of Dallas, investigations have been made. I don't know many of the details but my colleague probably will. He keeps track of that kind of thing."

"If she is proven to be Cave's sister will she have equal rank with him?"

"Certainly not. Cavesword is everything. But she will be equal to him on the human level though his inferior in truth. At least that appears to be the Dallas interpretation."

"She was very active, I suppose?"

"Right until the end. She traveled all over the world with Cavesword and, when she grew too old to travel, she took over the Residency of New York City, which she held until she died. As a matter of fact, I have a picture of her which I always carry. It was taken in the last years." He pulled out a steel-mesh wallet in which, protected by cellophane, was a photograph of Iris, the first I had seen in many many years. My hand shook as I held the picture up to the light.

For a split second I felt her presence, saw in the saddened face, framed by white hair, my summer love which had never been except in my own dreaming where I was whole and loved this creature whose luminous eyes had not altered with age, their expression the same as that night beside the western sea.

But then my fingers froze. The wallet fell to the ground. I fainted into what I supposed with my last vestige of consciousness to be death, to be nothing.

3

I awakened in my own bed with my old friend Dr. Raid beside me. He looked much concerned while, at the foot of the bed, stood Butler, very solemn and still. I resolved not to die with him in the room.

"My apologies, Mr. Butler," I said, surprised that I could speak at all. "I'm afraid I dropped your picture." I had no difficulty in remembering what had happened. It was as if I had suddenly shut my eyes and opened them again, several hours having passed instead of as many seconds. Time, I decided, was all nonsense.

"Think nothing of it. I'm only . . ."

"You must not strain yourself, Mr. Hudson," said the doctor. A few days in bed, plenty of liquids, a pill or two, and then I was left alone with a buzzer beside my bed which would summon the houseboy if I should have a coherent moment before taking a last turn for the worse. The next time, I think, will be the final one and though I detest the thought, these little rehearsals over the last few years – the brief strokes, the sudden flooding of parts of the brain with the blood of capillaries in preparation for that last arterial deluge – have got me used to the idea. My only complaint is that odd things are done to my memory by these strokes which, light as they have been, tend to alter those parts of the brain which hold the secrets of the past. I have found this week, while convalescing from Tuesday's collapse, that most of my childhood has been washed clean out of my memory. I knew of course that I was born on the banks of the Hudson but I cannot for the life of me recall what schools I attended; yet memories from college days on seem unimpaired, though I have had to reread this memoir

165

attentively to resume my train of thought, to refresh a dying memory. It is strange indeed to have lost some twenty years as though they had never been and, worse still, to be unable to find out about oneself in any case, since the will of others has effectively abolished one. I do not exist in the world and very soon (how soon I wonder?), I shall not exist even to myself, only this record a fragile proof that I once lived.

Now I am able to work again. Butler pays me a daily visit, as does the doctor. Both are very kind but both tend to treat me as a thing which no longer matters. I have been written off in their minds. I'm no longer really human since soon, perhaps in a few days, I shall not be one of them but one of the dead whose dust is in the air they breathe. Well, let it come. The fraternity of the dead, though nothing, is the larger kingdom.

I am able to sit up in bed (actually I can get around as well or as badly as before but it tires me too much to walk so I remain abed). Sunday is here at last, and from the excited bustle in the air, which I feel rather than hear, Butler's colleague must have arrived. I am not ready for him yet and I have hung a "Do Not Disturb" sign on the door, composed emphatically in four languages. It should keep them out for a few days.

I have a premonition of disaster which, though it is no doubt perfectly natural at my age with the last catastrophe almost upon me, seems to be of a penultimate nature, a final *human* crisis. All that I have heard from Butler about this young man, this colleague of his, disposes me to fear him. For although my existence has been kept a secret from the newer generations, the others, the older ones, the chief counselors are well aware of me. Though I have so far evaded their agents and though they undoubtedly assume that I am long since dead, it is still possible that a shrewd young man with a career in the making might grow suspicious, and one word to the older members of the hierarchy would be enough to start an inquisition which could end in assassination (ironic that I should fear *that* at this point!) or, more terrible, in a course of indoctrination where my apostasy would be reduced by drugs to conformity. It would be the most splendid triumph for Cave if, in my last days, I should recant. The best victory of all, the surrender of the original lutherist upon his deathbed.

Yet I have a trick or two up my sleeve and the game's not yet over. Should the new arrival prove to be the one I have so long awaited, I shall know how to act. I have planned for this day. My adversary will find me armed.

But now old days draw me back; the crisis approaches in my narrative.

4

The first summer was my last on the Hudson, at peace. Iris wrote me regularly from the Florida Keys. Short, brisk letters completely impersonal and devoted largely to what *he* was doing and saying. It seems that *he* was enchanted by the strangeness of the Keys, yet was anxious to begin traveling again. With some difficulty, I gathered between the lines, Iris had restrained him from starting out on a world tour. "He says he wants to see Saigon and Samarkand and so forth soon because he likes the names. I don't see how he can get away yet, though maybe in the fall after his tour. They say now he can make his talks on film all at once, which will mean of course he won't have to go through anything like last winter again." There followed more news, an inquiry into my health (in those days I was confident I should die early of a liver ailment; my liver now seems the one firm organ in my body; in any case, I enjoyed my hypochondria) and a reference to the various things I was writing for the instruction of converts and detractors both. I pushed the letter away, and looked out across the river.

I was alone, awaiting Clarissa for tea. I had actually prepared tea since she never drank alcohol and I myself was a non-drinker that summer when my liver rested (so powerful is imagination) like a brazen cannonball against the cage of bones.

I sat on my porch, which overlooked the lawn and the water; unlike most other houses on that river, mine had the railroad behind it instead of in front of it, an agreeable state of affairs; I don't mind the sound of trains but the sight of their tracks depresses me.

Beside me, among the tray of tea things, the manuscript of my dialogue lay neglected. I had not yet made up my mind whether or not to read it to Clarissa. Such things tended to bore her; yet, if she could be enticed into attention, her opinion would be useful. Such a long memory of old customs would be invaluable to me as I composed, with diligence rather than inspiration, an ethical system whose single virtue was that it tended to satisfy the needs of human beings as much as was possible without inviting chaos. I had, that morning over coffee, abolished marriage. During lunch, served me by my genteel but impoverished housekeeper (although servants still existed in those days in a few great houses, people like myself were obliged to engage the casual services of the haughty poor), I decided to leave marriage the way it was but make divorce much simpler. After lunch, suffering from a liver-inspired headache, I not only abolished marriage again but resolutely handed the children over to the impersonal mercies of the state.

Now, bemused, relaxed, my eyes upon the pale blue Catskills and the summer green, ears alert to the noise of motorboats like great waterbugs, I brooded upon the implications of what I was doing and, though I was secretly amused at my own confidence, I realized, too, that what I felt and did and wrote, though doubtless unorthodox to many, was, finally, not really the work of my own inspiration but a logical result of all that was in the world. A statement of the dreams of others which I could formulate only because I shared them. Cave regarded his own words as revelation when, actually, they only echoed the collective mind, a plausible articulation of what most men felt even though their conscious minds were corseted and constricted by familiar ways of thinking, often the opposite of what they truly believed.

Yet at this step I hesitated. There was no doubt that the children and the society would be the better for such an arrangement . . . and there was little doubt that our civilization was moving toward such a resolution. But there were parents who would want to retain their children and children who might be better cared for by their progenitors than by even the best-intentioned functionaries of the state. Would the state allow parents to keep their children if they wanted them? If not, it was tyrannous; if so, difficult in the extreme, for how could even the most enlightened board of analysts determine who should be allowed their children and who not? The answer, of course, was in the retraining of future generations. Let them grow up accepting as inevitable and right the surrender of babies to the state. Other cultures had done it and ours could too. But I was able to imagine, vividly, the numerous cruelties which would be perpetrated in the name of the whole, while the opportunity for tyranny in a civilization where all children were at the disposal of a government brought sharply to mind that image of the anthill society which has haunted the imagination of the thoughtful for at least a century.

I had got myself into a most gloomy state by the time Clarissa arrived, trailing across the lawn in an exotic ankle-length gown of gray which floated in yards behind her, like the diaphanous flags of some forgotten army.

"Your lawn is full of moles!" she shouted to me, pausing in her progress and scowling at a patch of turf. "And it needs cutting and more clover. *Always* more clover, remember that." She turned her back on me to stare at the river, which was as gray as her gown but, in its soft tidal motion, spangled with light like sequins on a vast train.

She had no criticism of the river when she at last turned and climbed the steps to the porch; she sat down with a gasp.

"I'm boiling! Tea? Hot tea to combat the heat."

I poured her a cup. "Not a hot day at all." Actually it was very warm. "If you didn't get yourself up as a Marie Corelli heroine, you'd be much cooler."

"Not very gallant today, are we?" Clarissa looked at me over her cup. "I've had this gown for five hundred years. There used to be a wimple, but I lost it moving."

"The material seems to be holding up quite well," and now that she had mentioned it, there was an archaic look to the texture of the gown, like those bits of cloth preserved under glass in museums.

"Silk lasts indefinitely, if one is tidy. Also I don't wear this much, as you can see, but with the devalued state of the dollar (an ominous sign, my dear, the beginning of the end!) I've been forced to redo a lot of old odds and ends I've kept for sentimental reasons. This is one of them and I'm very fond of it." She spoke deliberately, to forestall any further ungallantry.

"I just wondered if it was cool."

"It is cool. Ah, a letter from Iris." Clarissa had seen the letter beside my chair and, without asking permission, had seized it like a magpie and read it through quickly. "I admire a girl who types," she said, letting fall the letter. "I suppose they all do now though it seems like only yesterday that, if one did not open a tearoom, one typed, working for men, all of whom made advances. That was when we had to wear corsets and hatpins. One discouraged while the other protected." Clarissa chuckled at some obscene memory.

"I wonder if Paul can keep Cave from wandering off to some impossible place."

"I shouldn't be surprised." She picked at the tea sandwiches suspiciously, curling back the top slices of bread to see what was underneath. Tentatively, she bit into deviled ham; she chewed, swallowed; she was not disappointed. She wolfed another sandwich, talking all the while. "Poor Cave is a captive now. His disciples are in full command. Even Mohammed, as strong-headed as he was, finally ended up a perfect pawn in the hands

170

of Abu Bekr and the women, especially the women."

"I'm not so sure about Cave. He . . ."

"Does what they tell him, especially Iris."

"Iris? But I should have said she was the only one who *never* tried to influence him."

Clarissa laughed unpleasantly. A moth flew into her artificial auburn hair. Unerringly, she found it with one capable hand and quickly snuffed out its life in a puff of gray dust from broken wings. She wiped her fingers on a paper napkin. The day was full of moths, but none came near us again. "You are naive, Eugene," she said, her little murder done. "It's your nicest quality. In theory you are remarkably aware of human character; yet, when you're confronted with the most implausible appearance, you promptly take it for the reality."

I was irritated by this and also by the business of the sandwich, not to mention the murder of the moth. I looked at Clarissa with momentary dislike. "I was not aware . . . " I began, but she interrupted me with an airy wave of her hand.

"I forgot no one likes to be called naive. Calculating, dishonest, treacherous – people rather revel in those designations, but to be thought trusting. . . ." She clapped her hands as though to punctuate her meaning; then, after a full stop, she went on more soberly. "Iris is the one to look out for. Our own sweet, self-effacing, dedicated Iris. I adore her. I always have, but she's up to no good."

"I don't know what you're talking about."

"You will. You would if you weren't entirely blind to what they used to call human nature. Iris is acquiring Cave."

"Acquiring?"

"Exactly the word. She loves him for all sorts of reasons but she cannot have him in the usual sense (I found out all about that, by the way). Therefore, the only thing left for her to do is acquire him, to take his life in hers. You may think *she* may think that her slavish adoration is only humble love, but actually it's something far more significant, and dangerous."

"I don't see the danger, even accepting your hypothesis."

**171**

"It's no hypothesis and the danger is real. Iris will have him, and, through him, she'll have you all."

I did not begin to understand that day, and Clarissa, in her Pythoness way, was no help, muttering vague threats and imprecations with a mouth full of bread.

After my first jealousy at Iris's preference of Cave to me, a jealousy which I knew, even at the time, was unjustified and a little ludicrous, I had come to accept her devotion to Cave as a perfectly natural state of affairs. He was an extraordinary man and though he did not fulfill her in the usual sense, he gave her more than a mere lover might. He gave her a whole life and I envied her for having been able to seize so shrewdly upon this unique way out of ordinary life and into something more grand, more strange, more engaging. Though I could not follow her, I was able to appreciate her choice and admire the completeness of her days. That she was obscurely using Cave for her own ends, subverting him, did not seem possible, and I was annoyed by Clarissa's dark warnings. I directed the conversation into other waters.

"The children. I haven't decided what to do with them."

Clarissa came to a full halt. For a moment she forgot to chew. Then, with a look of pain, she swallowed. "*Your* children?"

"Any children, all children." I pointed to the manuscript on the table.

She understood. "I'm quite sure you have abolished marriage."

"As a matter of fact, yes, this morning."

"And now you don't know what to do about the children."

"Precisely. I . . . "

"Perfectly simple." Clarissa was brisk. This, apparently, was a problem she had already solved. "The next step is controlled breeding. Only those whose blood lines seem promising should be allowed to procreate. Now that oral contraceptives are so popular no one will make babies by accident . . . in fact, it should be a serious crime if someone does."

"Quite neat, but I wonder whether, psychologically, it's simple. There's the whole business of instinct, of the natural desire of a woman to want her own child after bearing it."

"All habit . . . . not innate. Children have been subordinate woman's weapon for centuries. They have had to develop certain traits which in other circumstances they would not have possessed. Rats, whom we closely resemble, though they suckle their young will, in moments of mild hunger or even exasperation, think nothing of eating an entire litter. You can condition human beings to accept any state of affairs as being perfectly natural."

"I don't doubt that. But how to break the habits of several thousand years?"

"I suppose there *are* ways. Look what Cave is doing. Of course making death popular is not so difficult since, finally, people want it to be nice. They do the real work or, rather, their terror does. In place of superstition, which they've nearly outgrown, he offers them madness."

"Now really, Clarissa . . ."

"I don't disapprove. I'm all for him, as you know. To make death preferable to life is of course utter folly but still a perfectly logical reaction for these poor bewildered savages who, having lost their old superstitions, are absolutely terrified at the prospect of nothing. They want to perpetuate their little personalities forever into space and time and now they've begun to realize the folly of that (who, after all, are they – are *we* – in creation?), they will follow desperately the first man who pulls the sting of death and Cave is that man, as I knew he would be."

"And after Cave?"

"I will not say what I see. I'm on the side of change, however, which makes me in perfect harmony with life." Clarissa chuckled. A fish leaped grayly in the river; out in the channel a barge glided by, the muffled noise of its engines like slow heartbeats.

"But you think it good for people to follow Cave? You think what he says is right?"

"Nothing is good. Nothing is right. But though Cave is wrong, it is a *new* wrong and so it is better than the old; in any case, he will keep the people amused, and boredom, finally, is the one monster the race will never conquer . . . the monster which will devour us in time. But now we're off the track. Mother love exists because we believe it exists. Believe it does not exist and it won't. That, I fear, is the general condition of 'the unchanging human heart.' Make these young girls feel that having babies is a patriotic duty as well as healthful therapy and they'll go through it blithely enough, without ever giving a second thought to the child they leave behind in the government nursery."

"But to get them to that state of acceptance . . ."

"Is the problem. I'm sure it will be solved in a few generations."

"You think I'm right to propose it?"

"Of course. It will happen anyway."

"Yet I'm disturbed at the thought of all that power in the hands of the state. They can make the children believe anything. Impose the most terrible tyranny. Blind at birth so that none might ever see anything again but what a few rulers, as ignorant as they, will want them to see. There'll be a time when all people are alike."

"Which is precisely the ideal society. No mysteries, no romantics, no discussions, no persecutions because there's no one to persecute. When all have received the same conditioning, it will be like . . ."

"Insects."

"Who have existed longer than ourselves and will outlast our race by many millennia."

"Is existence everything?"

"There is nothing else."

"Then likeness is the aim of human society?"

"Call it harmony. You think of yourself only as you are now dropped into the midst of a society of dull conformists. That's where you make your mistake. You'll not live to see it for if you did, you would be someone else, a part of it. No one of your disposition could possibly happen in such a society. There would be no rebellion against sameness because difference would not, in any important sense, exist, even as a proposition. You think: how terrible! But think again how wonderful it would be to belong to the pack, to the tribe, to the race, without guilt or anxiety or division."

"I cannot imagine it."

"No more can they imagine you."

"This will happen?"

"Yes, and you will have been a part of it."

"Through Cave?"

"Partly, yes. There will be others after him. His work will be distorted by others, but that's to be expected."

"I don't like your future, Clarissa."

"Nor does it like *you*, my dear. The idea of someone who is irritable and at odds with society, bitter and angry, separate from others. I shouldn't wonder but that you yourself might really be used as a perfect example of the old evil days."

"Virtue dies?"

"Virtue becomes the property of the race."

"Imagination is forbidden?"

"No, only channeled for the good of all."

"And this is a desirable world, the future you describe?"

"Desirable for whom? For you, no. For me, not really. For the people in it? Well, yes and no. They will not question their estate but they will suffer from a collective boredom which . . . but my lips are sealed. Your tea was delicious though the bread was not quite fresh. But then bachelors never keep house properly. I've gone on much too long. Do forget everything I've said. I am indiscreet. I can't help it." She rose, a cloud of gray suspended above the porch. I walked her across the lawn to the driveway where her car was parked. The breeze had died for the moment and the heat prickled me unpleasantly; my temples itched as the sweat started.

"Go on with it," she said as she got into her car. "You may as well be on the side of the future as against it. Not that it much matters anyway. When your adorable President Jefferson was in Paris he said. . ." But the noise of the car starting drowned the body of her anecdote. I caught only the end: ". . . that harmony was preferable. We were all amused. I was the only one who realized that he was serious." Dust swirled and Clarissa was gone down the drive at great speed, keeping, I noticed, to the wrong side of the road. I hoped this was an omen.

5

I got through an unusually sultry July without much interference from either Cave or the world. Paul paid me a quick visit to get the manuscript of the dialogues and I was reminded of those accounts of the progresses made by monarchs in other days, or rather of great ministers, for his party occupied four large cars which gleamed side by side in my driveway like glossy beasts while their contents, Paul and fourteen assistants, all strange to me save Stokharin, wandered disconsolately about the lawn until their departure.

Paul, though brisk, was cordial. "Trouble all over the map. But b-i-g t-r-o-u-b-l-e." He spelled it out with relish. Size was important, I knew, to a publicist, even to one turned evangelist.

"Is Cave disturbed by it?"

"Doesn't pay any attention. Haven't seen him but Iris keeps me posted. By the way we're hiring a plane the first week in August to go see him, Stokharin and me. Want to come along?"

I didn't but I said I would. I had no intention of being left out of anything. There was *my* work still to do.

"I'll let you know details. Is this hot stuff?" He waved the sheaf of papers I'd given him.

"Real hot," I said but my irony was too pale; only primary colors caught Paul's eye.

"I hope so. Got any new stunts?"

I told him, briefly, about my thoughts on marriage, or rather

Cave's thoughts. The literary device was for me to ask him certain questions and for him to answer them or at least to ask pointed questions in his turn. Cheerfully, I had committed Cave to my own point of view and I was somewhat nervous about his reaction, not to mention the others'. So far, only Clarissa knew and her approval was pleasant but perhaps frivolous: it carried little weight, I knew, with the rest.

Paul whistled. "You got us a tall order. I'm not sure we'll be able to handle that problem yet, if ever."

"I've done it carefully," I began.

Stokharin, who had been listening with interest, came to my aid. "In the Centers we, how you say, Paul? softpedal the family. We advise young boys to make love to the young girls without marrying or having babies. We speak of the family as a mere social unit, and of course society changes. I am most eager to study Mr. Luther's approach. Perhaps a little aid from those of us in clinical work . . ."

But then the dark sedans began to purr; nervous attendants whispered to Paul and I was soon left alone with the fragments of our brief conversation to examine and interpret at my leisure. I was surprised and pleased at Stokharin's unexpected support. I had thought of him as my chief antagonist. But then, my work finished, I tended roses and read Dio Cassius until the summons came in August.

6

The plane landed on a glare of blue water, more blinding even than the vivid sky about the sun itself, which made both elements seem to be a quivering blue fire in which was destroyed all of earth save a tiny smear of dusty faded green, the island of our destination.

The pilot maneuvered the plane against a bone-gray dock where, all alone, Iris stood, her hair tangled from the propellers' wind and her eyes hidden by dark glasses. Like explorers in a new country, Paul, Stokharin and I scrambled onto the dock, the heat closing in about us like blue canvas, stifling, palpable. I gasped and dropped my suitcase. Iris laughed and ran forward to greet us; she came first to me, an action which, even in my dazzled, shocked state, I realized and valued.

"Gene, you must get out of that suit this minute! And get some dark glasses or you'll go blind. Paul, how are you? It's good to see you, Doctor." And, in the chatter of greetings, she escorted us off the dock and across a narrow white beach to a grove of palm trees where the cottage stood.

To our delight, the interior was cooled by machinery. I sank into a wicker chair even as Cave pumped my hand. Iris laughed, "Leave him alone, John. He's smothered by the heat."

"No hat," said Cave solemnly after the first greeting which, in my relief, I'd not heard. "You'll get sunstroke."

Paul was now in charge. The heat which had enervated both Stokharin and me filled him with manic energy, like one of those reptiles that absorb vitality from the sun.

"What a great little place, Cave! Had no idea there were all the comforts of home down here, none at all. Don't suppose you go out much?"

Cave, unlike Iris, was not tanned though he had, for him, a good colour, unlike his usual sallowness. "I don't get too much sun," he admitted. "We go fishing sometimes, early in the morning. Most of the time I just hang around the house and look at the letters, and read some."

I noticed on the table beside me an enormous pile of travel magazines, tourist folders and atlases. I anticipated trouble.

Paul prowled restlessly about the modern living room with its shuttered sealed windows. Stokharin and I, like fish back in their own element after a brief excursion on land, gasped softly in our chairs while Iris told us of the Keys, and of their fishing trips. She was at her best here as she had been that other time in Spokane. Being out of doors, in Cave's exclusive company, brought her to life in a way the exciting busyness of New York did not. In the city she seemed like an object through which an electric current passed; here on this island, in the sun's glare, she unfolded, petal after petal, until the secret interior seemed almost exposed. I was conscious of her as a lovely woman and, without warning, I experienced desire. That sharp rare longing, which in me can reach no climax. Always before she had been a friend, a companion whose company I had jealously valued; her attention alone had been enough to satisfy me, but on this day I saw her as a man entire might and I plummeted into despair, talking of Plato.

"Of course there are other ways of casting dialogues, such as introducing the celebrated dead brought together for a chat in Limbo. But I thought that I should keep the talk to only two. Cave and myself . . . Socrates and Alcibiades." Alcibiades was precisely the wrong parallel but I left it uncorrected, noticing how delicately the hollow at the base of Iris's throat quivered with life's blood, and although I attempted, as I often had before with bitter success, to think of her as so much mortal flesh, the body and its beauty pulp and bone, beautiful only to a human eye (hideous, no doubt, to the eye of a geometric progression), that afternoon I was lost and I could not become, even for a moment, an abstract intelligence. Though I saw the bone, the dust, I saw her existing, triumphant in the present. I cursed the flaw in my own flesh and hated life.

"We liked it very much," she said, unaware of my passion and its attendant despair.

"You don't think it's too strong, do you? All morality, not to mention the churches, will be aligned against us."

"John was worried at first . . . not that opposition frightens him and it is *his* idea. I mean you wrote the dialogue but it reflects exactly what he's always thought." Though in love's agony, I looked at her sharply to make certain she was perfectly serious. She was. This helped soothe the pain. She had been hypnotized by Cave. I wondered how Clarissa could ever have thought it was the other way around.

"In a way we're already on record." Iris looked thoughtfully

179

across the room at Cave, who was showing Paul and Stokharin a large map of some strange country. "The Centers have helped a good many couples to adjust to one another without marriage and without guilt."

"But then there's the problem of what to do with the children when the family breaks up."

Iris sighed. "I'm afraid that's already a problem. Our Centers are taking care of a good many children already. A number, of course, go out for adoption to bored couples who need something to amuse them. I suppose we'll have to establish nurseries as a part of each Center until, finally, the government assumes the responsibility."

"*If* it becomes Cavite."

"When it becomes Cavite." She was powerful in her casualness.

"Meanwhile there are laws of adoption which vary from state to state and, if we're not careful, we're apt to come up against the law."

"Paul looks after us," she smiled. "Did you know that he has nearly a hundred lawyers on our payroll? All protecting us."

"From what?" I had not been aware of this.

"Lawsuits. Attempts by state legislatures to outlaw the Centers on the grounds of immorality and so on. The lawyers are kept busy all the time."

"Why haven't I read about any of this in the papers?"

"We've been able to keep things quiet. Paul is marvelous with the editors. Several have even joined us, by the way, secretly, of course."

"What's the membership now?"

Iris gestured. "No one knows. We have thirty Centers in the United States and each day they receive hundreds of new Cavites. I suspect there are at least four million by now."

I gasped, beginning to recover at last from the heat, from my unexpected crisis of love. "I had no idea things were going so fast."

"Too fast. We haven't enough trained people to look after

the Centers, and on top of that we must set up new Centers. Paul has broken the country up into districts, all very methodical: so many Centers per district, each with a Resident in charge. Stokharin is taking care of the clinical work."

"Where's the money coming from?"

"In bushels from heaven," Iris smiled. "We leave all that to Paul. I shouldn't be surprised if he counterfeits it. Anyway, I *must* get back to New York, to the school. I shouldn't really have gone off in the middle of everything, but I was tired and John wanted company so I came."

"How is he?"

"As you see, calm. I don't believe he ever considers any of our problems. He never mentions them; never reads the reports Paul sends him; doesn't even read the attacks from the churches. We get several a day, not to mention threatening mail. We now have full-time bodyguards."

"You think people are seriously threatening him?"

"I don't know how serious they are but we can't take chances. Fortunately, almost no one knows we're here and, so far, no cranks have got through from the mainland. Our groceries and mail are brought from the boat every other day from Key Largo. Otherwise, we're perfectly isolated."

I looked about me for some sign of the guards; there was none. A Cuban woman vacuuming in the next room was the only visible stranger.

Cave abandoned his maps and atlases long enough to tell me how much the dialogues pleased him.

"I wish I could put it down like you do. I can only say it when people listen."

"Do you think I've been accurate?"

Cave nodded solemnly. "Oh, yes. It's just like I've always said it, only written down." I realized that he had already assumed full responsibility (and credit, should there be any) for my composition. I accepted his presumption with amusement. Only Stokharin seemed aware of the humor of the situation. I caught him staring at me with a shrewd expression; he looked quickly away, mouth rigid as he tried not to smile. I liked him at that moment. We were the only ones who had not been possessed by Cave. I felt like a conspirator.

For several days we talked, or rather Paul talked. He had brought with him charts and statements and statistics and, though Cave did not bother to disguise his boredom, he listened most of the time and his questions, when they did occur, were apposite. The rest of us were fascinated by the extent of what Paul referred to as the "first operational phase."

Various projects had already been undertaken; others were put up to the directors for discussion. Thanks to Paul's emphatic personality, our meetings were more like those of account executives than the pious forgathering of a messiah's apostles – and already that word had been used in the press by the curious as well as by the devout. Cave was the messiah to several million Americans. But he was not come with fire to judge the world, not armed with the instruction of a super-natural being whose secret word had been given this favorite son. No, Cave was of another line. That of the prophets, of the teachers like Jesus before he became Christ, or Mohammed before he became Islam. In our age it was Cave's task to say the words all men awaited yet dared not speak or even attend without the overpowering authority of another who had, plausibly, assumed the guise of master. I could not help but wonder as I watched Cave in those heated conferences if the past had been like this.

Cave certainly had one advantage over his predecessors: modern communications. It took three centuries for Christianity to infect the world. It was to take Cave only three years to conquer Europe and the Americas.

But I did not have this foreknowledge in Florida. I only knew that Paul was handling an extraordinary business in a remarkable way. There was no plan so vast that he could not contemplate its execution with ease. He was exhausting in his energy and, though he did not possess much imagination, he was a splendid improvisor, using whatever themes were at hand to create his own dazzling contrapuntal effects.

We decided upon a weekly magazine to be distributed gratis to the Cavites (I was appointed editor though the actual work, of which I was entirely ignorant, was to be done by a crew already at work on the first issue). We would also send abroad certain films to be shown by Cavite lecturers. We then approved the itinerary of Cave's national tour in the fall (Cave was most alive during this discussion; suggesting cities he wanted particularly to see, reveling in the euphony of such names as Tallahassee). We also planned several dinners to be held in New York with newspaper editors and political figures, and we discussed the advisability of Cave's accepting an invitation to be questioned by the House Un-American Activities Committee, which had begun to show an interest in the progress of our Centers. It was decided that Cave delay meeting the committee until the time was propitious, or until he had received a subpoena. Paul, with his instinctive sense of the theatrical, did not want to have this crucial meeting take place without a most careful build-up.

We discussed the various steps taken or about to be taken by certain state legislatures against the Centers. The states involved were those with either a predominantly Catholic or a predominantly Baptist population. Since the Centers had been organized to conform with existing state and federal laws (the lawyers were earning their fees), Paul thought they would have a difficult time in closing any of them. The several laws which had been passed were all being appealed and he was confident of our vindication by the higher courts. Though the entrenched churches were now fighting us with every possible weapon of law and propaganda, we were fully protected, Paul felt, by the Bill of Rights even in its currently abrogated state.

Late in the afternoon after one of the day's conferences had ended, Iris and I swam in the Gulf, the water as warm as blood and the sky soft with evening. We stayed in the water for an hour, not talking, not really swimming, merely a part of the sea and the sky, two lives on a curved horizon, quite alone (for the others never ventured out). Only the bored bodyguard on the dock reminded us that the usual world had not slipped away in a sunny dream, leaving us isolated and content in that sea from which our life had come so long ago. Water to water, I thought comfortably as we crawled up on the beach like new-lunged creatures.

Iris undid her bathing cap and her hair, streaked blonde by the sun (and a little gray as well), fell about her shoulders. She sighed voluptuously. "If it would always be like this."

"If what?"

"Everything."

"Ah." I ran my hand along my legs and crystals of salt glittered and fell; we were both dusted with light. "You have your work," I added with some malice, though I was now under control; my crisis resolved after one sleepless night. I could now look at her without longing, without pain. Regret was another matter but regret was only a distant relative to anguish.

"I have that, too," she said. "The work uses everything while this is a narcotic. I float without a thought or a desire like . . . like an anemone."

"You don't know what an anemone is, do you?"

She laughed like a child. "How do you know I don't?"

"You said it like somebody reading a Latin inscription."

"What is it?"

I laughed, too. "I don't know. Perhaps something like a jellyfish. It has a lovely sound: sea anemone."

We were interrupted by a motorboat pulling into the dock. "It's the mail," said Iris. "We'd better go back to the house." While we collected towels, the guard on the dock helped the boatman unload groceries and mail.

Between a pair of palm trees, a yard from the door of the house, the bomb went off in a flash of light and gray smoke. A stinging spray of sand blinded Iris and me. The blast knocked me off balance and I fell backward onto the beach. For several minutes, I was quite blind, my eyes filled with tears, burned from the coral sand. When I was finally able to see again, Iris was already at the house trying to force open the door.

One of the palm trees looked as if it had been struck by lightning, all its fronds gone and its base smoldering. The windows of the house were broken and I recall wondering, foolishly, how the air conditioning could possibly work if the house was not sealed. The door was splintered and most of its paint had been burned off; it was also jammed, for Iris could not open it. Meanwhile, from a side door, the occupants of the house had begun to appear.

I limped toward the house, rubbing my eyes, aware that my left knee had been hurt. I was careful not to look at either the boatman or the guard, their remains strewn among the tin cans and letters in the bushes.

Paul was the first to speak. A torrent of rage which jolted us all out of fear and shock. Iris, after one look at the dead men, fled into the house. I stood stupidly beside the door, rolling my eyes to dislodge the sand.

Then the other guards came with blankets and gathered up the pieces of the two men. I turned away, aware for the first time that Cave was standing slightly apart, nearest the house. He was very pale. He spoke only once, half to himself, for Paul was still ranting. "Let it begin," said Cave softly. "Now, now."

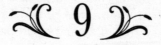

# 9

1

It began indeed, like the first recorded shot of a war. The day after the explosion, we left the island and Cave was flown to another retreat, this time in the center of New York City where, unique in all the world, there can exist true privacy, even invisibility.

The Cavite history of the next two years is publicly known and the private aspects of it are not particularly revealing. It was a time of expansion and of battle.

The opposition closed its ranks. Several attempts were made on all our lives and, six months after our return from Florida, we were all, except the indomitable Clarissa, forced to move into the brand-new Cavite Center, a quickly built but handsome building of yellow glass on Park Avenue. Here on the top floor, in the penthouse which was itself a mansion surrounded by Babylonian gardens and a wall of glass through which the encompassing city rose like stalagmites, Cave and Paul, Stokharin, Iris and I all lived with our bodyguards, never venturing out of the building, which resembled, during that time, a military headquarters with guards and adjutants and a maze of officials through whom both strangers and familiars were forced to pass before they could meet even myself, not to mention Cave.

In spite of the unnaturalness, it was, I think, the happiest time of my life. Except for brief excursions to the Hudson, I spent the entire two years in that one building, knowing at last the sort of security and serenity which monks must have known in their monasteries. I think the others were also content, except for Cave, who eventually grew so morose and bored by his confinement that Paul not only had to promise him a world tour but for his vicarious pleasure showed, night after night in the Center's auditorium, travel films which Cave devoured with eager eyes, asking for certain films to be halted at various interesting parts so that he might examine some landscape or building (never a human being, no matter how quaint). Favorite movies were played over and over again, long after the rest of us had gone to bed, leaving Cave and the projectionist alone with the bright shadows of distant places, alone save for the ubiquitous guards.

There were a number of attacks upon the building itself, but since all incoming mail and visitors were checked by machinery for hidden weapons, there was never a repetition of that island disaster which had had such a chilling effect on all of us. Pickets of course marched daily for two years in front of the Center's door and, on four separate occasions, mobs attempted to storm the building, only to be repulsed by our guards (the police, for the most part Catholic, did not unduly exert themselves in our defense; fortunately, the building had been constructed with the idea of defense).

The life in the Center was busy. In the penthouse each of us had an office and Cave had a large suite where he spent his days watching television and pondering journeys. He did not follow with much interest the doings of the organization, though he had begun to enjoy reading the attacks which regularly appeared against him in the newspapers. Bishop Winston was the leader of the non-Catholic opposition and his apologias and anathemas inspired us with admiration. He was, I think, conscious of being the last great spokesman of the Protestant churches and he fulfilled his historic function with wit and dignity, and we admired him tremendously. By this time, of course, our victory was in sight and we could show magnanimity to those who remained loyal to ancient systems.

GORE VIDAL

I was the one most concerned with answering the attacks since I was now an editor with an entire floor devoted to the *Cavite Journal* (we were not able to think up a better name). At first, as we had planned, it was published weekly and given away, but after the first year it became a daily newspaper, fat with advertising and sold on newsstands.

Besides my duties as editor, I was the official apologist and I was kept busy composing dialogues on various ethical matters, ranging from the virtues of cremation to fair business practices. Needless to say, I had a good deal of help and some of my most resounding effects were contrived by anonymous specialists. Each installment, however, of Cavite doctrine (or rationalization, as I preferred to think of my work) was received as eagerly by the expanding ranks of the faithful as it was condemned reflexively by the Catholic Church and the new league of Protestant Churches under Bishop Winston's leadership.

We sustained our most serious setback when, in the autumn of our first year in the new building, we were banned from the television networks through a series of technicalities created by Congress for our benefit and invoked without warning. It took Paul's lawyers a year to get the case through the courts, which finally reversed the government's ruling. Meanwhile, we counterattacked by creating hundreds of new Centers where films of Cave were shown regularly. Once a week he was televised for the Centers, where huge crowds gathered to see and hear him, and it was always Paul's claim that the government's spiteful action had been responsible for the sudden victory of Cavesword. Not being able to listen to their idol in their own homes, the Cavites and even the merely curious were forced to visit the Centers, where in the general mood of camaraderie and delight in the same Word, they were organized quite ruthlessly. Stokharin's clinics handled their personal problems. Other departments assumed the guidance and even the support, if necessary, of their children, while free medical and educational facilities were made available to all who applied.

At the end of the second year, there were more enrolled Cavites than any other single religious denomination, including the Roman Catholic. I published this fact and the accompanying statistics with a certain guilt which, needless to say, my fellow directors did not share. The result of this revelation was a special Congressional hearing.

In spite of the usual confusion attendant upon any of the vigorous old Congress's hearteningly incompetent investigations, this event was well staged, preparing the way politically, to draw the obvious parallel, for a new Constantine.

It took place in March, and it was the only official journey any of us, excepting Paul, made from our yellow citadel for two years. The entire proceedings were televised, a bit of unwisdom on the part of the hostile Congressmen, who in their understandable eagerness for publicity, overlooked their intended victim's complete mastery of that art. I did not go to Washington but I saw Cave and Paul and Iris off from the roof of the Center. Because of the crowds which had formed in the streets hoping for a glimpse of Cave, the original plan to fly to Washington aboard a chartered airplane was discarded at the last minute and two helicopters were ordered instead to pick up Cave and his party on the terrace in front of the penthouse, a mode of travel not then popular.

Paul saw to it that the departure was filmed. A dozen of us who were not going stood about among the trees and bushes while the helicopters hovered a few feet above the roof, their ladders dangling. Then Cave appeared with Paul and Iris while a camera crew recorded their farewell and departure. Cave looked as serene as ever, pale in his dark blue suit and white shirt, a small austere figure with downcast eyes. Iris was bright-faced from the excitement and cold, and a sharp wind tangled her hair.

"I'm terrified," she whispered fiercely in my ear as we shook hands for the camera.

"Paul seems in full command," I said, comfortingly. And Paul, not Cave, was making a short speech to the camera while Cave stood alone and still; then, in a gust of wind, they were gone and I went to my office to watch the hearings.

The official reason for the investigation was certain charges made by various churches that the Cavites were subverting Christian morality by championing free love and publicly decrying the eternal institution of marriage. This was the burden of the complaint against Cave which the committee most wished to contemplate since it was the strongest of the numerous allegations and, in their eyes, the most dangerous to the state, as well as the one most likely to get the largest amount of publicity. For some years the realm of public morals had been a favorite excursion ground for the Congress, and their tournaments at public expense were attended delightedly by everyone. This particular one, affecting as it did the head of the largest single religious establishment in the country, would, the Congressmen were quite sure, prove an irresistible spectacle. It was.

At first there was a good deal of confusion. Newspapermen stumbled over one another; flashbulbs were dropped; Congressmen could not get through the crowd to take their seats. To fill in, while these preliminaries were arranged, the camera was trained upon the crowd which was beginning to gather in front of the Capitol; a crowd which grew, as one watched, to Inaugural size. Though it was orderly, a troop of soldiers in trucks soon arrived as though by previous design, and they formed a cordon of fixed bayonets before the various entrances to the Capitol.

Here and there, against the gusty blue sky, banners with the single word "Cave," gold on blue, snapped. *In hoc signo* indeed!

Then the commentators, who had been exclaiming at some length on the size of the crowd, excitedly announced the arrival of Cave. A roar of sound filled the plaza. The banners were waved back and forth against the sky and I saw everywhere the theatrical hand of Paul Himmell.

The scene shifted to the House of Representatives entrance to the Capitol. Cave, wearing an overcoat but bareheaded, stepped out of the limousine. He was alone. Neither Paul nor

Iris was in sight. It was most effective that he should come like this, without equerries or counselors. He stood for a moment in the pillared entrance, aware of the crowd outside; even through the commentator's narrative one could hear, like the surf falling, Cave! Cave! Cave! For a moment it seemed that he might turn and go, not into the Capitol, but out onto the steps to the crowd. But then the chief of the Capitol guard, sensing perhaps that this might happen, gently steered him up the stairs.

The next shot was of the committee room where the hearings had at last begun. A somewhat phlegmatic Jesuit was testifying. His words were difficult to hear because of the noise in the committee room and the impotent shouts of the chairman. The commentator gave a brief résumé of the Jesuit's attack on Cave and then, in the midst of a particularly loud exchange between the chairman and the crowd, the clerk of the committee announced: "John Cave."

There was silence. The crowd parted to make way for him. Even the members of the committee craned to get a good look at him as he moved quietly, almost demurely, to the witness chair. The only movement in the room was that of the Papal Nuncio, who sat in the front rank of the audience. He crossed himself as Cave passed and shut his eyes.

Cave was respectful, almost inaudible. Several times he was asked to repeat his answers even though the room was remarkably still. At first Cave would answer only in monosyllables, not looking up, not meeting the gaze of his interrogators, who took heart at this, professionals themselves. Their voices, which had almost matched his for inaudibility, began to boom with confidence.

I waited for the lightning. The first intimation came when Cave looked up. For nearly five minutes he had not raised his eyes during the questioning. Suddenly I saw that he was trying to locate the camera. When at last he did, it was like a revelation. A shock went through me, and as well as I knew him, as few illusions as I had about him, I was arrested by his gaze, as if only he and I existed, as though he *were* I. All of those who watched him on television responded in the same fashion to that unique gaze.

But the committee was not aware that their intended victim had with one glance appropriated the eye of the world.

The subsequent catechism is too well known to record here. We used it as the main exposition of Cavesword, the one testament which contained the entire thing. It was almost as if the Congressmen had been given the necessary questions to ask, like those supporting actors whose roles are calculated to illuminate the genius of the star. Two of the seven members of the committee were Cavites. This was soon apparent. The other five were violent in their opposition. One as a Catholic, another as a Protestant, and two as materialistic lovers of the old order. Only one of the attackers, a Jew, made any real point. He argued the perniciousness of an organization which, if allowed to prosper, would replace the state and force all dissenters to conform; it was the Jew's contention that the state prospered most when no one system was sufficiently strong to dominate. I wanted to hear more of him but his Catholic colleague, a bull-voiced Irishman, drowned him out, winning the day for us.

Cave, to my astonishment, had memorized most of the dialogues I had written and he said my words with the same power that he said his own. I was startled by this. There had been no hint that such a thing might happen and I couldn't, for some time, determine the motive until I recalled Cave's reluctance to being quoted in print. He had apparently realized that now there would be a complete record of his testimony and so, for the sake of both literacy and consistency, he had committed to memory those words of mine which were thought to be his. At the great moment, however, at the peroration (by which time there were no more questions and Cave's voice alone was heard) he became himself, and spoke Cavesword.

Then, without the committee's leave, in the dazzled silence

which followed upon his last words, he rose abruptly and left the room. I switched off the television set. That week established Cavesword in the country and, except for various priests and ministers of the deserted gods, the United States was Cavite.

## 2

The desertion of the old establishments for the new resembled, at uneasy moments, revolution.

The Congressional committee, though anti-Cavite, did not dare even to censure him. Partly from the fear of the vast crowd which waited in the Capitol plaza and partly from the larger, more cogent awareness that it was political suicide for any popularly elected Representative to outrage a minority of such strength.

The hearing fizzled out after Cave's appearance, and though there were a few denunciatory speeches on the floor of Congress, no official action was taken. Shortly afterward the ban on Cave's television appearances was lifted, but by then it was too late and millions of people had got permanently into the habit of attending weekly meetings at the various Centers to listen to Cave on film and discuss with the Residents and their staffs points of doctrine . . . and doctrine it had become.

The second year in our yellow citadel was even more active than the first. It was decided that Cave would make no personal appearances anywhere. According to Paul, the mystery would be kept intact and the legend would grow under the most auspicious circumstances. He did not reveal his actual motive in Cave's presence. But he explained himself to me late one afternoon in my office.

"Get him in front of a really hostile crowd and there'd be no telling what might happen." Paul was restlessly marching about the room in his shirtsleeves; a blunt cigar in his mouth gave him the appearance of a lower-echelon politician.

"There's never been a hostile audience yet," I reminded him. "Except for the Congressional hearings, and I thought he handled himself quite well with them."

"With your script in his head." Paul chuckled and stopped his march to the filing cabinet by way of that television set which dominated every office and home. "What I mean is, he's never been in a debate. He's never had a tough opponent, a heckler. The Congressmen were pretty mild and even though they weren't friendly they stuck to easy issues. But what would happen if Bishop Winston got him up before an audience? Winston's a lot smarter and he's nearly as good in public."

"I suppose Cave would hypnotize him, too."

"Not on your life." Paul threw himself into a chair of flimsy chrome and plastic. "Winston's been trying to arrange a debate for over two years. He issues challenges every Sunday on his program (got a big audience, too, though not close to ours. I checked the ratings)."

"Does Cave want to give it a try?"

"He's oblivious to such things. I suppose he would if he thought about it. Anyway it's to our advantage to keep him out of sight. Let them see only a television image, hear only his recorded voice. It's wonderful copy! Big time." He was out of the chair and playing with the knob of the television set. The screen was suddenly filled with a romantic scene, a pulsating green grotto with water falling in a thin white line; so perfected had the machine become that it was actually like looking through a window, the illusion of depth quite perfect and the colors true. A warm deep voice off-screen suggested the virtues of a well-known carbonated drink. Paul turned the switch off. I was relieved since I, alone in America, was unable to think or work or even relax while the screen was bright with some other place.

"He won't like it. He expects next year, at the latest, to start his world tour."

"Perhaps then," said Paul thinly. "Anyway, the longer we put it off the better. Did you know we turn away a thousand people a day who come here just to get a glimpse of him?"

"They see him at the Center meetings."

"Only our own people, the ones in training to be Residents. I keep those sessions carefully screened. Every now and then some outsider gets in but it's rare."

I glanced at the tear-sheet of my next day's editorial. It contained, among other useful statistics, the quite incredible figures of Cavite membership in the world. Dubiously, I read off the figure which Paul had given me at a directors' meeting.

"It's about right," he said complacently, coming to a full stop at the files. "We don't actually know the figures of places without proper Centers like the Latin countries where we are undergoing a bit of persecution. But the statistics for this country are exact."

"It's hard to believe." I looked at the figure which represented so many human beings, so much diversity, all touched by one man. "Less than three years . . ."

"Three more years and we'll have most of Europe too."

"Why, I wonder?"

"Why?" Paul slammed shut the cabinet drawer which he'd been examining. He looked at me sharply. "You of all people ask why? Cavesword . . . and all your words too, did the trick. That's what. We've said what they wanted to hear. Just the opposite of my old game of publicity where we said what we wanted them to hear. This time it's just the other way around and it's big, ah, it's big."

I could agree with that but I pressed him further. "I know what's happened, of course, and your theory is certainly correct if only because had we said the opposite of what they wanted to hear nothing would have happened. But the question in my mind, the real 'why,' is Cave and us. Why we of all the people in the world? Cavesword, between us and any school of philosophy, is not new. Others have said it more eloquently. In the past it was a reasonably popular heresy which the early popes stamped out . . ."

"Timing! The right man at the right time saying the right thing. Remember the piece you did on Mohammed . . . "

"I stole most of it."

"So what? Most effective. You figured how only at that one moment in Arabian political history could such a man have appeared."

I smiled. "That is always the folly of the 'one unique moment.' For all I know such a man could have appeared in any of a hundred other Arab generations."

"But he never did except that one time, which proves the point."

I let it go. Paul was at best not the ideal partner in the perennial conversation. "There is no doubt that Cave's the man," I said, neutrally. "Not the last of the line but at least the most effective, considering the shortness of the mission so far."

"We have the means. The old people didn't. Every man, woman, and child in this country can see Cave for themselves, and at the same moment. I don't suppose ten thousand people saw Christ in action. It took a generation for news of him to travel from one country to the next."

"Parallels break down," I agreed. "It's the reason I wonder so continually about Cave and ourselves and what we are doing in the world."

"We're doing good. The people are losing their fear of death. Last month there were twelve hundred suicides in this country directly attributable to Cavesword. And these people didn't kill themselves because they were unhappy, they killed themselves because he had made it easy, even desirable. Now you know there's never been anybody like that before in history, anywhere."

"Certainly not!" I was startled by the figure he had quoted. In our *Journal* we were always reporting various prominent suicides, and though I had given orders to minimize these voluntary deaths, I had been forced every now and then to record the details of one or another of them. But I'd had no idea there had been so many. I asked Paul if he was quite sure of the number.

"Oh yes." He was blithe. "At least that many we know of."

"I wonder if it's wise."

"Wise? What's that got to do with it? It's logical. It's the proof of Cavesword. Death is fine so why not die?"

"Why not live?"

"It's the same thing."

"I would say not."

"Well, you ought to play it up a little more anyway. I meant to talk about it at the last directors' meeting but there wasn't time."

"Does Cave know about this? About the extent . . ."

"Sure he does." Paul headed for the door. "He thinks it's fine. Proves what he says and it gives other people nerve. This thing is working."

There was no doubt about that, of course. It is hard to give precisely the sense of those two years when the main work was done in a series of toppling waves which swept into history the remaining edifices of other faiths and institutions. I had few firsthand impressions of the country for I seldom stirred from our headquarters.

I had sold the house on the river. I had cut off all contacts with old friends. My life was Cave. I edited the *Journal*, or rather presided over the editors. I discussed points of doctrine with the various Residents who came to see me in the yellow tower. They were devoted men and their enthusiasm was heartening, if not always communicable to me. Each week further commentaries on Cavesword were published and I found there was no time to read them all. I contented myself, finally, with synopses prepared for me by the *Journal*'s staff. I felt like a television emperor keeping abreast of contemporary letters.

Once a week we all dined with Cave. Except for that informal occasion we seldom saw him. Though he complained continually about his captivity (and it was exactly that; we were all captives to some degree), he was cheerful enough. Paul saw to it that he was kept busy all day addressing Residents and Communicators, answering their questions, inspiring them by the mere fact of his presence. It was quite common for strangers to faint upon seeing him for the first time, as a man and not as a figure on a bit of film. He was good-natured, though occasionally embarrassed by the chosen groups which were admitted to him. He seldom talked privately to any of them, however, and he showed not the faintest interest in their problems, not even bothering to learn their names. He was only interested in where they were from and Paul, aware of this, as an added inducement to keep Cave amenable, took to including in each group at least one Cavite from some far place like Malaya or Ceylon.

Iris was busiest of all. She had become, without design or preparation, the head of all the Cavite schools throughout the country where the various Communicators of Cavesword were trained, thousands of them each year, in a course which included not only Cavesword but history and psychology as well. There were also special classes in television production and acting. Television, ultimately, was the key. It was the primary instrument of communication. Later, with a subservient government and the aid of mental therapists and new drugs, television became less necessary, but in the beginning it was everything.

Clarissa's role was, as always, enigmatic. She appeared when she pleased and she disappeared when she pleased. I discovered that her position among the directors was due to her possession of the largest single block of stock, dating back to the first days. During the crucial two or three years, however, she was often with us merely for protection, since all our lives had been proscribed by the last remnants of the old churches, which as their dominion shrank fought more and more recklessly to destroy us.

Stokharin spent his days much like Iris, instructing the Communicators and Center therapists in psychology. His power over Paul had fortunately waned and he was far more likable. Paul was "freed," Stokharin would say with some satisfaction, by therapy . . . and a new father image.

Less than two years after the Congressional hearing, Paul, in his devious way, entered politics. In the following Congressional elections, without much overt campaigning on our part the majority of those elected to both Houses of the Congress were either Cavite or sympathetic.

3

At last I have met him. Early this evening I went downstairs to see the manager about an item on my bill which was incorrect. I had thought that I should be safe, for this was the time when most of the hotel guests are bathing and preparing for dinner. Unfortunately, I encountered Butler and his newly arrived colleague in the lobby. I suddenly found myself attempting, by an effort of will, very simply to vanish into smoke like one of those magicians in a child's book. But I remained all too visible. I stopped halfway across the lobby and waited for them.

They came toward me, Butler murmuring greetings and introductions to Communicator Jessup (soon to be Resident of Luxor "when we get under way"): "And this, Jack, is the Mr. Hudson I told you about."

The Resident-to-be shook my hand firmly. He was not more than thirty, a lean, dark-eyed mulatto whose features and coloring appealed to me, used as I now am to the Arabs: beside him, Butler looked more red and gross than ever.

"Butler has told me how useful you've been to us," said Jessup. His voice was a little high, but he did not have the trick of overarticulation which used to be so common among educated Negroes in earlier times, a peculiarity they shared with Baptist clergymen and professional poets.

"I've done what I could, little as it is," I said ceremoniously. Then, without protest, I allowed them to lead me out onto the terrace which overlooked the setting sun and the muddy river.

"We planned to see you when Jack, here, arrived," said Butler expansively as we sat down, a tray of gin and ice and tonic water set before us by a waiter who was used now to

American ways. "But you had the sign on your door so I told Jack we'd better wait till Mr. Hudson is feeling better. You *are* okay now, aren't you?"

"Somewhat better," I said, enjoying the British gin. I'd had none since I left Cairo. "At my age one is either dead or all right. I seem not to be dead."

"How I envy you!" said Jessup solemnly.

"Envy me?" For a moment I did not quite understand.

"To be so near the blessed state! Not to see the sun again and feel the body quivering with corrupt life. Oh, what I should give to be as old as you!"

"You could always commit suicide," I said irritably, forgetting my role as an amiable soft-headed old cretin.

This stopped him for only the space of a single surprised breath. "Cavesway is not possible for his servants," he said at last, patiently. "You have not perhaps followed his logic as carefully as you might had you been living in the civilized world." He looked at me with bright eyes inscrutably focused.

Why are you here? I wanted to ask furiously, *finally*, but I only nodded my head meekly and said, "So much had changed since I came out here. I do recall, though, that Cavesway was considered desirable for all."

"It is. But not for his servants who must, through living, sacrifice their comfort. It is our humiliation, our martyrdom on his behalf. Even the humblest man or woman can avail themselves of Cavesway, unlike us his servants, who must live, disgusting as the prospect is, made bearable only by the knowledge that we are doing his work, communicating his word."

"What courage it must take to give up Cavesway!" I intoned with reverent awe.

"It is the least we can do for him."

The bright sun resembled that red-gold disc which sits on the brow of Horus. The hot wind of Numidia stirred the dry foliage about us. I could smell the metallic odor of the Nile. A muezzin called, high and toneless in the evening.

"Before I slip off into the better state," I said at last,

emboldened by gin, "I should like to know as much as possible about the new world the Cavites have made. I left the United States shortly after Cave took his way. I have never been back."

"How soon after?" The question came too fast. I gripped the arms of my chair tightly.

"Two years after, I think," I said. "I came to Cairo for the digging at Sakharra."

"How could you have missed those exciting years?" Jessup's voice became zealous. "I was not even born then, and I've always cursed my bad luck. I used to go about talking to complete strangers who had been alive in those great years. Of course most were laymen and knew little about the things I had studied but they could tell me how the sky looked the day he took his way. And, every now and then, it was possible to meet someone who had seen him."

"Not many laymen ever saw him," I said. "I remember with what secrecy all his movements were enveloped. I was in New York much of the time when he was there."

"In New York!" Jessup sighed voluptuously.

"You saw him too, didn't you, Mr. Hudson?" Butler was obviously eager that I make a good impression.

"Oh yes, I saw him the day he was in Washington. One of his few public appearances! I was very devout in those days. I am now too, of course," I added hastily. "But in those days when it was all new, one was – well – exalted by Cavesword. I made a special trip to Washington just to get a glimpse of him." I played as resolutely as possible upon their passionate faith.

"Did you really see him?"

I shook my head sadly. "Only a quick blur as he drove away. The crowd was too big and the police were all around him."

"I have of course relived that moment in the library, watching the films, but actually to have been there that day . . ." Jessup's voice trailed off as he contemplated the extent of my good fortune.

"Then afterward, after his death, I left for Egypt and I've never been back."

"You missed great days."

"I'm sure of that. Yet I feel the best days were before, when I was in New York and each week there would be a new revelation of his wisdom."

"You are quite right," said Jessup, pouring himself more gin. "Yours was the finer time even though those of us who feel drawn to the Mother must declare that later days possessed some virtue too, on her account."

"Mother?" I knew of course before he answered what had happened.

"As Cave was the father of our knowledge, so Iris is its mother," said Jessup. He looked at Butler with a half-smile. "Of course there are some, the majority in fact, of the Communicators who deprecate our allegiance to the Mother, not realizing that it enhances rather than detracts from Cave. After all, the Word and the Way are entirely his."

Butler chuckled. "There's been a little family dispute," he said. "We keep it out of the press because it really isn't the concern of anybody but us, Cave's servants. Don't mind talking to you about it since you'll be dead soon anyway and up here we're all in the same boat, all Cavites. Anyway, some of the younger fellows, the bright ones like Jessup, have got attached to Iris, not that we don't all love her equally. It's just that they've got in the habit of talking about death being the womb again, all that kind of stuff without any real basis in Cave."

"It runs all through Cave's work, Bill. It's implicit in all that he said." Jessup was amiable but I sensed a hardness in his tone. It had come to this, I thought.

"Well, we won't argue about it," said Butler, turning to me with a smile. "You should see what these Irisians can do with a Cavite text. By the time they finish you don't know whether you're coming or going."

"Were you at all active in the Mission?" asked Jessup, abruptly changing the subject.

I shook my head. "I was one of the early admirers of Cave but I'm afraid I had very little contact with any of his people. I tried once or twice to get in to see him, when they were in the yellow tower, but it was impossible. Only the Residents and people like that ever saw him personally."

"He was busy in those days," said Jessup, nodding. "He must have dictated nearly two million words in the last three years of his life."

"You think he wrote all those books and dialogues himself?"

"Of course he did." Jessup sounded surprised. "Haven't you read Iris's account of the way he worked? The way he would dictate for hours at a time, oblivious of everything but Cavesword."

"I suppose I missed all that," I mumbled. "In those days it was always assumed that he had a staff who did the work for him."

"The lutherists," said Jessup, nodding. "They were extremely subtle in their methods, but of course they couldn't distort the truth for very long . . ."

"Oh," said Butler. "Mr. Hudson asked me the other day if I knew what the word 'lutherist' came from and I said I didn't know. I must have forgotten, for I have a feeling it was taught us, back in the old days when we primitives were turned out, before you bright young fellows came along to show us how to do Caveswork."

Jessup smiled. "We're not that bumptious," he said. "As for lutherist, it's a word based on the name of one of the first followers of Cave. I don't know his other name or even much about him. As far as I remember, the episode was never even recorded. Much too disagreeable, and of course we don't like to dwell on our failures."

"I wonder what it was that he did," I asked, my voice trembling despite all efforts to control it.

"He was a nonconformist of some kind. He quarreled with Iris, they say."

"I wonder what happened to him," said Butler. "Did they send him through indoctrination?"

"No, as far as I know . . ." Jessup paused. When he spoke again his voice was thoughtful. "According to the story I heard –

legend really – he disappeared. They never found him and though we've wisely removed all record of him, his name is still used to describe our failures. Those among us, that is, who refuse Cavesword despite indoctrination. Somewhere, they say, he is living, in hiding, waiting to undo Cavesword. As Cave was the Antichrist, so Luther, or another like him, will attempt to destroy us."

"Not much chance of that." Butler's voice was confident. "Anyway, if he was a contemporary of Cave he must be dead by now."

"Not necessarily. After all, Mr. Hudson was a contemporary and *he* is still alive." Jessup looked at me then. His eyes, in a burst of obsidian light, caught the sun's last rays. I think he knows.

### 4

There is not much time left and I must proceed as swiftly as possible to the death of Cave and my own exile.

The year of Cave's death was not only a year of triumph but one of terror as well. The counteroffensive reached its peak in those busy months, and we were all in danger of our lives.

In the South, groups of Baptists stormed the new Centers, demolishing them and killing, in several instances, the Residents. Despite our protests and threats of reprisal, many state governments refused to protect the Cavite Centers and Paul was forced to enlist a small army to defend our establishments in those areas which were still dominated by the old religions. Several attempts were made to destroy our New York headquarters. Fortunately, they were discovered before any damage could be done, though one fanatic, a Catholic, got as far as Paul's office, where he threw a grenade into a wastebasket, killing himself and slightly scratching Paul, who as usual had been traveling nervously about the room, out of range at the proper moment.

The election of a Cavite-dominated Congress eased things for us considerably, though it made our enemies all the more desperate.

Paul fought back. Bishop Winston, the most eloquent of the Christian prelates and the most dangerous to us, had died, giving rise to the rumor, soon afterward confirmed by Cavite authority to be a fact, that he had killed himself and that, therefore, he had finally renounced Christ and taken to himself Cavesword.

Many of the clergy of the Protestant sects, aware that their parishioners and authority were falling away, became, quietly, without gloating on our part, Cavite Residents and Communicators.

The bloodiest persecutions, however, did not occur in North America. The Latin countries provided the world with a series of massacres remarkable even in that murderous century. Yet it was fact that in the year of Cave's death, Italy was half-Cavite and France, England and Germany were nearly all Cavite. Only Spain and parts of Latin America held out, imprisoning, executing, deporting Cavites against the inevitable day when our Communicators, undismayed, proud in their martyrdom, would succeed in their assaults upon these last citadels of paganism.

On a hot day in August, our third and last autumn in the yellow tower, we dined on the terrace of Cave's penthouse overlooking the city. The bright sky shuddered with heat.

Clarissa had just come from abroad, where she had been enjoying herself hugely under the guise of an official tour of reconnaissance. She sat wearing a large picture hat beneath the striped awning that sheltered our glass-topped table from the sun's rays. Cave insisted on eating out-of-doors as often as possible, even though the rest of us preferred the cool interior where we were not disturbed by either heat or by the clouds of soot which floated above the imperial city, impartially lighting upon all who ventured out into the open.

It was our first "family dinner" in some months (Paul insisted on regarding us as a family, and the metaphors which he derived from this one conceit used even to irritate the imperturbable Cave). At the end of the table sat Clarissa, with Paul and me on either side of her; at the other end sat Cave, with Iris and Stokharin on either side of him. Early in the dinner, when the conversation was particular, Iris and I talked privately.

"I suppose we'll be leaving soon," she said. A gull missed the awning by inches.

"I haven't heard anything about it. Who's leaving . . . and why?"

"John thinks we've all been here too long; he thinks we're too remote."

"He's quite right about that." I blew soot off my plate. "But where are we to go? After all, there's a good chance that if any of us shows his head to the grateful populace someone will blow it off."

"That's a risk we have to take. But John is right. We must get out and see the people . . . talk to them direct." Her voice was urgent. I looked at her thoughtfully, seeing the change that three years of extraordinary activity had wrought. She was overweight and her face, as sometimes happens in the first access of weight, was smooth, without lines. That wonderful sharpness, her old fineness, was entirely gone and the new Iris, the busy, efficient Iris, had become like . . . like . . . I groped for the comparison, the memory of someone similar I had known in the past, but the ghost did not materialize; and so haunted, faintly distrait, I talked to the new Iris I did not really know.

"I'll be only too happy to leave," I said, helping myself to the salad which was being served us by one of the Eurasian servants whom Paul, in an exotic mood, had engaged to look after the penthouse and the person of Cave. "I don't think I've been away from here half a dozen times in two years."

"It's been awfully hard," Iris agreed. Her eyes shifted regularly to Cave, like an anxious parent's. "Of course I've had more chance than anyone to get out but I haven't seen nearly as much as I ought. It's my job, really, to look at all the Centers, to supervise in person all the schools, but of course I can't if Paul insists on turning every trip I take into a kind of pageant."

"It's for your own protection."

"I think we're much safer than Paul thinks. The country's almost entirely Cavite."

"All the more reason to be careful. The die-hards are on their last legs; they're desperate."

"Well, we must take our chances. John says he won't stay here another autumn. September is his best month, you know. It was in September that he first spoke Cavesword."

"What does Paul say?" I looked down the table at our ringmaster, who was telling Clarissa what she had seen in Europe.

Iris frowned. "He's doing everything he can to keep us here . . . I can't think why. John's greatest work has been done face to face with people, yet Paul acts as if he didn't dare let him out in public. We have quarreled about this for over a year, Paul and I."

"He's quite right. I'd be nervous to go about in public without some sort of protection. You should see the murderous letters I get at the *Journal.*"

"We've nothing to fear," said Iris flatly. "And we have everything to gain by mixing with people. We could easily grow out of touch, marooned in this tower."

"Oh, it's not that bad." To my surprise, I found myself defending our monastic life. "Everyone comes here. Cave speaks to groups of the faithful every day. I sit like some disheveled hen over a large newspaper and I couldn't be more instructed, more engaged in life, while you dash around the country almost as much as Paul does."

"But only seeing the Centers, only meeting the Cavites. I have no other life any more." I looked at her curiously. There was no bitterness in her voice, yet there was a certain wistfulness which I had never noticed before.

"Do you regret all this, Iris?" I asked. It had been three years since I had spoken to her of personal matters. We had become, in a sense, the offices which we held: our symbolic selves paralyzing all else within, true precedent achieved at a great cost. Now a fissure had suddenly appeared in the monument which Iris had become, and through the flow I heard again, briefly, the voice of the girl I had met on the bank of the Hudson in the spring of a lost year.

"I never knew it would be like this," she said almost whispering, her eyes on Cave while she spoke to me. "I never thought my life would be as alone as this, all work."

"Yet you wanted it. You *do* want it. Direction, meaning, you wanted all that and now you have it. The magic worked, Iris. Your magician was real."

"But I sometimes wonder if *I* am real any more." The words, though softly spoken, fell between us like rounded stones, smooth and hard.

"It's too late," I said, mercilessly. "You are what you wanted to be. Live it out, Iris. There is nothing else."

"You're dead too," she said at last, her voice regaining its usual authority.

"Speaking of dead," said Cave, suddenly turning toward us (I hoped he had not heard all our conversation), "Stokharin here has come up with a wonderful scheme."

Even Clarissa fell silent. We all did on those rare occasions when Cave spoke on social occasions. Cave looked cheerfully about the table for a moment. Stokharin beamed with pleasure at the accolade.

"You've probably all heard about the suicides as a result of Cavesword." Cave had very early got into the habit of speaking of himself in the third person whenever a point of doctrine was involved. "Paul's been collecting the monthly figures and each month they double. Of course they're not accurate since there are a good many deaths due to Cavesword which we don't hear about. Anyway, Stokharin has perfected a painless death by poison, a new compound which kills within an hour and is delightful to take."

208

"I have combined certain narcotics which together insure a highly exhilarated state before the end, as well as most pleasant fantasies." Stokharin smiled complacently.

Cave continued. "I've already worked out some of the practical details for putting this into action. There are still a lot of wrinkles, but we can iron them out in time. One of the big problems of present-day *unorganized* suicide is the mess it causes for the people unfortunate enough to be left behind. There are legal complications; there is occasionally grief in old-fashioned family groups; there is also a general social disturbance which tends to give suicide, at least among the reactionaries, a bad name.

"Our plan is simple. We will provide at each Center full facilities for those who have listened to Cavesword and have responded to it by taking the better way. There will be a number of comfortable rooms where the suicidalist may receive his friends for a last visit. We'll provide legal assistance to put his affairs in order. Not everyone of course will be worthy of us. Those who choose death merely to evade responsibility will be censured and restrained. But the deserving, those whose lives have been devoted and orderly, may come to us and receive the gift."

I was appalled. Before I could control myself I had said: "But the law! You just can't let people kill themselves . . . "

"Why not?" Cave looked at me coldly and I saw, in the eyes of the others, concern and hostility. I had anticipated something like this ever since my talk with Paul, but I had not thought it would come so swiftly or so boldly.

Paul spoke for Cave. "We've got the Congress and the Congress will make a law for us. For the time being, it *is* against the statutes, but we've been assured by our lawyers that there isn't much chance of their being invoked, except perhaps in the remaining pockets of Christianity where we'll go slow until we do have the necessary laws to protect us."

At that moment the line which from the very beginning had been visibly drawn between me and them became a wall apparent to everyone. Even Clarissa, my usual ally, fearless and sharp, did not speak out. They looked at me, all of them awaiting a sign; even Cave regarded me with curiosity.

My hand shook and I was forced to seize the edge of the table to steady myself. The sensation of cold glass and iron gave me a sudden courage. I brought Cave's life to its end.

I turned to him and said, quietly, with all the firmness I could summon: "Then you will have to die as well as they, and soon."

There was a shocked silence. Iris shut her eyes. Paul gasped and sat back abruptly in his chair. Cave turned white but he did not flinch. His eyes did not waver. They seized on mine, terrible and remote, full of power; with an effort, I looked past him. I still feared his gaze.

"What did you say?" The voice was curiously mild yet it increased rather than diminished the tension. We had reached the crisis, without a plan.

"You have removed the fear of death, for which future generations will thank you, as I do. But you have gone too far . . . all of you." I looked about me at the pale faces; a faint wisp of new moon curled in the pale sky above. "Life is to be lived until the flesh no longer supports the life within. The meaning of life, Cave, is more life, not death. The enemy of life is death, an enemy not to be feared but no less hostile for all that, no less dangerous, no less wrong when the living choose it instead of life, either for themselves or for others. You've been able to dispell our fear of the common adversary; that was your great work in the world. Now you want to go further, to make love to this enemy we no longer fear, to mate with death, and it is here that you, all of you, become enemies of life."

"Stop it!" Iris's voice was high and clear. I did not look at her. All that I could do now was to force the climax.

"But sooner or later every act of human folly creates its own opposition. This will too, more soon than late, for if one can make any generality about human beings it is that they want *not* to die. You cannot stampede them into death for long. They are enthusiastic now. They may not be soon . . . unless of course there is some supreme example before them, one which you, Cave, can alone supply. *You* will have to die by your own hand to show the virtue and the truth of all that you have said."

I had gone as far as I could. I glanced at Iris while I spoke: she had grown white and old-looking and, while I watched her, I realized whom it was she resembled, the obscure nagging memory which had disturbed me all through dinner. She was like my mother, a woman long dead, one whose gentle blurred features had been strikingly similar to that frightened face which now stared at me as though I were a murderer.

Paul was the one who answered me. "You're out of your mind, Gene," he said, when my meaning had at last penetrated to them all. "It doesn't follow in the least that Cave must die because others want to. The main work is still ahead of him. This country is only a corner of the world. There's some of Europe and most of Asia and Africa still ahead of us. How can you even suggest he quit now and die?"

"The work will be done whether he lives or not, as you certainly know. He's given it the first impetus. The rest is up to the others, to the ambitious, the inspired. We've met enough of *them* these last few years. They're quite capable of finishing the work without us."

"But it's nothing without Cave."

I shrugged. I was suddenly relieved as the restraint of three furious years went in a rush. "I am as devoted to Cave as anyone," I said (and I was, I think, honest). "I don't want him to die but all of you in your madness have made it impossible for him to live. He's gone now to the limit, to the last boundary. He is the son of death and each of you supports him. I don't, for it was my wish to make life better, not death desirable. I never really believed it would come to this. That you, Cave, would speak for death, and against life." I raised my eyes to his. To my astonishment he had lowered his lids as though to hide from me, to shut me out. His head was shaking oddly from left to right and his lips were pressed tight together.

211

I struck again, without mercy. "But don't stop now. You've got your wish. By all means, build palaces if you like for those who choose to die in your name. But remember that you will be their victim, too. The victim of their passionate trust. They will force you to lead the way and *you* must be death's lover, Cave."

He opened his eyes and I was shocked to see them full of tears. "I am not afraid," he said.

# ❧ 10 ❧

## 1

A few days after our disastrous dinner, Clarissa came to me in my office. It was our first private meeting since her return from Europe. It was also my first meeting with any one of the directors for, since the scene on the penthouse terrace, none had come near me, not even Paul, whom I usually saw at least once a day.

Clarissa looked tired. She sat down heavily in the chair beside my desk and looked at me oddly. "Recriminations?" I asked cheerfully. The recent outburst had restored me to perfect health and equanimity. I was prepared for anything, especially battle.

"You're an absolute fool and you know it," she said at last. "I suppose there are wires in here, recording everything we say."

"I shouldn't be surprised. Fortunately, I have no secrets."

"There's no doubt of that." She glared at me. "There was no need to rush things."

"You mean you anticipated this?"

"What else? Where else could it lead? The same thing happened to Jesus, you know. They kept pushing him to claim the kingdom. Finally, they pushed too hard and he was killed. It was the killing which perpetuated the legend."

"And a number of other things."

"In any case, it's gone too far. Also, I don't think you even begin to see what you've done."

"Done? I've merely brought the whole thing into the open and put myself on record as being opposed to this . . . this passion for death."

"That of course is nonsense. Just because a few nitwits . . ."

"A few? Have you seen the statistics? Every month there are a few hundred more, and as soon as Stokharin gets going with his damned roadhouses for would-be suicides we may find that . . ."

"I always assumed Paul made up the statistics. But even if they *are* true, even if a few hundred thousand people decide to slip away every year, I am in favor of it. There are too many people as it is and most of them aren't worth the room they take up. I suspect all this is just one of nature's little devices to reduce the population, like pederasty on those Greek islands."

"You're outrageous."

"I'm perfectly rational, which is more than I can say for you. Anyway, the reason I've come to see you today is, first, to warn you and, second, to say goodbye."

"Goodbye? You're not . . ."

"Going to kill myself?" She laughed. "Not in a hundred years! Though I must say lately I've begun to feel old. No. I'm going away. I've told Paul that I've had my fun, that you're all on your own and that I want no part of what's to come."

"Where will you go?"

"Who knows? Now for the warning. Paul of course is furious at you and so is Iris."

"Perfectly understandable. What did he say?"

"Nothing good. I talked to him this morning. I won't enrage you by repeating all the expletives. It's enough to say he's eager to get you out of the way. He feels you've been a malcontent all along."

"He'll have trouble getting me to take Stokharin's magic pill."

"He may not leave it up to you," said Clarissa significantly, and inadvertently I shuddered. I had of course wondered if they would dare go so far. I had doubted it but the matter-of-fact Clarissa enlightened me. "Watch out for him, especially if he becomes friendly. You must remember that with the country Cavite and with Paul in charge of the organization you haven't much chance."

"I'll take what I have."

Clarissa looked at me without, I could see, much hope. "What you don't know, and this is my last good deed, for in a sense I'm responsible for getting you into this, is that you accidentally gave the game away."

"What do you mean?"

"I mean that Paul has been planning for over a year to do away with Cave. He feels that Cave's usefulness is over. Also he's uneasy about letting him loose in the world. Paul wants full control of the establishment and he can't have it while Cave lives. Paul also realizes – he's much cleverer than you've ever thought, by the way – that the Cavites need a symbol, some great sacrifice, and obviously Cave's suicide is the answer. It is Paul's intention either to persuade Cave to kill himself or else to do it for him and then announce that Cave, of his own free will, chose to die."

I had the brief sensation of a man drowning. "How do you know all this?"

"I have two eyes. And Iris told me."

"She knows too?"

"Of course she knows! Why else do you think she's so anxious to get Cave away from this place? She knows Paul can have him killed at any time and no one would be the wiser."

I grunted with amazement. I understood now what it was that had happened on the terrace. I felt a perfect fool. Of them all I alone had been unaware of what was going on beneath the surface and, in my folly, I had detonated the situation without knowing it. "*He* knows too?" I asked weakly.

"Of course he does. He's on his guard every minute against Paul."

"Why has no one ever told me this?"

Clarissa shrugged. "They had no idea which side you'd take. They still don't know. Paul believes that you are with him and though he curses you for an impetuous fool, he's decided that perhaps it's a good idea now to bring all this into the open, at least among ourselves. He hopes for a majority vote in the directors' meeting to force Cave to kill himself."

"And Cave?"

"Has no wish to die, sensible man."

"I am a fool."

"What I've always told you, dear." Clarissa smiled at me. "I will say, though, that you are the only one of the lot who has acted for an impersonal reason, and certainly none of them understands you except me. I am on your side, in a way. Voluntary deaths don't alarm me the way they do you, but this obsession of Cave's, of death being preferable to life, may have ghastly consequences."

"What can I do?"

"I haven't the faintest idea. It's enough that you were warned in advance."

"What would *you* do?"

"Exactly what I'm going to do. Take a long trip."

"I mean if you were I."

She sighed. "Save your life, if possible. That's all you can do."

"I have a few weapons, you know. I have the *Journal* and I'm a director. I have friends in every Center." This was almost true. I had made a point of knowing as many Residents as possible. "I also have Iris and Cave on my side since I'm willing to do all I can to keep him alive, that he *not* become a supreme symbol."

"I wish you luck." Clarissa was most cynical. She rose. "Now that I've done my bit of informing, I'm off."

"Europe?"

"None of your business. But I *will* tell you I won't go back there. They've gone quite mad too. In Madrid I pretended to be a Catholic and I watched and I watched them put Cavites up

216

before firing squads. Of course our people, despite persecution, are having a wonderfully exciting time with passwords and peculiar college fraternity handclasps and so on." She collected her gloves and handbag from the floor where, as usual, she had strewn them. "Well, now goodbye" She gave me a kiss; then she was gone.

## 2

Events moved rapidly. I took to bolting my bedroom door at night, and during the day I was careful always to have one or another of my assistants near me. It was a strange sensation to be living in a modern city with all its police and courts and yet to fear that in a crisis there would be no succor, no one to turn to for aid and protection. We were a separate government within the nation, beyond the law.

The day after Clarissa had said goodbye, Paul appeared in my office. I was surrounded by editors, but at a look from him and a gesture from me they withdrew. We had each kept our secret, evidently, for none of those close to us in that building suspected that there had been a fatal division.

"I seem to be in disgrace," I said, my forefinger delicately caressing the buzzer which I had built into the arm of my chair so that I might summon aid in the event that a visitor proved to be either a bore or a maniac, two types curiously drawn to enterprises such as ours.

"I wouldn't say that." Paul sat in a chair close to my own; I recall thinking, a little madly, that elephants are supposed to be at their most dangerous when they are perfectly still. Paul was noticeably controlled. Usually he managed to cross the room at least once for every full sentence; now he sat looking at me, his face without expression.

"I've seen no one since our dinner except Clarissa," I explained; then I added earnestly: "I wonder where she plans to go. She didn't . . ."

217

"You've almost wrecked everything," he said, his voice tight, unfamiliar in its tension.

"I didn't want to," I said, inaccurately. I was at the moment more terrified than I had ever been either before or since. I could get no real grip on him. The surface he presented me was as unyielding as a prison wall.

"Who told you? Iris? Cave? Or were you spying?" Each question was fired at me like a bullet.

"Spying on whom?"

"On me, damn you!" Then it broke. The taut line of control which had held in check his anger and his fear broke all at once and the torrent flowed, reckless and overpowering: "You meddling idiot! You spied on me. You found out. You thought you'd be able to stall things by springing it like that. Well, you failed." I recall thinking, quite calmly, how much I preferred his face in the congested ugliness of rage to its ordinary banality of expression. I was relieved, too, by the storm. I could handle him when he was out of control. I considered my counter-offensive while he shouted at me, accused me of hostility to him, of deviationism from Cavesword and of numerous other crimes. He stopped finally, for lack of breath.

"I gather," I said, my voice shaking a little from excitement, "that at some point recently you decided that Cave should apply Cavesword to himself and die, providing us with a splendid example, an undying (I mean no pun) symbol."

"You know you found out and decided to get in on the act, to force my hand. Now he'll never do it."

That was it, then. I was relieved to know. "Cave has refused to kill himself?"

"You bet your sweet life he has." Paul was beginning to recover his usual poise. "Your little scene gave him the excuse he needed: 'Gene's right.'" Paul imitated Cave's voice with startling accuracy and malice. 'Gene's right. I never did mean for everybody to kill themselves off, where'd the world be if *that* happened? Just a few people. That's all.' And he's damned if he's going to be one of them. 'Hate to set that sort of example.' "

"Well, you'll have to try something else, then."

"Why did you do it?" Paul's voice became petulant. "Did Iris put you up to it?"

"Nobody put me up to it."

"You mean to sit there and try to make me believe that it just occurred to you, like that, to suggest Cave would have to kill himself if he encouraged suicide?"

"I mean that it occurred to me exactly like that." I looked at Paul with vivid loathing. "Can't you understand an obvious causal relationship? With this plan of Stokharin's you'll make it impossible for Cave *not* to commit suicide, and when he does, you will have an international death cult which I shall do my best to combat."

Paul's hands began nervously to play with his tie, his lapels. I wondered if he had come armed. I placed my finger lightly upon the buzzer. Implacably, we faced one another.

"You are not truly Cavesword," was all that he said.

"We won't argue about that. I'm merely explaining to you why I said what I did and why I intend to keep Cave alive as long as possible. Alive and hostile to you, to your peculiar interpretation of his Word."

Paul looked suddenly disconsolate. "I've done what I thought best. I feel Cave should show all of us the way. I feel it's both logical and necessary to the Establishment that he give back his life publicly."

"But he doesn't want to."

"That is the part I can't understand. Cavesword is that death is not to be feared but embraced, yet he, the man who has really changed the world, refuses to die."

"Perhaps he feels he has more work to do. More places to see. Perhaps, Paul, he doesn't trust you, doesn't want to leave you in control of the Establishment."

"I'm willing to get out if that's all that's stopping him." But the insincerity of his protestation was too apparent for either of us to contemplate it for long.

"I don't care what his motives are. I don't care if he himself is terrified of dying (and I have a hunch that that is the real reason for his hesitancy), but I *do* know that I don't want him dead by his own hand."

"You're quite sure of that?"

"Absolutely sure. I'm a director of the Establishment and don't forget it. Iris, Cave, and I are against you and Stokharin. You may control the organization but we have Cave himself." I gathered courage in my desperation. I purposely sounded as though I were in warm concert with the others.

"I realize all that." Paul was suddenly meek, conciliatory, treacherous. "But you must allow me as much sincerity as you withhold for yourself. I want to do what's best. I think he should die and I've done everything to persuade him. He was near agreement when you upset everything."

"For which I'm happy, though it was something of an accident. Are you sure that it is only for the sake of Cavesword you want him dead?"

"What other reason?" He looked at me indignantly. I could not be sure whether he was telling the truth or not. I doubted it.

"Many other reasons. For one thing you would be his heir, in complete control of the Establishment; and that of course is something worth inheriting."

Paul shrugged convincingly. "I'm as much in charge now as I would be with him dead," he said with a certain truth. "I'm interested in Cavesword, not in Cave. If his death enhances and establishes the Word more securely then I must convince him that he must die."

"There is another way," I said, smiling at the pleasant thought.

"Another way?"

"To convince us of your dedication and sincerity to Cavesword."

220

"What's that?"

"You kill *yourself*, Paul."

There was a long silence. I pressed the buzzer and my secretary came in. Without a word, Paul left.

Immediately afterwards, I took the private elevator to Cave's penthouse. Two guards stopped me while I was announced by a third. After a short delay I was admitted to Cave's study, where Iris received me.

"I know what's happening," I said. "Where is he?"

"Obviously you do." Her voice was cold. She did not ask me to sit down. Awkwardly, I faced her at the room's centre.

"We must stop him."

"John? Stop him from what?"

"Doing what Paul wants him to do."

"And what you want as well."

"You're mistaken. I thought I made myself clear the other night. But though my timing was apparently bad, under *no* circumstances do I want him to die."

"You made your speech to force him."

"And Paul thinks I made it to stop him." I couldn't help smiling. "I am, it seems, everyone's enemy."

"Paul has told me everything. How you and he and Stokharin all decided, without consulting us, that John should die."

I was astonished at Paul's boldness. Could he really be moving so swiftly? How else explain such a prodigious lie? I told her quickly and urgently what I had said to Paul and he to me. She heard me to the end without expressing either belief or disbelief. When I had finished she turned away from me and went to the window where, through yellow glass, the city rose upon the band of horizon.

"It's too late," she said, evenly. "I hadn't expected this. Perhaps you're telling me the truth. If you are, you've made a terrible mistake." She turned about suddenly, with a precision almost military. "He's going to do it."

The awful words fell like a weight upon a scale. I reached for a chair and sat down, all strength gone. "Stop him." I said, all that I could say. "Stop him."

"It's too late for that." She took pity on me. "I think you're telling me the truth." She came over to where I was sitting and looked down at me gently. "I'm sorry I accused you. I should have realized Paul was lying."

"*You* can stop him."

"I can't. I've tried but I can't." Her control was extraordinary. I did not then guess the reason for her calm, her strength.

"Then I must try." I stood up.

"You can't do anything. He won't see you. He won't see anyone but me."

"I thought he told Paul he agreed with me, that he didn't want to . . . to countenance all this, that he . . ."

"At first he took your side, if it is really what you feel. Then he thought about it and this morning he decided to go ahead with Paul's plan."

I was confused. "Does Paul know?"

Iris smiled wanly. "John is reserving for himself the pleasure of doing what he must do without Paul's assistance."

"Or knowledge?"

Iris shrugged. "Paul will find out about it this evening, I suppose. There will be an announcement. John's secretary is getting it ready now . . . one for the public and another for the Establishment."

"When will it happen?"

"Tomorrow. I go with him, Gene."

"You? You're not going to die too?"

"I don't see that it makes much difference what I do when John dies."

"You can't leave us now. You can't leave Paul in charge of everything. He's a dangerous man. Why, if . . ."

"You'll be able to handle him." It was perfectly apparent to me that she was no longer interested in me or in the others; not even in the fate of the work we had begun.

"It's finished, if you go too," I said bleakly. "Together we

222

could control Paul; alone, I wouldn't last ten days. Iris, let me talk to him."

"I can't. I won't."

I contemplated pushing by her and searching the penthouse, but there were guards everywhere and I had no wish to be shot on such an errand.

She guessed my thought and said quickly, "There's no possible way for you or anyone to get through to him. Sometime tonight or tomorrow he will leave and that's the end."

"He won't do it here?" This surprised me.

She shook her head. "He wants to go off alone, away from everyone. I'm to be with him until the end. Then I'll send the body back here for burial, but he'll leave full instructions."

"You mean I'm never to see either of you again? Just like that, you both go?"

"Just like this." For the first time she displayed some warmth. "I've cared for you, Gene," she said gently. "I even think that of us all you were the one most nearly right in your approach to John. I think you understood him better than he did himself. Try to hold on after we go. Try to keep it away from Paul."

"As if I could!" I turned from her bitterly, filled with unexpected grief. I did not want to lose her presence even though I had lost her or, rather, never possessed more of her than that one bright instant on the California coast when we had both realized with the unexpected clarity of the lovers we were not that our lives had come to the same point at the same moment. The knowledge of this confluence was the only splendor I had ever known, the single hope, the unique passion of my life.

"Don't miss me. I couldn't bear that." She put her hand on my arm. I walked away, not able to bear her touch. Then they came.

Paul and Stokharin were in the study. Iris gasped and stepped back when she saw them. I spun about just as Paul shouted, "It won't work, Iris! Give it up."

"Get out of here, Paul." Her voice was strong. "You have no right here."

"I have as much right as you. Now tell me whose idea it was. Yours? Or was it John's? Or Gene's? Since he seems to enjoy playing both sides."

"Get out. All of you." She moved to the old-fashioned bell cord which hung beside Cave's desk.

"Don't bother," said Paul. "No one will come."

Iris, her eyes wide now with fear, tugged the cord twice. The second time it broke off in her hand. There was no response.

Paul looked grim. "I'm sorry to have to do it this way but you've left me no choice. You can't leave, either of you."

"You've read . . ."

"I saw the release. It won't work."

"Why not? It's what you've wanted all along. Everything will be yours. There'll be nobody to stop you. John will be dead and I'll be gone for good. You'll never see me again. Why must you interfere?" She spoke quickly and plausibly, but the false proportion was evident now, even to me. The desperate plan was tumbling down at Paul's assault.

"Iris. I'm not a complete fool. I know perfectly well that Cave has no intention of killing himself and that . . ."

"Why do you think I'm going with him? To send you the body back for the ceremony which you'll perform right here, publicly . . ."

"Iris." He looked at her for a long moment. Then: "If you two leave as planned tonight (I've canceled the helicopter, by the way) there will be no body, no embalming, no ceremony. Only a mystery which might very well undo all our work. I can't allow that. Cave must die here, before morning. We might have put it off but your announcement has already leaked out. There'll be a million people out there in the street tomorrow. We'll have to show them Cave's body."

Iris swayed. I moved quickly to her side and held her arm. "It's three to two, Paul," I said. "I assume we're still directors. Three of us have agreed that Cave and Iris leave. That's final." But my bluff was humiliatingly weak; it was ignored.

"The penthouse," said Paul softly, "is empty . . . just the five of us here. The Doctor and I are armed. Take us in to him."

"No." Iris moved instinctively, fatally, to the door that led to Cave, as if to guard it with her body.

There was a brief scuffle, ending with Iris and myself, considerably disheveled, facing two guns. With an apology, Stokharin pushed us through the door.

In a small sunroom we found Cave sitting before a television screen, watching the installation of a new Resident in Boston. He looked up with surprise at our entrance. "I thought I said . . ." he began, but Iris interrupted him.

"They want to kill you, John."

Cave got to his feet, face pale, eyes glaring. Even Paul was shaken by that glance. "You read my last statement?" Cave spoke sharply, without apparent fear.

"That's why we've come," said Paul. He and Stokharin moved, as though by previous accord, to opposite ends of the little room, leaving the three of us together, vulnerable at its center. "You must do it here." Paul signaled Stokharin, who produced a small metal box which he tossed to Cave.

"Some of the new pills," he said nervously. "Very nice. We use peppermint in the outer layer and . . ."

"Take it, John."

"I'll get some water," said Stokharin. But Paul waved to him to keep his place.

Cave smiled coldly. "I will not take it. Now both of you get out of here before I call the guards."

"No more guards," said Paul. "We've seen to that. Now, please, don't make it any more difficult than it is. Take the pill."

"If you read my statement you know that . . ."

"You intend to take a pleasant trip around the world incognito with Iris. Yes, I know. As your friend, I wish you could do it. But, for one thing, sooner or later you'd be recognized, and for another we must have proof . . . we must have a body."

"Iris will bring the body back," said Cave. He was still quite calm. "I choose to do it this way and there's nothing more to be said. You'll have the Establishment all to yourself and I will be a most satisfactory figure upon which to build a world religion." It was the only time in my experience with Cave that I ever heard him strike the ironic note.

"Leave us alone, Paul. You have what you want. Now let us go." Iris begged, but Paul had no eyes for anyone but Cave.

"Take it, John," he repeated softly. "Take Cavesway."

"Not for you." Cave hurled the metal box at Paul's head and Stokharin fired. There was one almost bland moment when we all stood, politely, in a circle and watched Cave, a look of wonder on his face, touch his shoulder where the blood had begun to flow through a hole in the jacket.

Then Iris turned fiercely on Paul, knocking him off balance. while Cave ran to the door. Stokharin, his hand shaking and his face silver with fear, fired three times, each time hitting Cave, who quivered but did not fall; instead, he got through the door and into the study. As Stokharin hurried after him, I threw myself upon him expecting death at any moment; but it did not come, for Stokharin had collapsed. He dropped his gun and hid his face in his hands, rocking back and forth on the floor, sobbing. Free of Iris's fierce grip, Paul got to Cave before I did.

Cave lay in the corridor only a few feet from the elevator. He had fallen on his face and lay now in his own blood, his hands working at the floor as though trying to dig himself a grave in the hard stone. I turned him on his back and he opened his eyes. "Iris?" he asked. His voice was ordinary though his breathing was harsh and uneven.

"Here I am." Iris knelt down beside him, ignoring Paul.

Cave whispered something to Iris. Then a flow of blood, like the full moon's tide, poured from his mouth. He was dead.

"Cavesway," said Paul at last when the silence had been used up. The phrase he had prepared for this moment was plainly inadequate for the reality at our feet.

"*Your* way," said Iris as she stood up. She looked at Paul calmly, as though they had only just met. "*Your* way," she repeated.

In the other room Stokharin moaned.

## 1

Now the work was complete. Cavesword and Cavesway formed a perfect design and all the rest would greatly follow, or so Paul assumed. I believe if I had been he I should have killed both Iris and myself the same day, removing at one stroke witnesses and opposition. But he did not have the courage, and I also think he underestimated us, to his own future sorrow.

Iris and I were left alone in the penthouse. Paul, after shaking Stokharin into a semblance of calm, bundled Cave's body into a blanket and then, with the Doctor's help, placed it in the private elevator.

The next twenty-four hours were a grim carnival. The body of Cave, beautifully arranged and painted, lay in the central auditorium of the Center as thousands filed by to see him. Paul's speech over the corpse was telecast around the world.

Iris and I kept to our separate rooms, both by choice and from necessity, since gentle guards stood before our doors and refused, apologetically, to let us out.

I watched the services over television while my chief editors visited me one by one, unaware of what had happened and ignoring the presence of the guards. It was assumed that I was too shocked by grief to go to the office. Needless to say, I did not mention to any of them what had happened. At first I had thought it best to expose Paul as a murderer and a fraud, but on second thought (the second thought which followed all *too* swiftly upon the first, as Paul had no doubt assumed it would),

228

I did not want to risk the ruin of our work. Instead, I decided to wait, to study Paul's destruction, an event which I had grimly vowed would take place as soon as possible. He could not now get rid of either Iris or me in the near future and all we needed, I was sure, was a week or two. I was convinced of this though I had no specific plan. Iris had more influence, more prestige in the Establishment, than Paul, and I figured, correctly as later events corroborated, that Cave's death would enhance her position. As for myself, I was not without influence.

I kept my lines of communication clear the next few days during what was virtually a house arrest. The editors came to me regularly and I continued to compose editorials. The explanation for my confinement was, according to a bulletin signed by Stokharin, a mild heart condition. Everyone was most kind. But I was alarmed when I heard of the diagnosis. It meant that with one of Stokharin's pellets in my food death would be ascribed to coronary occlusion, the result of strain attendant upon Cave's death. I had less time than I thought. I made plans.

Paul's funeral oration was competent though less than inspiring. The Chief Resident of Dallas, one of the great new figures of the Establishment, made an even finer speech over the corpse. I listened attentively, judging from what was said and what was not said the wind's direction. Cavesway was now the heart of the doctrine. Death was to be embraced with passion; life was the criminal, death the better reality; consciousness was an evil which, in death's oblivion, met its true fate . . . man's one perfect virtuous act was the sacrifice of his own consciousness to the pure nothing from which, by grim accident, it had come into being. The Chief Resident of Dallas was most eloquent and chilling.

Even sequestered in my room, I caught some of the excitement which circled the globe like a lightning storm. Thirty-five hundred suicides were reported within forty-eight hours of Cave's death. The statisticians lost count of the number of people who fought to get inside the building to see Cave in death. From my window I could see that Park Avenue had been roped off for a dozen blocks. People swarmed like ants toward the gates of the tower.

I sent messages to Iris but received none, nor, for that matter, did I have any assurance that she had got mine. I followed Paul's adventures on television and from the reports of my editors who visited me regularly, despite Stokharin's orders.

On the third day, I was allowed to go to my office, Paul having decided that it would be thought odd if I were to die so soon after Cave. No doubt he was also relieved to discover that I had not revealed to my friends what had happened. Now that he had established the fact of my weak heart, my death could be engineered most plausibly at any time.

I did not see him face to face until the fourth day when John Cave's ashes were to be distributed over the United States. Stokharin, Paul and I sat in the back seat of a limousine at the head of a motorcade which, beginning at the tower, terminated at the airport where the jet plane which would sprinkle the ashes over New York, Seattle, Chicago and Los Angeles was waiting, along with a vast crowd and the President of the United States, an official Christian but known to incline, as Presidents do, toward the majority. Cavites were the majority and had been for almost two years.

I was startled to find Paul and Stokharin in the same automobile. It had been my understanding that we were to travel separately in the motorcade. They were most cordial.

"Sorry to hear you've been sick, Gene," Paul said with an ingenuous grin. "Mustn't strain the old ticker."

"I'm sure the good Doctor will be able to cure me," I said cheerfully.

They both laughed loudly. The car pulled away from the tower and drove down Park Avenue at the head of a long procession. Crowds lined the street as we drove slowly by. They were curiously still, as though they hardly knew how to react.

This was a funeral, yet Cavesway was glorious. Some cheered. Most simply stared and pointed at our car, recognizing Paul. I suddenly realized why they were so interested in this particular car. On the floor, at Paul's feet, was what looked like a large flowerpot covered with gold foil.

"Are those the ashes?"

Paul nodded. "Did an extra quick job, too, I'm glad to say. We didn't want any slipup."

"Where's Iris?"

"I was going to ask *you* that." Paul looked at me sharply. "She disappeared yesterday and it's very embarrassing for all of us, very inconsiderate too. She knew I especially wanted her at the ceremony. She knows that everyone will expect to see her."

"I think she took the idea of Cavesway most illogically," said Stokharin. His usual sang-froid had returned, the breakdown forgotten. "She should be grateful to us for making all this possible, despite Cave's weakness."

I ignored Stokharin. I looked at Paul, who was beaming at the crowd, acknowledging their waves with nods of his head. "What will you do now?"

"You heard the ceremony?"

"Yes."

"Well, just that. Cavesway has become universal. Even the economists in Washington have privately thanked us for what we're doing to reduce the population. There's a theory that by numerous voluntary deaths wars might decrease since – or so the proposition goes – they are nature's way of checking population."

"Perhaps you're right." I assumed a troubled expression as I made the first move of my counteroffensive.

Paul looked away from the crowd to regard me shrewdly. "You don't think I trust you, do you?"

I shrugged. "Why not? I can't change Cavesway now."

Paul grunted. I could see that he did not credit this spurious *volte-face*; nevertheless, an end to my active opposition would force him to revise his plans. This would, I hoped, give me the time I needed. I pressed on. "I think we can compromise. Short of rigging my death, which would cause suspicion, you must continue to put up with me for a while. You've nothing to fear from me since you control the Establishment and since the one weapon I have against you I will not use."

"You mean. . ."

"My having witnessed the murder of Cave. If I had wanted to I could have revealed this before the cremation. An autopsy would certainly have ruined everything for you."

"Why didn't you?" I could see that Paul was genuinely interested in my motives.

"Because it would have meant the end of the work. I saw no reason to avenge Cave at such a cost. You must remember he was not a god to me, any more than you are."

The twist of a blunt knife had the calculated effect. "What a cold devil you are!" said Paul, almost admiringly. "I wish I could believe you."

"There's no reason not to. I was opposed to the principle of suicide. It is now firmly established. We must go on from there."

"Then tell me where Iris is."

"I haven't any idea. As you know, I've been trying to get in touch with her for days. Your people intercepted everything. How *did* she manage to get away?"

"One of the guards let her out. I thought he was one of our boys but it seems she worked on him and he left with her. I've alerted all the Centers; so far no one's seen her."

Just before Grand Central Terminal, the crowd began to roar with excitement and Paul held up the jar of ashes. The crowd went wild and tried to break through the police lines. The cortege drove a bit faster and Paul set the ashes down. He looked triumphant but tired, as though he'd not slept in a month. One eyelid, I saw, was twitching with fatigue.

"When are we to have a directors' meeting?" I asked as we crossed the bridge which spanned the river. "We're still legally a company. We must elect a new board chairman."

"As soon as we find Iris," said Paul. "I think we should all be there, don't you? Two to two."

"Perhaps three to one on the main things," I said, allowing this to penetrate, aware that his quick mind would study all the possibilities and arrive at a position so subtle and unexpected as to be of use to me if I, in turn, were quick enough to seize my opportunity.

At the airport, a detachment of airborne troops was drawn up before a festooned reviewing stand. Nearby the Marine Band played incongruous marches, while in the center of the stand, surrounded by cameras and dignitaries, stood the smiling President of the United States.

2

The next day while I was examining the various accounts of the last ceremony, the chief editor came into my office, his face blazing with excitement. "Iris Mortimer!" was all he could say.

"Iris? Where?"

"Dallas." He exploded the name in exhalation. Apparently, word had come from our office there that Iris had, a few hours before, denounced Paul for having ignored Cave's last wishes to be embalmed and that, as a result of this and other infidelities to Cavesword, she, as ranking director and with the full concurrence of the Chief Resident of Dallas, was calling a Council of Residents to be held the following week at Dallas, to determine the future course of the Establishment.

I almost laughed aloud with pleasure. I had not believed she would show such vigor and daring. I had feared that she might choose to vanish into obscurity, her life ended with Cave. Even at my most optimistic, I had not dreamed she would act so boldly, exploiting a rivalry between Paul and the Chief Resident of Dallas, the premier member of the Council of Residents, a group that until now had existed for purely ceremonial reasons, exerting no influence upon the board of directors which, while Cave lived, was directed by Paul.

I moved swiftly. The *Journal* was at that moment going to press. I scribbled a brief announcement of the approaching Council of Residents, and I referred to Iris as Cave's spiritual heir. By telephone, I ordered a box to be cut out of the first page. I had not acted a moment too soon, for a few minutes after my telephone call to the compositor, Paul came to my office, furious. He slammed the door behind him.

"You knew this was going to happen."

"I wish I had."

He paced the floor quickly, eyes shining. "I've sent out an order countermanding Iris. I've also removed the Resident at Dallas. I'm still in charge of the Establishment. I control the funds and I've told every damned Resident in this country that if he goes to Dallas I'll cut off his Center without a penny."

"It won't work." I smiled amiably at Paul. "Your only hold over the Establishment is legal. You are the vice president of the corporation and now, at least for the interim, you're in charge. Fine. But since you've become so devoted to the letter of the law you can't act without consulting your directors and two of them will be in Dallas, reorganizing."

He cursed me for some minutes. Then abruptly he stopped. "You won't go to Dallas. You're going to be here for the directors' meeting that will cut off every Resident who attends that circus. We own the damned Centers. We can appoint whom we like. You're going to help ratify my new appointments."

I pressed the buzzer in my chair. A secretary came in. I told her to get me a reservation on the next plane to Dallas; then, before she had closed the door behind her, I was halfway through it. I turned to look back at Paul, who stood now quite alone in the office. "You had better come too." I said. "It's all over."

3

The new Establishment was many months in the making. The Council of seven hundred Residents from all parts of the world sat in general session once a week and in various committees the rest of the time. Iris was everywhere at once, advising, encouraging, proposing. We had adjoining suites in the huge white marble Center, which had now become (and was to remain) the capitol of the Cavite Establishment.

The Residents were an extraordinary crew, ranging from wild-eyed zealots to urbane, thoughtful men. None had been in the least disturbed by Paul's threats, and with Iris and myself as chief stockholders (Clarissa had turned her voting shares over to Iris, I discovered), we dissolved the old company and a new organization was fashioned, one governed by the Council of Residents, who in turn chose an heir to Cave and an administrative assistant to direct the affairs of the Establishment. Iris was unanimously appointed Guardian of Cavesword, while the Chief Resident of Dallas undertook Paul's old administrative duties. From a constitutional point of view the Council was in perfect agreement, accepting Iris's guidance without demur.

I myself was something of a hero for having committed the *Journal* at a crucial moment to the Dallas synod. I was made an honorary Resident (Poughkeepsie was given to me as a titular Center) and appointed to the Executive Committee, which was composed of Iris, Dallas, two elected Residents and myself.

We worked harmoniously for some weeks. Each day we would issue bulletins to the news services which had congregated in the city, reporting our progress devotedly.

Paul arrived in the second week. He came secretly and unannounced. I have no idea what it was that he said to Iris or what she said to him; all I know is that a few hours after their meeting in the Center, he took Cavesway of his own free will and to my astonishment.

I had not believed it possible, I said, when Iris told me,

shortly after the Center announced the presence of Paul Himmell among the dead for that week (regular lists were published of those who had used the Center's facilities to take Cavesway); in fact, so quietly was it handled that very little was made of it in the press, which did not even report the event until ten days after it had taken place.

"We may have misunderstood Paul." Iris was serene. In the last year her figure had become thick and maternal, while her hair was streaked with premature white. We were alone in the Committee Room, waiting for our fellow committeemen who were not due for some minutes. The August sun shone gold upon the mahogany table, illuminating like a Byzantine mosaic the painting of Cave that hung behind her chair.

"He really did do it himself?" I looked at her suspiciously. She smiled softly, with amusement.

"He was persuaded," she said. "But he did it himself, of his own free will."

"Not forced?"

"I swear not. He was more sincere than I'd ever thought. He believed in Cavesway." How naturally she said that word which she had so desperately tried to keep from ever existing.

"Had you really planned to go away?" I asked. "The two of you?"

Iris looked at me, suddenly alert, impersonal. "That's all finished, Gene. We must keep on in the present. I never think now of anything but Cavesword and Cavesway. It does no good to think of what might have been."

And that was the most we were ever to say to one another about the crisis in our lives. We talked of the present and made plans. Stokharin had disappeared at the same time Paul flew to Dallas and we both decided it was wisest to forget him. Certainly he would not trouble us again. There was no talk of vengeance.

The committee members, important and proud, joined us and we took up the day's problem, which by some irony was the standardization of facilities for Cavesway in the different

Centers. Quietly, without raising our voices, in a most good-humored way, we broke neatly in half on Cavesway. I and one other Resident objected to the emphasis on death. Dallas and the fourth member were in favor of expanding the facilities, both physically and psychologically, until every Cavite could take Cavesway at the moment when he felt his social usefulness ebbing. We argued reasonably with one another until it became apparent that there was no possible ground for compromise.

It was put to vote and Iris broke the tie by endorsing Cavesway.

4

This morning as I finished the lines above I suffered a mild stroke . . . a particularly unusual one since I did not become, as far as I know, unconscious. I was rereading my somewhat telescoped account of the Council of Dallas when, without warning, the blow fell. A capillary burst in my brain and I felt as though I were losing my mind in one last fantastic burst of images. The pain was negligible, no worse than a headache, but the sensation of letting go one's conscious mind was terrifying. I tried to call for help, but I was too weak. For one long giddy moment I thought: I am dying: this is the way it is. Even in my anguish I was curious, waiting for that approach of winged darkness which years ago I once experienced when I fainted and which I have always since imagined to be like death's swift entrance.

But then my body recovered from the assault. The wall was breached, the enemy is in the city, but the citadel is still intact and I live.

Weakly I got up, poured myself a jigger of brandy and then, having drunk it all at once, fell across my bed and slept and did not dream, a rare blessing in these feverish last days.

I was awakened by the sensation of being watched. I opened

my eyes and saw Jessup above me, looking like a bronze figure of Anubis. "I'm sorry . . . didn't mean to disturb you. Your door was open."

"Perfectly all right," I said, as smoothly as I could, drugged with sleep. I pulled myself up against the pillows. "Excuse me for not getting up, but I'm still a little weak from my illness."

"I wanted to see you," said Jessup, sitting down in the chair beside the bed. "I hope you don't mind my coming in like this."

"Not at all. How do you find Luxor?" I wanted to delay as long as possible the questions which I was quite sure he would want to ask me.

"The people are not so fixed in error as we'd been warned. There's a great curiosity about Cavesword." His eyes had been taking in the details of the room with some interest; to my horror I recalled that I had left the manuscript of my work on the table instead of hiding it as usual in the washstand. He saw it. "Your . . . memoirs?" He looked at me with a polite interest which I was sure disguised foreknowledge.

"A record of my excavations," I said, in a voice which descended the scale to a whisper. "I do it for my own amusement, to pass the time."

"I should enjoy reading it."

"You exaggerate, in your kindness," I said, pushing myself higher on the bed, preparing if necessary for a sudden spring.

"Not at all. If it is about Egypt, I should read it. There are no contemporary accounts of this country . . . by one of us."

"I'm afraid the details of findings in the valley yonder," I gestured toward Libya and the last acres of the kings, "won't be of much use to you. I avoid all mention of people less than two millennia dead."

"Even so." But Jessup did not pursue the subject. I relaxed a little.

"I must tell you," he said suddenly, "that I was suspicious of you."

Now I thought, now it comes; then I was amused. Right at

the end they arrive, when it was too late for them, or for me. "What form did your suspicion take?" My fear left me in one last flurry, like a bird departing in a cold wind for another latitude, leaving the branch which held it all summer through to freeze.

"I thought you might be the one we have so often heard of . . . in legend, that is. The enemy of Cave."

"Which enemy?"

"The nameless one, or at least we know a part of his name if lutherist is derived from it."

"What made you suspect me?"

"Because were I an enemy of Cave and were I forced to disappear, I should come to just such a town in just such a country as this."

"Perfectly logical," I agreed. "But there are many towns in the Arab League, in Asia too. Why suppose one old man to be this mythical villain?"

Jessup smiled. "Intuition, I'm afraid. A terrible admission from one who has been trained in the logic of Caveword. It seemed exactly right. You're the right age, the right nationality. In any case, I telephoned Dallas about you."

I took this calmly. "You talked to the Chief Resident himself?"

"Of course not." Jessup was surprised at my suggestion. "One just doesn't call the Chief Resident like that. Only senior Residents ever talk to him personally. No, I talked to an old friend of mine who is one of the five principal assistants to the Historian General. We were in school together and his specialty is the deviationists of the early days."

"And what did you learn from this scholar?"

Jessup gave me a most charming smile. "Nothing at all. There was no such person as I thought existed, as a number of people thought existed. It was all a legend, a perfectly natural one for gossip to invent. There was a good deal of trouble at the beginning, especially over Cavesway. There was even a minority at Dallas that refused to accept the principle of

Cavesway, without which of course there could be no Establishment. According to the stories one heard as recently as my university days, ten years ago, the original lutherist had led the opposition to Iris, in Council and out. For a time it looked as though the Establishment might be broken in two (this you must remember since you were contemporary to it; fortunately, our Historical Office has tended more and more to view it in the long perspective, and popular works on Cave now make no reference to it); in any case, there was an open break and the minority was soon absorbed by the majority."

"Painlessly?" I mocked him. Could he be telling the truth? Or was this a trap?

Jessup shrugged. "These things are never without pain. It is said that an attempt was made on our Mother Iris's life during the ceremony of Cave's ashes. We still continue it, you know."

"Continue what?"

"The symbolic gathering of the ashes. But of course you know the origin of all that. There was a grave misinterpretation of Cave's last wishes. His ashes were scattered over the United States when it was his wish to be embalmed and preserved. Every year, Iris would travel to the four cities over which the ashes had been distributed and collect a bit of dust in each city to symbolize her obedience to Cavesword in all things. At Seattle, during this annual ceremony, a group of lutherists tried to assassinate her."

"I remember," I said. I had had no hand in that dark episode, but it provided the Establishment with the excuse they needed. My partisans were thrown in prison all over the country. The government, which by then was entirely Cavite, handed several thousand over to the Centers, where they were indoctrinated, ending the heresy for good. Iris herself had secretly arranged for my escape . . . but Jessup could know nothing of this.

"Of course you know these things, perhaps even better than I since you were alive then. Forgive me. I have got into the bad Residential habit of explaining the obvious. An occupational disease." He was disarming. "The point I'm trying to make is that my suspicions of you were unworthy and unfounded since there was no leader of the lutherists to escape; all involved responded nicely to indoctrination and that was the end of it. The story I heard in school was a popular one. The sort that often evolves, like Lucifer and the old Christian God, for instance. For white there must be black, that kind of thing. Except that Cave never had a major antagonist, other than in legend."

"I see. Tell me, then, if there was no real leader to the lutherists, how did they come by their name?"

His answer was prompt. "Martin Luther. My friend in the H. O. told me this morning over the telephone. Someone tried to make an analogy, that's all, and the name stuck, though as a rule the use of any words or concepts derived from the dead religions is frowned upon. You know the story of Martin Luther? It seems that he . . ."

"I know the story of Martin Luther," I answered, more sharply than I intended.

"Now I've tired you." Jessup was sympathetic. He got to his feet. "I just wanted to tell you about my suspicions, that's all. I thought it might amuse you and perhaps bring us closer together, for I'd very much like to be your friend, not only for the help you can give me here but also because of your memories of the old days when Cave and Iris, his Mother, still lived."

"Iris was at least five years younger than Cave."

"Everyone knows that, my friend. She was his *spiritual* Mother, as she is ours. 'From the dark womb of unbeing we emerge in the awful light of consciousness from which the only virtuous escape is Cavesway.' I quote from Iris's last testament. It was found among her papers after her death."

"Did *she* take Cavesway?"

Jessup frowned. "It is said that she died of pneumonia, but had death *not* come upon her unexpectedly it was well known that she would have taken Cavesway. There has been

241

considerable debate over this at Dallas. I hear from highly placed people that before many years have passed they will promulgate a new interpretation, applying only to Iris, which will establish that intent and fact are the same, that though she died of pneumonia she *intended* to take Cavesway and, therefore, took Cavesway in spirit and therefore in fact."

"A most inspiring definition."

"It is beautifully clear, though perhaps difficult for an untrained mind. May I read your memoir?" His eyes strayed curiously to the table.

"When it's finished," I said. "I should be most curious to see how it strikes you."

"Well, I won't take up any more of your time. I hope you'll let me come to see you."

"Nothing could give me more pleasure." And then, with a pat on my shoulder and a kind suggestion that should I choose Cavesway he would be willing to administer the latest drug, Jessup departed.

I remained very still for some minutes, holding my breath for long intervals, trying to die. Then, in a sudden rage, I hurled my pillow across the room and beat the mattress with my fists: it was over. All was at an end except my own miserable life, which will be gone soon enough. My name erased; my work subverted; all that I most detested regnant in the world. I could have wept had there been one tear left in me. Now there is nothing I can do but finish this narrative . . . for its own sake since it will be thought, I know, the ravings of a madman when Jessup reads it, as he surely will after I am dead.

I have tried now for several hours to describe my last meeting with Iris but I find that my memory is at last seriously impaired, the result, no doubt, of that tiny vein's eruption this morning in my brain. It is all a jumble. I think there were several years in which I was in opposition. I think that I had considerable support and I am almost sure that, until the attempted assassination of Iris at Seattle, I was close to dominating the Council of Residents. But the idiotic attempt on her life ruined everything. She knew of course that I had had nothing to do with it, but she was a resolute leader and she took this opportunity to annihilate my party. I believe we met for the last time in a garden. A garden very like the one where we first met in California. No, on the banks of the Hudson . . . I must reread what I have written to refresh my memory. It is all beginning to fade rapidly.

In any case, we met in a garden in the late autumn when all the trees were bare. She was white-haired then, though neither of us was much over forty.

I believe that she wept a little. After all, we were the last who had been close to Cave, heirs become adversaries, she victrix and I vanquished. I never loved her more than at that last moment. Of this I am sure. We talked of possible places of exile. She had arranged for my passage on a ship to Alexandria under the name of Richard Hudson (yes, she who erased my name, in her compassion, gave me a new one). She did not want, however, to know where I intended to go from there.

"It would be a temptation to the others," she said. I remember that one sentence and I do remember the appearance of the garden, though its location I have quite forgotten: there was a high wall around it and the smell of smoldering leaves was acrid. From the mouth of a satyr no water fell in a mossy pool.

Ah yes! The question and the answer. That's it, of course. The key. I had nearly lost it. Before I left, I asked her what it was that Cave had said to her when he was dying, the words the rest of us had not heard. At first she hesitated but then, secure in her power and confident of her own course, she told me: "He said: 'Gene was right.'" I remember looking at her with shock, waiting for her to continue, to make some apology for her reckless falsification of Cave's life and death. But she said no more. There was, I suppose, no explanation she might have made. Without a word, I left the garden. My real life had ended.

There's more to it than this but I cannot get it straight.

Something has happened to my memory. I wonder if perhaps I have not dreamed all this: a long nightmare drawing to its bitter close among the dry ruins of an ancient world.

It is late now. I still live, though I am exhausted and indifferent to everything except that violent living sun whose morning light has just this moment begun to strike upon the western hills across the river: all that is left, all that ever was, the red fire.

I shall not take Cavesway even though I die in pain and confusion. Anubis must wait for me in the valley until the last, and even then I shall struggle in his arms, for I know now that life, my life, was more valuable than I knew, more significant and virtuous than the other's was in her bleak victory.

Though my memory is going from me rapidly the meaning is clear and unmistakable and I see the pattern whole at last, marked in giant strokes upon the air: I was he whom the world awaited. I was that figure, that messiah whose work might have been the world's delight and liberation. But the villain death once more undid me, and to him belongs the moment's triumph. Yet life continues, though I do not. Time bends upon itself. The morning breaks. Now I will stop, for it is day.